MANSFIELD

C.K. Stead was Professor of English at the University of Auckland until 1986. In 1984, he was awarded the CBE for services to New Zealand literature. He is the renowned author of poetry, of literary criticism and of short stories. He edited the Penguin Modern Classics *Letters and Journals of Katherine Mansfield* (1977). *Mansfield* is his tenth novel.

ALSO BY C.K. STEAD

Fiction

Smith's Dream
Five for the Symbol (stories)
All Visitors Ashore
The Death of the Body
Sister Hollywood
The End of the Century at the End of the World
The Singing Whakapapa
Villa Vittoria
The Blind Blonde with Candles in her Hair (stories)
Talking About O'Dwyer
The Secret History of Modernism

Poetry

Whether the Will is Free
Crossing the Bar
Quesada
Walking Westward
Geographies
Poems of a Decade
Paris
Between
Voices
Straw into Gold: Poems New and Selected
The Right Thing
Dog

Criticism

The New Poetic
In the Glass Case: Essays on New Zealand Literature
Pound, Yeats, Eliot and the Modernist Movement
Answering to the Language
The Writer at Work
Kin of Place: Essays on 20 New Zealand Writers

Edited

Oxford New Zealand Short Stories (second series)
Measure for Measure, A Casebook
The Penguin Letters & Journals of Katherine Mansfield
The Collected Stories of Maurice Duggan
The Faber Book of Contemporary South Pacific Stories
Werner Forman's New Zealand

C.K. Stead

MANSFIELD

𝒱

VINTAGE

Published by Vintage 2004

2 4 6 8 10 9 7 5 3 1

Copyright © C.K. Stead 2004

First published in Great Britain in 2004 by
The Harvill Press

Vintage
Random House, 20 Vauxhall Bridge Road,
London SW1V 2SA

Random House Australia (Pty) Limited
20 Alfred Street, Milsons Point, Sydney
New South Wales 2061, Australia

Random House New Zealand Limited
18 Poland Road, Glenfield,
Auckland 10, New Zealand

Random House (Pty) Limited
Endulini, 5A Jubilee Road, Parktown 2193,
South Africa

The Random House Group Limited Reg. No. 954009
www.randomhouse.co.uk/vintage

A CIP catalogue record for this book
is available from the British Library

ISBN 0 099 46865 4

Printed and bound in Great Britain by
Bookmarque Ltd, Croydon, Surrey

Acknowledgements

MY GRATEFUL THANKS TO THOSE WHO PROVIDED ACCOMMODATION WHILE I was writing this novel in 2002: Margaret Stead and Guy Clayton in Maida Vale, Perry (Rory) Anderson in Islington, Robin and Elizabeth Marleyn in Bristol and Cornwall, Sveriges Forfattarforbund (the Swedish Writers' Union) in Stockholm, Lars and Carin Ardelius on the island of Gotland, Yvonne Riley in Notting Hill Gate, Anthony and Ann Thwaite in Paddington, Massimo and Angela Bacigalupo in Rapallo and Tony and Pat Axelrad in Uzès.

Also to librarians from whom I received help at the Alexander Turnbull Library, Wellington, the Library of the University of Auckland and the British Library.

And special thanks, as always, to my publisher and good friend, Christopher MacLehose.

This is a work of fiction, and therefore employs imagination, guesswork and contrivance. Like every historical novel, it fills as best it can – and sometimes also is glad to exploit – gaps in the record. Occasionally, for the sake of an orderly narrative, it makes very small alterations to the actual sequence of incident. None of the characters is invented, and all major events, occasions and relationships are as near to documented 'truth' as I could make them. Brief quotations from, and paraphrases of, letters from and to Katherine Mansfield, and of journal entries, are authentic, but the long letter to Frederick Goodyear in Chapter Eleven, though based on known facts, is invented. The letter Katherine writes to Jack in Chapter One has its counterpart in John [i.e. Jack] Middleton Murry's novel *Still Life*. For Londoners puzzled about Devonshire Street running from Queen Square to Theobald's Road I should explain that it was heavily bombed in the Second World War and subsequently re-named Boswell Street.

C.K.S.

PROLOGUE

London — Summer 1917

HE MUST HAVE HEARD HER COMING AFTER HIM. SHE GUESSED he would want to escape; yet part of him (a large part) would feel he should not, that it would be a rudeness; and another, smaller, part would be curious, would want to wait for her, walk with her. His shyness might win out if she did nothing but clatter along behind losing ground, so she called: "Oh Mr Eliot."

She panted up to where he stood awkwardly, leaning to one side. She put a hand on his lapel, as if steadying herself. In fact steadying herself. But it was a mistake and she removed it. "Mr Eliot," she breathed.

"Mrs Murry," he breathed back. And after that, while she was wondering whether she should explain that she was not yet Mrs Murry, only soon to be, and that she was, meanwhile, Murry's mistress and handmaiden (the thought of saying it amused her), he said: "So you decided to leave too."

"I took my chance. You made an opening."

"Oh dear." His concern was real. "I do hope I didn't break up the party."

"No fear of that. Captain Graves is in full flight."

There was an awkward moment before he said, "It's such a lovely night I thought I might walk for a while. But you will be wanting . . ."

"You want to be alone. You're a poet, after all. There might be poems out there." She waved at the night sky, briefly clear over the river.

"Not at all. If you would care to walk with me . . ."

She was not sure in what spirit this was uttered, but she responded: "I should like nothing better."

So they turned and walked sedately through the faintly misty night under alternating light and shadow from the street lamps. Below the parapet on their right, the Thames made the quiet but forceful undertone of river-flow and tide moving in unison. Ahead, a pattern of not altogether distinct lights sketched the Hammersmith Bridge.

"I felt I just had to escape," she said. "Captain Graves has so many opinions; and they come at one so hard."

"He's been wounded," Eliot said.

"And won medals," she acknowledged. "Or *a* medal. An important one. MM. Or MMM." She hummed it, "Mmmmmmmm . . ." but Tom Eliot didn't smile.

"I think it was the MC," he said.

"And you think his MC excuses . . ."

"I'm sure he wouldn't think he needed excusing."

"No of course not." She looked at him resolutely. "And I don't."

"You don't . . ."

"Excuse him."

"Oh . . . I see. No, well . . ."

Graves had been loud, argumentative, dogmatic, disagreeable. She said, "I disliked him – *so* much."

She felt Tom Eliot wince at the intensity of it, but she carried right on. "I don't mind that he thinks Homer was a woman, though I can't believe it myself. Can you imagine a woman inventing all

2

that butchery when Ulysses comes home? Not just the suitors. Even the serving women get sliced up. But never mind. It's an amusing idea. And then he says he can't read Milton. That's all right too. Captain Graves can read someone else. You, Mr Eliot. Or that Shelton, he likes so much."

"Skelton," Eliot corrected.

"Skelton. You're right. And then he thinks the French are misers and thieves who water the British troops' beer. Well, I suppose they are, and they do. If beer's something you care about – which clearly the French don't – I can see that it matters."

Eliot remained stubbornly silent, which had the effect of making her go stubbornly on. "He's one of those *smug* soldiers who can't open their mouths without hinting that we pampered civilians haven't the faintest idea what it's like over there. But it was his story about forcing frightened men up to the line at the point of a revolver made me decide to dislike him. I went cold all over. It's one thing to be heroic yourself – not to care whether you live or die. But to require it of others . . ."

They had stopped again under a street lamp and were looking down at the fast-moving water. She noticed in the half-light, not for the first time, how darkly handsome the American was, with his intelligent eyes, his slightly beaked nose, his fastidious nostrils and fine mouth.

"I'm sorry," she said. "I'm as bad as he is. The war's not a good subject for me."

Eliot shook his head. "You have nothing to apologise for."

They watched the river in silence. "I thought Jack Hutchinson was very rude to you this evening," she said. "Going on like that about America . . ."

"Oh, I go on about America myself."

"*Do* you?" She was surprised that Tom Eliot would "go on"

about anything. But then, why not? "Yes, of course," she said. "One does. I go on about my own . . ." She hesitated. "New Zealand. You know I'm . . ."

He nodded gravely. Yes, he knew.

"But that doesn't mean I'm happy to hear someone else telling me about its deficiencies."

"Well, you know how it is. Casualty figures are running so high – everyone's feeling it. Hutchinson thinks America should have come in sooner. He thinks we're going to be there at the last moment, when the hard fighting's been done, and we'll take an undeserved share of the spoils. Uncle Sam with his nose in the victory trough."

"Did you want America in the war?"

He looked down at his feet. She looked too and thought his black shoes with their rounded toes were not as elegant as the rest of his clothing, despite their curves of stitching and the trouble he – or someone – had taken to shine them. He said gravely, "I'm told I wouldn't pass the medical."

It wasn't an answer. And why would he not pass? Was he blaming his feet? Were they flat? One heard of men failing the medical for that reason, which didn't seem a good and sufficient one. Her Jack Murry had got some kind of exemption because an obliging doctor had written "TB?" on his report, although he must have known Jack was suffering from nothing more than a cold on the chest. She was glad of it; but it was strange when seriously wounded men were being sent back to fight a second, even sometimes a third, time. Captain Graves's wound had been so serious he'd been reported dead. His parents had received a letter from his commanding officer informing them of it and expressing regret. His lungs were still bad. Yet he seemed to expect he would be sent back to fight again. Even to relish the prospect.

4

She said, "Jack Hutchinson should be over there himself if he's so keen." Hutchinson was a very large, strong-looking man. He'd stood at the head of the table this evening wearing a white apron, carving the meat and hectoring them, the red of his face growing darker, while Tom Eliot, silently accepting these blows and declining to put up any defence of America, grew correspondingly pale.

"He reminds me of a butcher," she said. "He's like a character out of Dickens. I'm not surprised his wife prefers Clive Bell."

Eliot's laugh was uneasy. She could see that he didn't wish to speak unkindly of their host; and their hostess's liaison with Bell was not to be touched either. "Speaking of homelands," he said, "did you know that I sometimes use Apteryx as a pseudonym?"

"Apteryx?"

"You don't know the word? It's the Latin name for a New Zealand bird – the kiwi."

It was meant to please her, and it did. She shook her head at him, smiling. "The erudite Mr Eliot. I'm surprised you know there's a kiwi let alone its Latin name."

"I saw one in the London zoo. The Latin name was on the cage. I wrote to my cousin about it. Our letters are very silly. I told her I'd given it a bun."

Katherine murmured, "I think they feed at night." And then, more quietly, "When buns are in bed."

She glanced at him and yes, he thought it funny. "So you write as Apteryx. It's quite a word, isn't it? Apt. Tricks. It's good. It suits you."

"And it's flightless – that's really why I chose it. It suits my pose, you see. The anti-Romantic modern."

Yes, she did see. And she would have to think again about his "It suits my pose". It made her think of a phrase she'd lingered over in a poem in his just published book, *Prufrock and Other Observations* – about "preparing a face to meet the faces that you meet". Only a few weeks ago she'd read the title poem, "The Love Song of J. Alfred Prufrock", to the literary group that gathered for weekends at Lady Ottoline Morrell's country house, Garsington Manor, not far from Oxford. Katherine was a good reader – she was confident of that – and she felt the reading had created a stir. She wondered whether Eliot knew this had happened. She would have liked to tell him, but it wouldn't do – would seem too consciously ingratiating. And if he didn't know now, he would sooner or later hear of it.

They were walking again. She stopped a moment and breathed deeply. There had been a faintly bitter smell of privet but now it was something different, nicer. "Rosemary?" she suggested. "Or lavender?"

"The City's been full of flowers this month. It seems early to have such humid weather."

"You brought Mary flowers this evening. They were beautiful."

"They were beautiful when I bought them. They'd been home with me on the tram. I think they were rather the worse for wear by the time I got them here."

"Mary told me you're a banker."

"I'm employed at Lloyds," he acknowledged. "I got the job on the false claim someone made for me that I know a number of European languages. I deal with the balance sheets of foreign banks."

"A banking linguist."

"A banker with dictionaries."

"My father's a banker," she said. "Well, no, he's a businessman. But he's Chairman of the Bank of New Zealand. I used to say

6

he's the richest man in New Zealand and the meanest, but of course it isn't true. Not even half true – neither very rich nor very mean. It's just that . . . I suppose he's the sort of father who makes the sort of daughter I am want to say such things." She took a breath and began again. "He just doesn't understand my wanting to write modern stories."

"Your father and mine might get on very well," Eliot said.

She thought not, but didn't say. She imagined a father more sophisticated than hers, but also more severe, with a Founding Fathers kind of severity.

"Do you think of going home?" he asked.

"To New Zealand? Oh, I think of it, not always with pleasure. But sometimes, yes. What about you?"

"I've not been here long. And my wife's English."

"There are so many good reasons for living in deepest darkest London."

"And so many for escaping from one's family."

Ah yes, *that* was true, she thought, recognising in the same instant that she was full of contradictions. How she missed the family and the homeland she'd been so desperate to leave behind.

"If one could live in a house like Jack and Mary Hutchinson's," she said, "one would not have much to complain of. London would be very tolerable at River House. That's to say, if one could live there and not be Jack and Mary."

Eliot frowned up at the sky. "If one could live there and not be *oneself*," he said. "*That* would be first-rate."

This interested her so much she was not sure how to reply. "Not to be oneself," she said, very quietly. "That idea – it's too much of a challenge for me. I think I want to be myself. Yes, I'm sure I do. But I'd like to be so much better at it."

"I did admire the decorations," he said.

They came to a green, with a park bench under a street light. "We must find our ways home," she said, conscious he would feel it wrong, impolite, to be the one to bring their conversation and their walk to an end. "I think it will be a taxi for me. But first, could we sit here for just a moment do you think?"

"Of course." He wiped dew from the surface with his handkerchief before she sat down. She was still thinking about his unguarded moment when he'd expressed pleasure at the thought of not being himself. "If you lived out here," she said, "you and Mrs Eliot could go dancing at the Hammersmith Palais."

"Yes, we could." He looked at her, checking, she supposed, that he wasn't being mocked. "So you know about our dancing."

"Lady Ottoline mentioned it – with admiration."

"Ballroom is Vivien's passion. But she's good at any kind. Not just good. Excellent. She has such grace."

"Lady Ottoline believes you're very good too."

"That's because Vivien says so. Wifely encouragement rather than strict truth. I do enjoy it, but she's the dancer. She keeps it up – learns the new steps. She has a dancing lesson this evening – otherwise she would have come."

"She *does* keep it up. But that's good. I thought she might have been unwell."

The anxious look she'd seen at intervals crossed his face again. "Her health is precarious. But just for the moment – no, she's well." He spoke tenderly and Katherine was touched.

"And what about your . . . About Murry?" She thought he'd been about to say "your husband"; so perhaps he did, after all, know that they were not man and wife: that she was for the time being still Mrs Bowden. And then she thought, Of course he does. They all knew one another's business, these literary people; and despite his primness, and what Virginia Woolf liked to call his "four-piece suit", Tom Eliot was probably as much a gossip as the rest.

"Jack and I are living apart," she explained. "Just in the meantime. We're not far from one another. I'm in Chelsea, he's in Fulham. He comes to me in the evenings and we cook supper together and read one another our work."

This didn't, of course, explain why they had not come to dinner as a couple, and she was glad Eliot hadn't asked where Jack was, because if he had she would have found it difficult not to say (now she'd thought of it) that she didn't have the faintest idea, he might be taking dancing lessons with Mrs Eliot.

The truth was she'd chosen to treat the Hutchinsons' invitation as if it was intended for her alone – and perhaps it had been. She just wasn't sure, and hadn't enquired. Sometimes it was good to be solo. She didn't enjoy it, not entirely, but it woke her up, made her alert, made her see things and fired her to write.

"You don't dance?" Eliot asked.

"I like ballroom dancing. But not . . . I don't have your wife's talent for it. Music when I was young – that was where I had, well . . . at least a certain competence. I played the cello. I liked to sing. I was in an opera chorus once."

"I heard you were an actress."

She laughed. "Who told you that?"

"I think it was Bertie . . ." He stopped and there was that look of anxiety again before he added, as if he didn't want to say the name, or didn't want it heard: "Bertrand Russell."

"Of course, you two are friends." He didn't respond, and she went on, "I've done some acting for the movies. Just walk-on parts, crowd scenes. It's a way of making money. Desperation Alley really. When all else fails you queue up and take what you can get."

"Really? But it must be interesting."

"You wouldn't believe how cold I've been standing around on a draughty set in a flimsy evening gown waiting for the camera to start rolling." As she said this she thought, flimsy, filmsy. She glanced at Eliot. No, on the whole it wasn't the kind of thing you said to him.

Over dinner Captain Graves had spoken dismissively, even angrily, of the campaign Bertie Russell was waging against the war. Graves's friend and fellow-poet, Siegfried Sassoon, was going to issue a public statement as a decorated officer, saying he would not return to the Front because he was convinced the fighting was being needlessly prolonged. An argument had raged around the table, Graves blaming Russell for encouraging Sassoon. It wasn't a question of whether Sassoon's statement was right or wrong, Graves had insisted. What mattered was that it could have no effect except to get his friend into trouble.

. Katherine knew something about this drama; had been involved in it and thought it better to say nothing. To Eliot now she said, changing the subject, "I caught sight of you and Russell in the street once. I think it was in the Strand. I thought of a funny sentence – at least, it seemed funny to me."

She expected he would ask what it was, but he simply looked at her – trying to appear encouraging, she thought, but in reality apprehensive, and silent. "Well, never mind," she said. "I often amuse myself and no one else is amused. Do you find that? One is one's own best company?"

He shook his head slightly and asked, "What was the sentence?"

"Oh, well . . . It's because Bertie's short, you see. No taller than I am."

"And you are?"

"I'm five foot three and a half."

Eliot nodded gravely.

"The half is very important," she said. "Nothing must be wasted." And when he didn't laugh: "Very well, the sentence. It was . . . It went, 'Mr T. S. Eliot is six feet tall. And the Hon. Bertrand Russell is . . . not.'"

She looked for his response. His eyes were keen but there was only the faintest smile. "No? There you are, you see? Too subtle. Or too silly. It depends on that pause between the 'is' and the 'not'. You didn't find it at all funny, did you?"

"I did,' he said; and he seemed to mean it. "It's just that I don't laugh out loud. It's the kind of thing Vivien says. You're not unlike her, you know. I don't say clever things. I never think of them. I wish I did, but they just don't occur to me until it's too late."

"Oh but you don't have to be clever if you're a genius."

He laughed – a quick dismissive snort – and she imagined in the half-light she could see that he was blushing. "Perhaps you don't if you are," he said. "But since in my case it's *not* the case . . ."

"And besides you do say clever things. Wicked things. Murry read me something you wrote about Tennyson. You said he had a large dull brain like a farmhouse clock."

He smiled. "Sometimes I've been known to *write* clever things. It's just that they don't come to me in conversation."

"If you were with me they would," she said, with a rush of reckless confidence.

He looked at her with interest, and didn't reply.

ONE

Winter 1915 – Katherine

ON THE WAY TO LONDON KATHERINE TRIED FIRST TO FOCUS ON, or even somehow to be drawn right into, the flying landscape and the lulling accompaniment of train-clatter. Trees and fields and hills and sky for the eye; and for the ear the clickety-clack clickety-clack clickety-clack of wheels and rails.

Patches of snow that had lain about a few weeks ago were melted and the sun shone, but it was a winter sun and the trees knew better than to take the least notice of it. They were dead to the world . . .

She stopped herself because this giving trees and fields – giving *things* – thoughts and a language was all very well in writing stories. You are not in a story, Katya, she told herself (taking for herself a story-like name, however); you are in the real world, and you want to make a better fist of it this time.

But this didn't work either. The thought of her French soldier came back – Francis Carco, not just a soldier but a writer, a poet, with a novel published that lifted a lid on some of Paris's dark and secret places. And he was a friend of Colette's! Oh heavens, imagine if she too could become Colette's friend: it was an absurd idea, and one that ought to make no difference at all to the value she placed on Carco's love, but it did. Colette's novels more than spoke to her; they whispered in her ear. There was something about them, intimate and direct, that she could find nowhere else.

She repeated to herself a phrase from Carco's latest letter – "*Je vous aime chaque jour d'avantage.*" "Every day I love you more." But *vous* not *tu* in what was, after all, a love letter? – and for several hundred clickety-clacks she escaped into thoughts about the subtleties of the French language. She remembered the rule: an intimate statement would be *tu*, not *vous* – but evidently not always. This *vous* seemed formal, literary perhaps, certainly respectful – *propre*. He was signalling (she decided) that he was not treating her, or their growing intimacy, as *easy*, something to be taken for granted. She remembered in Paris hearing a husband and wife addressing one another as *vous* but not in a tone that had been in the least cold. She would ask Jack about it.

No of course she would *not* ask Jack. Another habit to be broken.

It was necessary just for a moment (and a moment, she knew, was all she could sustain) to switch off emotion – all of it, shut it down – and ask herself what on earth it was she wanted. What was her purpose? Why this obsession with Carco, Jack's friend really, who had not impressed her so very much when they had, all three, been in Paris? But his image had remained with her, growing like some mad overfed weed in the garden of her mind, while he wrote letters that had become (in response, she had to acknowledge, to the warmth of her own) increasingly love letters – no other way of describing them.

"*Kathérine, je ne veux que vous. Vous êtes et vous serez toute ma vie.*" "I want only you. You are and will be my whole life." It was a bit much, a bit hard to swallow, though she'd swallowed it happily on first reading. She'd told him she was in love with him – had told Jack too – but how could she be? There was so little to build upon: only those Paris memories of a charming Frenchman, not tall, not quite handsome – perhaps what the French would call "*joli-laid*": appealingly ill-favoured.

Witty, amusing, knowing, clever, a writer like herself, and like herself from the South Pacific, so they had been able to reminisce (excluding Jack who, however, seemed incapable of jealousy) about warm beaches and wild coasts, she pretending that New Zealand was "one of those islands", spoken of in the same breath as semi-tropical New Caledonia.

It must be because I want an adventure, she told herself; want copy. I'm a predator – am I? But so is he.

But if that was true, it wasn't all. Why, if it were no more than her old search for sensation, had she felt guilty, unfaithful, when she and Jack made love two nights ago? In the dark she'd tried to imagine it was Carco, not Jack at all, but that had only made the infidelity seem worse.

She had *submitted* – that was the word she'd heard Jack use of her, speaking to their friend Campbell. He'd meant, she thought, that when they made love these days it was only because he wanted to – and that was true. It wasn't that she ever felt it as an invasion, or unpleasant. It was easy to submit, just as it was easy to have cake pressed on you when really you weren't hungry. But she had not felt for Jack – not for a long time – the strong desire she felt when she'd thought, in these recent weeks, of Carco. So she'd submitted; but it had been, each time, what she thought of as the *adieu* submission. She made love to Jack always thinking, This might be the last time – and if it is, *I won't care*.

But now she remembered another recent time when she and Jack had made love and then had lain together in silence, she feeling that they were saying goodbye, separating, but loving one another more rather than less because of it. And then she'd asked what he was thinking and he'd said he'd been imagining Lawrence telling him she was gone for ever, and that he'd accepted it and not felt the expected anguish. From the way he told this she could see that he had no idea how painful it was to her, how disillusioning.

There was a hunger in her for something more expansive than her life with Jack. It was like the novel he was working on, *Still Life*: every time he mentioned God, or his hero's soul, or "the truths of the spirit", she felt the walls closing in. It wasn't that he was a "believer" in any of the orthodoxies – not devoutly anyway. He was just devoutly *serious* – about what he thought might be "inside" things, and especially inside himself. There was a whole other world out there, a world of people and things, plants and animals, of "trees and stones and books in the running brooks", and Jack wouldn't look at it.

These were uncomfortable thoughts, accompanied by strong twinges of pity for him, and guilt. She could be resolute when she thought of him as in some way authoritative, her lover, senior, the Man. But when she focused too long on his failings, and his image shrank to boy-size, to brother or (even) child, then up rose the loyal Katherine, the fierce protector, the mother. She wept for him, hated herself for her own cruelty, and wanted only to shield him.

She should have been helping him as writer, encouraging him, as unfailingly he helped and encouraged her; but the pages of *Still Life* he'd read to her were so laboured, humourless, *boring*, they made her want to mock; they made her *angry*, as if by writing badly he was letting down the side. They made her anxious, thinking her own aspirations to write fiction might be as ill-founded as his.

That was why, despite the turmoil, the furious arguments and absurd sentimental reconciliations of their friends D. H. Lawrence and Frieda, it had been reassuring to have them nearby; to be part of a community with them. Because Lawrence on the page, or talking about writing, was real, powerful. He was mad – perhaps congenitally, perhaps driven mad by Frieda and by the wartime harassment and surveillance he was subject to on account of having a German wife. But he was a writer as Jack would never be.

So they'd had their little community at Cholesbury – the D. H. Lawrences close at hand in one cottage, the Gilbert Cannans in their windmill nearby; other friends – Freddie Good-year, Rupert Brooke, Koteliansky, the Gordon Campbells – coming and going. They'd had their "great Dostoevsky nights" when Campbell told her she was "at her worst" because she always out-quoted and out-argued him. There had been their long exchanges with the Lawrences about men and women and sex, sometimes absurd, often solemn, sometimes funny, occasionally enlightening – but *free*, no holds barred, the kind of serious talk she'd always craved. And they had their own writing, and talk of writing.

Yet still here she was running away from it, not following their friends in their move to Sussex, as Lawrence wanted, but going in pursuit of the Frenchman whom the mocking part of herself was already calling "my Napoléon", and "the little Corporal".

What was wrong with her? There was no answer; or there were many answers. There was the war for example. Did that explain it? She looked up at the swaying compartment and of course there were uniforms, two of them, two moustaches, two caps, two long coats – officers carrying with them the mysterious knowledge of what it was like, *really* like, "at the Front". If she'd been a man she would have wanted to go, to be part of it, to find out, to experience the fear and exhilaration and triumph over self – if that was what it was (and why did they never say?). For a moment she amused herself, first with the idea of asking them ("Excuse me, gentlemen, but do tell me, *What is it like at the Front?*") and then with the fantasy that "*at the Front*" was a fiction, nothing more than a secret society, a club where soldiers went and met with the enemy, and joked about civilians, and together made up stories, all linked together into one big story called "the Great War", which they brought home and pretended to be reluctant to tell, so friends and families and neighbours and reporters had to squeeze hard to get a few drops from the lemon of their secret and unspeakable experience.

She remembered the excitements of those first days of war when they had wandered about the streets of London believing they were living in something called History – a war that would involve (so it was said) many millions of men; feeling, even, that there was Right on their side, Justice in their cause, because England's declaration stood not only for solidarity with *la belle France* but more, for the defence of "little Belgium", a child in a fairy story invaded by the Giant Hun.

Then, for a time, excitement had turned to alarm when it seemed that France might be lost; that this might be 1870 all over again. The German army had got to within thirty miles of Paris, and the Kaiser announced he would spend his birthday there. But his birthday passed, the invasion was stopped, even pushed back in places, and now the war seemed stalled for ever along that line referred to always as "the Front".

Francis Carco (she liked to say his name giving her Parisian r, and the final syllable, full measure) was a soldier. He was in "*la zone des armées*" where only soldiers and residents were permitted. I'll do the impossible, she'd thought; I'll go there. She'd meant it too, though she didn't believe she would succeed.

The train was pulling into Paddington, and almost at once she saw her brother Leslie, searching for her in the crowd pouring out on to the platform. She held back a moment, watching him through the glass. How fine he seemed to her – still the little boy she'd known with their mother's sleepy eyes and wavy hair, but now a handsome 21-year-old, here in London because he'd resolved not to be an Anzac soldier but to join up with a British regiment. He'd been accepted for officer training and would soon be going to Oxford to take his course.

His serious young face broke into smiles as he picked her out. She embraced him. "Do I embarrass you if I tell you, little brother, that you've grown into a very good-looking fellow?"

"Flattery? I can stand it if you can."

"Oh but I'm telling the truth."

"Well, if it's truth you want I'll have to drop the routine compliments and just say you're a fascinating creature and a pleasure to look at."

"That will do," she said. "Thank you. Now follow me and stay close."

She found them a Lyons Teashop not far away and they settled in a corner. She ordered a pot of tea, and cakes which she knew he would like, and would pay for.

"Have you written?" she asked, meaning to their parents in New Zealand. It was something they'd discussed already.

"I told them you and Jack have an assignment in Paris. Oh, and while I remember . . ." He took two banknotes from his wallet. "You're sure ten pounds is enough?" It was to pay her fare and for her few days in Paris.

"It's more than enough, and awfully generous. I'll see you get it back."

He shrugged. "When these stories you write from France make you rich and famous."

"You didn't tell them I was borrowing . . ."

"Of course not, Katie."

"It's just that if you did they mightn't believe the story about Paris."

"The story . . . Oh." He thought about this. "But there is an assignment."

She put her hand over his where it lay on the table. "No there isn't, Bogey." Did he mind if she called him by his old pet name? It seemed he hadn't noticed. She hadn't meant to tell him the truth, but she'd been uncomfortable lying to him – especially lying and taking his money. "I made that up."

He shrugged. "So you're going on spec. Freelance. You hope to . . ." His voice trailed away, not sure what she might hope to do, and finding no confirmation in those sibling eyes.

"I'm going alone. Jack's in Cholesbury. I hope to meet my lover."

"Your lover. I see." His tone was neutral, his expression stern, a very youthful headmaster, perhaps, who felt he'd been taken advantage of.

"He's French," she said, reacting to the headmaster, thinking (not without a certain relish), that that might make it worse. And then, to make the worse a little better: "A soldier."

"You told me you and Jack . . ."

"Were more in love than ever. I know. I'm sorry. It's not true. I think it's all over between us. We've had three idyllic years . . ." She felt tears start and saw that Leslie saw them; but he didn't respond with sympathy. She dabbed her eyes and sat up straight. "You won't tell the parents."

19

"I didn't come all this way to spy for the family." His tone was reproachful. And then pompous: "I came because there's a war to be fought."

"I've offended you."

"No I don't think so. But evidently you don't trust me . . ."

"Evidently I do, Boge, or I wouldn't have told you now." They looked at one another. "Listen," she said. "I knew you wouldn't find it easy lying to them. So *I* lied to *you*. I'm better at it. I've had more practice. Now you've written the letter and I'm telling you the truth. See? Trusting you with it."

He nodded. Yes he did see, though whether he saw the reason was less certain, and perhaps it was better if he didn't, since the reason was unworthily financial. Six years ago, pregnant, Katherine had married George Bowden only to provide respectability for herself and legitimacy for the child that was not his – then had walked out on him without explaining herself, after which she'd gone to Bavaria where there had been a miscarriage, so the Mrs Bowden manoeuvre had proved unnecessary. I put the i-s-c into marriage, she said to herself, but not to anyone else. The pain of it all, including the loss of the child which, despite her circumstances, she had very much wanted to have, had hardened her.

Their mother knew – had come racing over (if those seven weeks by sea could be called racing); had in fact travelled with her to Bavaria, put her in a *pension* there, and left. How much she had told the father Katherine wasn't sure; but both parents knew she was now living with Jack Murry "out of wedlock", intending to marry him once a divorce from Bowden was achieved. Already she suspected, from hints dropped during that hideous and quarrelsome sojourn in Germany, that she might have been cut out of her mother's will. She depended on an allowance from her father. That too might be cut off if they learned of her present adventure.

So she'd told Leslie what she wanted her parents to hear.

"You didn't mention D. H. Lawrence, did you, Boge?"

Leslie shook his head. The cakes had arrived and his mouth was full.

"Not that they'd be likely to have heard of him out there, or be able to get their hands on his books. But one learns to be careful."

"Is he so shocking, Katie? His work, I mean. His books."

"Lawrence is brilliant," she said, and felt the tremor of her own enthusiasm. "But there's all this fuss about his frankness. Relations between men and women. He's ahead of his time, that's all. If our little mother knew Jack and I were friends with the Lawrences, it would just be something else to worry her."

"Is it true he ran off with his professor's wife?"

Katherine frowned. "Who told you that?"

"Aunt Belle." Leslie was staying with their mother's sister in Surrey. "She said you told her."

"Did I? Damn!"

He waited for her to explain.

"Frieda was married to a Professor Weekley. She's German. An aristocrat." He seemed impressed by that, and she wasn't able to resist adding, "She's like a big German cake, Bogey. Lots of butter and not a lot of brain."

He seemed to have got over the shock of discovering she'd used him to convey untruths to the family. The young head-master face was gone. He looked cheerful again, and in good appetite.

"I must say you do get up to all kinds of tricks, Katie."

"I'm forgiven?"

21

"Of course, darling."

They spent the rest of the day together, walking about London and talking about Wellington. It was as if each acted as the other's guide. She took him about in fact, he led her back in memory and imagination. That night, when she lay wide awake letting her mind take its own direction, it was as if she'd spent those hours in air fresh as the first Washday of creation, under high blue-and-white skies, seeing shirts and blouses filled to bursting by the Wellington wind, pegged out and tugging to get away from green gardens and white weatherboard houses which propped themselves against steepnesses that everywhere dived into the sea – into the beautiful harbour from which she'd sailed out seven years before. That was her past and she felt no need to return to it; but it helped free her of present bonds.

Next evening she wrote to Jack:

Dear Jack,

I'm going away to be with Carco. I know this will hurt you, but not very much really. (If I could be sure it would hurt you more I might have less reason for going.) I hope you won't magnify it because that would do no good and would only put us against one another, which neither of us wants.

And you mustn't think – perhaps you wouldn't in any case – that you have failed me. You haven't. Nor have I failed you. Sitting here looking out on the London night, considering, I know that I am not being rash or impulsive or even unfair to you.

Part of me says I should "explain myself" to you, but I might do it badly. Or I might do it well and still you might misunderstand – wilfully – and I would resent that. I want there to be no resentment between us. Let my actions speak for me, not my words. My actions *do* speak for me; and you do understand them, even if they give you pain.

You had better tell people quite frankly about it, but don't tell them more than is really necessary. I'm quite ready to face the music, but I don't see why it should be a brass band.

I don't know whether, or when, I will come back. If I don't I will send you a list of my things that I especially want you to send me, some of which I perhaps should have with me now. They will include the framed photograph of my family, of course, and the ivory-handled umbrella, that are in the panel drawer of my desk. Also the music in the piano seat. But more of that later.

Au'voir – or perhaps adieu. Who knows?

    I am your

      Katya.

A week or so later she was in Paris, in the Quai aux Fleurs on the Ile de la Cité. Carco had written to his concierge instructing her to give Katherine a key to his apartment, and the old woman (who perhaps was not so old, merely battered by a hard life) had looked at her with suspicion and, at moments, with a fierce, sidelong hostility, but had done as instructed, not daring to challenge the bold cold manner Katherine could adopt when it was needed. Money would have made a difference but Katherine had none to spare.

She'd had her hair cut short, and went about, collar turned up, in a Burberry with military buttons bought for this expedition, looking, she thought, like a little soldier. "You'll soon be at the Front," she told her reflection in a shop window. "And have no fear – I'll be at the Back."

She was excited to be in Paris again, but it was not all pleasure. Her responses were extreme. She was thrilled by the city's beauties, disturbed by its darker corners where the poor lurked and seemed to threaten an assault either on her mind (the women and children) or on her person (the men). At the Fountain of the Medicis in the Luxembourg Gardens she found herself weeping copiously and without cause. Notre Dame, so imposing from the outside, and which she had once visited in a spirit of reverence, seemed horrible, the forests of candles in its murmuring-echoey interior deeply sinister, its smell the smell of death, but faded, cold, as if death itself had died there a long time ago. The disappointed God, His tormented Son, the Son's grieving Mother, the variously wounded, tortured or suffering saints, looked down at her. Quite pointedly it was at her they looked, to her they pointed out their wounded heads and hearts. Old women in black headscarves humbled themselves and mumbled prayers and propitiations. Priests lurked in corners and looked at her with unfriendly eyes. Frightened, and embarrassed at her fright, she retreated to the street, breathed deep, and welcomed such light and air as the winter afternoon had on offer.

It was the time in Bavaria that came back to her in such moments – the same excitement at being in a foreign place, the same fear tending towards horror, the same longing for companionship and love, the same rebellious will to hit back at what hurt or disgusted her.

Her fears, she knew, were less real than those the soldiers faced not many miles away, but they faced theirs together. She was alone. It was a mood she accepted, couldn't reject, wouldn't run away from. It was what had produced her first book, *In a German Pension*, and now, desperate four years later that there should be a second, and somehow "blocked" from producing it, she accepted the discomforts. If they were necessary to the process, then so be it.

There was a café not far from Carco's apartment to which he had taken her and Jack and their friend Freddie Goodyear. She went there now with her *cahier*, found herself a corner table, looked, listened, silently practised her French, drank the purplish coffee (which made her slightly *drunk* – was that possible?), took note of everything – the dirty and ragged tricolour in the window; the waiter's too-long apron; the dry scrape of his fingernails as he scooped up her *sous*; his strangely sweet sweat-smell; the greasy cloth with which he wiped tables; the way he stood, when there was nothing else to do, as if posing for photographs of "the scene of the crime". No one could have taken the role of waiter more seriously. But there was an element of theatre too, a hint of self-mockery.

At the *caisse* a pale thin woman sat with her back to the window and her head mostly turned to the street, watching the crowds go by. The light from out there seemed to shine, not around, but through her. Katherine noted her down as the Sometime Virgin, Mary. She laughed at that. What a difference a comma can make!

Next morning there was a letter from Carco. He had found a room in Gray where she could stay a few nights. He offered instructions and would wait for the train in the hope she could get through. But the town, he reminded her, was out of bounds to visitors. She would encounter obstacles, might have to talk her way through, risked being turned back, could even come under suspicion of spying. There was a risk for him too, but he would take it if she would. He loved her and wanted her and would be waiting.

She tried to read his letter with a certain disengagement. He was, and she knew it, a young soldier arranging for himself a *lit garni* – but with what elegance, what charm. If there was a dash of cynicism in the mix, she must forgive it, acknowledging that there might be a dash of the same in hers. Her decision was already made. She was wanted. It was war. She would go.

Carco's concierge seemed to guess what was going on and entered into the spirit of the adventure. Perhaps it was because she was glad to see "*la maîtresse de Caporal Carco*" (as Katherine had heard herself described on the echoing stairs) leave. Or was it because the *maîtresse* was going to give *bon courage* to a French soldier, and this patriotic self-sacrifice could only be applauded? Whatever the reason, the concierge woke her at six in the morning, had her *petit déjeuner* ready, and was watching as she departed along the *quai*.

Carts and drays were clattering on the bridges; a little tug hauling a line of sand-barges hooted up from the river; the fresh morning air opened up the stale rooms of her lungs. Down into the Métro she rushed and reached the Gare d'Austerlitz minutes before nine when her train was due to leave.

The journey was slow, with stops that seemed random, unscheduled. The countryside appeared waterlogged, glinting and shining under an unseasonably warm sun. Soldiers in the carriage leaned out and talked, when they could, to others working on the line or guarding bridges and canals. The exchanges were so rapid and so deep in the throat she could pick up only a word here and there; but they were cheerful fellows, and had no doubts about being on the side that would win. Even the wounded sitting in the sun outside a hospital waved their bandaged arms at their comrades, exchanging shouts and smiles. War, it seemed, was no bad thing.

She saw a platoon of German prisoners, fifteen or twenty in ragged overcoats, shuffling along a country road under guard. In Bavaria she had whipped up a great dislike of Germans and had mocked them in her book; but that had been another time, another place, a different story. She was glad if the war was going to be quickly won. She hoped these poor fellows would be sent home soon to their wives and mothers.

The train pulled into Châteaudun just after one. There was time for coffee and a croissant.

The train for the little town of Gray, was smaller, slower. The woman opposite her in the compartment watched her, curious. She appeared harmless, but her interest, those glances that seemed to invite conversation, made Katherine anxious. She preferred for the moment not to speak, not to have her foreign accent noted.

She kept her head down, reading and re-reading the letter that was supposed to explain and excuse her journey. Carco had written it for her. It came from her "aunt" in Gray who was ill and longed for a visit from her *chère Kathérine*. It had the right postmark, but she wouldn't herself have believed it. Weren't girl-friends often caught trying to get through to see their soldiers?

They pulled into the station. Those not in uniform were directed to line up in the waiting room. Two officers sat, each at a table, checking papers and reasons for being in the War Zone. Very imposing they looked with their whiskers and their Turkish cigarettes. When Katherine's turn came she presented her passport and the letter. She did her "pretty" smile and thought it probably looked, as it felt, like a grimace of pain.

"You are English," the officer said, speaking in French. "And your aunt is French?"

"My uncle is French," she replied, and restrained herself from saying, And that is *la plume de ma tante*.

"Ah, your uncle." Yes, he saw the point of that. "So your aunt is English. But why then did she not write in English?"

"Why not indeed, *mon Colonel*. She has lived here a very long time."

He was not a colonel, and he liked it that she addressed him as one. Still he wasn't satisfied, and took her passport to the other, who glanced at it, stared at her, decided (she thought) that she was quite passable to look at, and clean enough to be let loose on the soldiery of France. She was waved on in a manner that seemed to say, Don't imagine for a moment, young English lady, that we are fooled.

And he was there, Francis Carco, in the road outside the station, looking indeed like Napoleon at the gates of Moscow, waiting for her and pretending not to be. He was in his uniform and carrying a postman's bag. That was his job in the army – postman to a unit that baked his regiment's bread. It was not glorious, or didn't seem so to one raised in the British tradition. But who could say? The French took bread so seriously, and letters hardly less so.

As instructed in his letters she behaved as if she didn't know him, only slowing as she approached but not looking at him. Under his breath he sang, "Follow. There's a cab."

She followed.

He stopped, stood aside, letting her go by. "Up there beside the house. By the toll bridge."

She walked on towards the cab and climbed in. He followed, getting in on the toll-house side, hidden from the road. The driver, under prior instruction, whipped the horse away. The doors flapped like elephant ears. Katherine reached for one,

Carco for the other, and they slammed them shut.

Through the town streets now, at a fast clip, Carco sitting on the floor out of sight (soldiers were not supposed to travel by cab) while Katherine sang,

> "Down the road
> Away went Polly
> With a step so jolly
> That I knew she'd win."

He had to return to his duties but there was time to introduce her to her landlady and see her safely to the room he'd taken in a house not far from the barracks.

"*Bienvenu, mon bébé*," he said, kissing her when the door was shut on them – a long kiss. And then, in his best English: "I will be back very soon, don't fear. This is just 'ullo and goodbye, *n'est ce pas?*"

"Oh yes, especially 'ullo," she replied, laughing at him, but also with relief, with happiness. She'd done it! She was with him. She was in the War Zone, one where (even better) no war was apparent – no broken houses (such a nice suburban street, this one), not even the distant pounding of guns. In fact a few distant poundings would have been welcome, just to embellish the story she would tell her friends, and was already telling in her head.

It was a pretty room, simple, white, with mignonettes (the flower) on the wallpaper, mignonette (the lace) around two enormous square pillows that lay over the bolster, blue daisies on the clock's big homely face, wallflowers in the garden outside the window. The sun was shining. She wanted to write to Jack and tell him of her triumph – but how could she write to say that running away to be with another man was making her happy? Still she drafted a letter in her *cahier* that would never be sent, calling him "Jaggle dearest" and feeling, as she wrote it, a tightening of the throat and the prickle of tears.

After that she wrote to Frieda. It was another letter that would probably not be sent, because Lawrence disapproved of her leaving, and had taken Jack's side. Besides, Lawrence was insane about the war and would think her behaviour frivolous. To tell him where she was might send him into one of his rages.

That evening, under a lantern in a restaurant that was really a barn, they dined on onion soup followed by a little dish of cold peppery sausage, then cutlets and *frites*, and finally *crème au caramel* – all of it served with one, then a second, carafe of the local *rouge*, most of which Carco drank. He talked, sometimes in English, mostly in French. She listened and was happy.

He spoke of his childhood in Noumea, of the fruit and flowers in the garden of the family house, the papaya and mango trees that shaded its verandah and the rooms at the front; of running wild with the native children; of palms thrashing and bending double and roofs lifting off in a hurricane; of swimming in glass-clear swelling and falling ocean-water among brightly coloured reef fish. He talked about the convicts on the island, the mixture of pity, fear and liking he felt for them as a child; about the family's "Kanaka" cook and servant, the freed-convict gardener, the maid who had come out from France to be near her convict husband.

Then, almost without pause, but as if that was enough nostalgia and romanticism, he told her that Paris was where he belonged; that he would never go back. *Jamais.*

"We are brother and sister," she said, thinking of Wellington. "One can't go back to childhood because it isn't there."

"Only in words," he said.

"Have you written about it? Will you?"

He shrugged and shook his head, very French, dismissive. By

30

"going back to it in words" he meant it was something to talk about, not to write about – not for him, anyway. His novel (like her, he had published just one book) was set in Paris, breathed Paris – especially Montmartre – its streets and cafés, its low-life characters, its weather. "Paris to me is what the Pacific was for Gauguin. It is my region of romance. It is what fires me to write. I can't imagine that will ever change."

"I know what you mean," she said. "But when you talk about the Pacific you make it sound new – even to me. You make it sound like a subject for fiction."

"Then *you* must write about it, *mon amie*. I give it to you. It's yours."

They spent the night talking (a great deal), making love (effortlessly, cosily), and, she supposed, sleeping, though it was never more than a half-sleep. She had not been mistaken about Carco. He was so at ease, natural, clever, entertaining. There was something feminine about him – not just his small neatly rounded body, his long curly eyelashes and soft wavy-brown hair, his particularity about washing and scenting himself and doing his hair, and the fine bangle he wore on his arm. In his personality he was not what she thought of as a "Pa-man" – one whose strong masculinity could make her love him against all the odds including her better judgment. But he was a man, one who knew how to please her in pleasing himself.

He hated the war almost as much as Lawrence did, though he spoke about it quite differently. It was folly, waste, incompetence, error – and consequent grief. He didn't take readily to the discipline, to accepting orders shouted at him by men he considered his inferiors. It made him angry, encroached on his freedom and his comfort. It was bad for Europe, and should have been avoided.

"But France must be defended," she objected. "Mustn't it?"

He shrugged – a huge French shrug that acknowledged the point, but grudgingly. "*Oui, bien sûr. Il faut la défendre.*"

They made love as (she thought) a brother and sister might if making love were something brothers and sisters did. This too reminded her of Bavaria – the good part of that bad time, when she and her Polish lover, Floryan Sobieniowski, had curled up together in a bed over which were scattered books of fiction and poetry in Russian, German, French, while he taught her mournful Polish songs, crooning them into her ear, and she sang, when it was her turn, the English songs of her childhood. Later, following her to London, Floryan had turned, first jealous lover, and then faintly sinister "old friend", visitor and sponger. But she couldn't forget it was his love had rescued her from the despair of that time; and he who had introduced her to the works of Chekhov – a double gift. With Floryan she had lived dangerously, and had lived to regret it. She was living dangerously now, with Carco, but this time, she told herself, it would be all right. She had learned. She would do better.

Carco too was a singer. He had street songs from Marseilles, gypsy ballads, songs he'd learned from the convicts in his childhood, popular songs of the moment, even some that were his own compositions. "My family name is Carcopino," he told her. "We are from Corsica. The Italian in me sings, the Frenchman writes. The French are only good for singing in church."

Her happiness persisted through the night and was with her in the morning, even though at some half-waking moment in the small hours it had come to her that what Carco felt for her was affection, gratitude, goodwill and good fellowship; that he was not, despite the protestations of his letters, in love with her

at all, and that (consequently? – she asked herself was it a consequence and was unsure) she was not in love with him. It was a
recognition which, she decided, cleared the air, made the whole
business between them simpler, cleaner. This was an adventure.
It was not an earthquake, not the destruction of the old city
requiring the building of a new.

When morning brought pale light back into the room, and
she could pick out the flowers, first on the wallpaper, then on
the clock face, it was she who was wide awake, she who nudged
and cajoled him to get out of the warm bed. He was tired, reluctant, said he was lazy, that he was unwell (she was not surprised
– he had drunk so much of that robust red), but he was persuaded
to let her, at the count of three, roll him out on to the floor
where – courageous, naked – he staggered to his feet, washed
and shaved in cold water, and put himself, piece by piece, back
into his blue and red uniform.

"*Au'voir ma petite.*" It was done. He was launched again.

He kissed her, waved from the door and was gone. She saw
him pass the window on the path to the gate. Off to war – and
he would be back at noon! The world had changed so little. It
was like being a wife, a Frenchman's wife. Her postman would
come home for lunch – and a little siesta perhaps?

Another day, another night, another day. The magic held. It held
too well. She basked in it, did not want it to end, did not want
to go back to awkward English Jack with his class consciousness,
his bow legs, his sensitive soul and laborious novel. It was their
talk – hers and Carco's – of books, of childhood, of the Pacific
then and of Paris-and-London now; of the future of the novel;
of the novels they, each of them, would write. It was the sense of
common ground and at the same time the foreignness. It was his

ease with her, his songs and puns – and a charm that seemed almost impersonal. It was the sex too, with its power to reach beyond physical limits, to compel. So she found herself beginning to think, failing to stop herself from thinking, might it not go on longer? For years? For a lifetime?

The question was out of bounds – she knew that. This had never been part of the contract. It was wartime. Carco was a soldier. Somewhere out there, if you went far enough, the silence would come to an end. There would be the boom of artillery, rattle of machine guns, glint of rifle barrels and bayonets; the groans of the wounded and the colour of blood. She had to believe in it, as one had to believe in death, or that the earth went around the sun. It was out there somewhere, the war, and at any moment he, her little corporal, postman to an army of bakers, might be caught up in it.

Or was all that (if that indeed was what he would say) just an excuse, an evasion? Hadn't he written saying that he loved her, that he wanted her, and only her, in his life?

They were in the barn again, their favoured, indeed their only, restaurant ("*sympa*", he called it), where the boy who ran about doing little jobs, and the woman who waited on the tables, and the chef who appeared at the door to the kitchen, late, when the rush was over, all greeted them warmly, personally, on some French principle that three days established a "regular".

Somewhere between the *plat du jour* and the day's variation on *crème brûlée* that was to follow, she asked did he love her and he said (of course – what else?) that he did.

She asked what it meant and he said it meant she was very dear to him.

But what did *that* mean she asked, and he asked what did it mean to her.

34

She said it might mean something about the future, and he cast his eyes to the ceiling and sighed.

If he had only sighed and (for example) looked down at his hands on the table – it would not have mattered; it might have suggested sadness – as if to ask what, in such times as these, could one say about the what-was-to-come? But eyes cast towards the ceiling – that was quite another matter. That spoiled it all; ended the idyll. She could not forgive his eyes – would never forgive them.

"You're bored with me," she said.

He said he was not, but it was spoken without conviction.

"Your voice."

"My voice?"

"Bored. Exasperated. I know that voice."

No. He insisted not.

She said, "You can tell me the truth. I'm not a child."

He shook his head. "Such questions, they . . ."

"Bore you."

"A man is what he does. You can see what I am. I am a man who loves you."

"In the night – in bed."

"In the night and in the morning and in between." He smiled very nicely. She should have left it there, but she couldn't. "Please, Francis . . ."

"These inquisitions," he said. "Why do women do it?"

Women. To use that word was a mistake, almost as unforgivable as the eyes cast towards the ceiling. It meant (or so she argued) that for him she had passed already into a category. She was a woman, one of many. One of his women. Yes, he was bored.

The quarrel, or debate (because at times it took an intellectual turn) went on through the night. They half made it up, made love (and not half-heartedly – rather well in fact), and returned to it. In its latter hours he dozed in the long intervals when she was talking. Finally he was answering in his sleep.

Next morning she planned to say just one thing to him. It was something that had come to her in the dark, bitter hours of his sleep: "To me, Carco, you have been a drug, a poison. Fortunately you are also the antidote."

But – whether because it was unjust, or too studied – in the full light of morning she decided in favour of silence. It was he who spoke. "*Ecoute*, Kathérine. I am sorry that I have disappointed you. I want to say that you have not disappointed me."

She'd resolved that she would not speak to him again – not ever; not in this life or the next – if there should be a next, and if they should find themselves in the same place, which she allowed herself to think unlikely. That was how she'd put it to herself as the sun had begun to pick out the flowers on the clock face – and she stuck to it, but with difficulty. "Your little speech was very charming," she wanted to say, with heavy irony; but she only thought it – and reproached herself. He had made her a very nice compliment, which almost made up for the fact that he had not fallen in love with her.

At the post office she found it was still possible to send a telegram to England. She sent one to Jack. The tone was peremptory – but why not? If Jack had only stirred himself, had stood up for his rights instead of behaving like a doormat . . .

She stopped herself there. If Jack had been more decisive she might not have had this adventure which in the long term, when the pain had gone, it would be hard to regret.

She would be coming home (the message told him), travelling all day to Paris and on to Dieppe, and taking the night crossing.

She would be at Victoria in the morning. She would be grateful if he would please meet her there. But he should not assume she was returning to him. That was something yet to be decided.

TWO

Spring 1915 – Katherine

THREE WEEKS LATER SHE WAS AT THE FERRY RAIL AGAIN, CROSSING the Channel on the night sailing, Folkestone to Boulogne, looking out over the black oily-calm swell, and up at a misty drizzle floating like fine gauze curtains through the rigging lights. She had come on deck from the Ladies' Cabin. Later she would try to sleep, stretched out on one of its hard, sprigged couches; but for now it was too cosy down there, too many hats and skirts and boots and boxes, too much feminine chatter and fuss, everything being disassembled for a night that would not last until morning. She was glad to be out in the air, excited to be alone and to be travelling again. She was afraid – there was always fear, but not too much this time; just enough to make her feel alive, quick, alert.

Jack had seen her off at Victoria. It was all over with Carco. She was clear about that, and had even written him a thank-you letter. "Thank you for having me," she'd written, almost certain he would recognise the double entendre. The thanks were genuine, and the apology that went with it; but she'd wanted also to ask whether his offer that she could use his apartment in Paris was still open.

"Forgive my high dudgeon," she'd written, and then crossed it out. His English wasn't up to that. "Forgive my marching out and hardly saying goodbye. The truth is, *mon cher*, you have only yourself to blame. For a man whose intentions are strictly limited to the moment and the matter in hand, you make yourself altogether too charming; and parting's 'sweet sorrow' is something I never had much talent for."

She'd regained her composure and could write that, more or less truthfully. She and soldier Carco (postman Carco) were an episode, something to be enjoyed, not to be spoiled by demands for more. She'd gone to him wanting not to love but to be loved. It wasn't easy to achieve. She had failed again, briefly, but she'd recovered.

Carco, of course, was incapable of switching off the vocabulary of seduction even when there was no serious intent. He had written back saying that he missed her; that she was the summit of his *escalier d'amour*, and so on. But on the matter of the apartment he'd been all specifics and generous practicality. It was hers whenever she should want it after 20 March, the date when a friend who had it at the moment would be leaving. He would instruct the concierge to expect her, and give her any help she might need. In the same letter he'd told her it was possible he might soon be sent to Turkey, though he didn't want to go, and would resist if he could, possibly by seeking a transfer to a different regiment or even to another service.

So she was able – or she hoped she was – to return to Paris now without upsetting Jack any further. Since her return from Gray they'd slept in separate rooms. She'd wanted to be back with him, not for the sex (though that might have been nice) but for the reassurance; but she'd thought she should wait to be asked. It was possible that Jack wanted it too, but hadn't the courage to suggest it. On the other hand he might have been punishing her. With Jack you couldn't be sure. Why had he made so little fuss about Carco? He was attached to her, she sometimes thought, not because he wanted to be, but because that was where he found himself, and anything so decisive, so demanding, as a break would have been beyond him.

She stared up at the stars which flickered through a thinning of the mist and cloud that had persisted since London. Thinking of Jack like this made her love him again. She loved him best when they were apart. She could feel it already, invading, taking control. She could see him breaking a brioche in half when they'd had coffee at Victoria, padding the doughy centre with two fingers. It was something he did with buns too, his head slightly on one side. It was so *him*, so utterly *Jack*, she had to go back indoors to escape from it.

All was tranquil now in the Ladies' Cabin, some women sitting in comfortable chairs dozing or holding murmured conversations; others stretched out on the couches. She found a space in a corner and settled there under her Burberry. Sure she would not sleep, she fell asleep almost at once. When her own coughing woke her some hours later it was 4 a.m. and she heard the stewardess, coming down from the deck, saying that a British destroyer was signalling the All Clear, that the mist had cleared and the French coast could be made out.

Katherine washed her face, tidied herself, brushed her hair (still short from the military cut she'd chosen for her visit to Carco) and went on deck again. She loved this time of day, before even the first of the light arrived, but when you felt it was there in the wings, waiting. Everything seemed washed, renewed, young. She could just make out the town of Boulogne, the meagre lights and the outline of hills behind.

Down on the wharf uniformed officials moved about the area where the gangway was just now being hoisted to the lower deck. She went down, carrying her bag.

"*C'est tout, Madame?*" the Customs man asked.

"*C'est tout, Monsieur*" – and he chalked his mysterious squiggle and waved her on through the wide echoing shed and towards the station platform where she found the buffet and bought herself coffee.

Soon she was climbing aboard the train, finding a comfortable corner in the tall, padded carriage, exchanging friendly remarks with her fellow-passengers. There was the stationmaster's wave of his little red flag, the whistle-blast, the last banging of doors, the grinding of reluctant iron, and they were edging away from the platform.

She settled back to watch the sun come up over the wide fields of France, seeing it already beginning to strike on the stripped white upper branches of birch and willow along the edges of the track.

Not many days later she was sitting in the Café d'Harcourt with Beatrice Hastings, now living in Montparnasse and writing for *The New Age* in London a Paris column which she signed Alice Morning. They had known one another first when they were both writing for that paper, and Beatrice had been the editor's mistress. Katherine from New Zealand, Beatrice from South Africa – they'd egged one another on in their pose of toughness and wit, saying, and sometimes believing, that they were the two cleverest young women in Britain.

Beatrice was explaining now that she had just ended an affair with an Italian painter and was starting one with a Spaniard. The Italian's name was Amedeo Modigliani (she called him Dedo) and the Spaniard, Pablo Picasso. "Pablo is more exciting," she said, "but it won't last. He doesn't understand my jokes, but when he begins to, he'll be off."

41

Katherine knew a little about M. Picasso. When Jack had been editing his first literary magazine he'd got permission to include one of his sketches as an illustration. "Isn't he becoming famous?" she asked.

Bea shrugged. "People buy his work. He's very attached to me. An excellent lover." She closed her eyes. "Dedo may kill him of course. Dedo's violent and jealous." She considered a moment. "Yes, it could happen."

Beatrice had been an exquisite creature and was still delicately beautiful, like a fine work on paper just starting to fade from too much exposure to light.

"For an orderly woman, Bea, you lead a very disorderly life."

Katherine had visited her apartment and found it charming – two spacious rooms, both opening on to a small yellow-gravelled courtyard with shrubs and flowers in pots and baskets; everything tidy and tasteful. She had also been shown the wooden bed-head with its carved notches representing, or so Beatrice claimed, her count of lovers.

"Disorderly?" Beatrice waved that away. "Weren't we always said to be alike?"

She held up her straw handbag. "This is Pablo's work." The picture painted on its flat outer surface suggested a table covered with a cloth, grey with a pattern of red stars, and on the cloth a dish of grapes and a glass of red wine. Picasso had written into the painting, so that it was part of the composition, the words "*En reconnaissance éternelle*".

"I don't know whether he's mad or a genius. But his colours . . . Just look at them, K. I'd make love to a horse if it could do colours like that."

"Is he a horse?"

They caught one another's eye and laughed. Bea said, "I think a cow really. Pablo has bovine eyes. Very soft, very beautiful."

She looked around the café, taking proper note of it for the first time. "You like this place, Katya?"

"D'you know why I suggested we come here? I'll tell you."

The story Katherine told was Jack's. This was the café he'd come to every evening when he was first in Paris, an Oxford undergraduate, poor (a scholarship boy) and out of England for the very first time.

"It's come up in the world since then," Katherine said. "Jack used to come here to look at the street girls. One, very bold and brassy, attached herself to him, but there was another he was really interested in. He used to let the brassy one pretend he was hers, but he was refusing to get into bed with her and – typical Jack! – dreaming about the one who looked young and innocent and vulnerable. Of course she can't have been innocent at all, and she soon got him. But he was a virgin, you see, and it took some contrivance."

Katherine hesitated, and then added by way of an aside, "I had the same problem when I first knew him. In the end I just said, 'Why don't you make me your mistress.'"

"Mistress." Bea repeated. "Very proper."

"This little Marguérite pretended to be ill and sent a friend here one evening to find him. He went immediately, thinking she must be at death's door – which I think might have suited him quite as well. She was in bed, and soon he was in with her. *Voilà tout*. Our little lad lost his clean sheet. But of *course*, Jack being Jack, he lost his head as well."

"Fell in love." Bea's voice was comically factual and grave.

"Fell in love," Katherine confirmed. "He used to go on to me about how much he'd loved her, how she took a job as a seamstress – a seamstress! D'you believe that? – it's so *literary*.

43

And how they might have married, but he abandoned her; the pain of it, the guilt, Paris, the intensity of young love . . . He tells me all this and of course it doesn't occur to him that I'm thinking, 'He never loved *me* like that.'"

"But Katya . . . First love and all that."

"Of course. Yes. Agonising. But you know . . ." She shrugged. "In matters of the heart . . ."

"Matters of the heart." Bea picked the phrase up and inspected it. "Your heart's got nothing to do with it, Katherine. I remember when you and Jack first crossed the Channel, you had another lover in tow. A young writer. Frederick . . ."

"Oh that was Freddie Goodyear. He wasn't a lover. He just wanted to be but he didn't know how to tell me. Yes, he tagged along with us. He used to come down and stay with us at Runcton too, before he went off to India. I liked Freddie very much. But he was too shy to make his move."

"You paid him a lot of attention."

"Did I? I suppose so. He was so quick and clever. He always laughed at my jokes."

"And now you've been unfaithful with Carco. Please don't tell me you're serious about Jack. I don't believe it."

"I'm serious. I *am*. I fall in and out of love with Jack. It's like learning to ride a bicycle."

After a moment she went on, "In any case, I'm here to write. I'm serious about that, too. I'm doing it. I've made a start."

Bea met her eyes, nodded, and looked down at her hands on the table. "You know what I think you should write."

"More in my *German Pension* style. No, I won't do it, Bea. I'm more ambitious than that."

"The road to hell is paved with literary ambitions."

"The road, yes. But satire's the short-cut. It's the laundry chute."

"Brilliant stories, Katya. I still laugh when I think of them. With this war, and anti-German feeling, haven't publishers been after you?"

"They have, yes. But I won't. No reprint until I've done something better. If I'm going to make my mark at all, it has to be the right mark, and the *German Pension*'s not it."

Katherine walked back to Carco's apartment that evening, made herself tea, and drank it watching lights reflected on the lovely curve of the river. She'd made her way home through back streets and alleys, where ugly people sold, or failed to sell, ugly used objects from stalls and tables. There was no letter from Jack and she stood at the window now, dry-eyed, telling herself that she didn't care, that it didn't matter. The sky was pure violet and the river had turned the colour of the violet's leaves.

She went back to her desk, read over the day's new pages, made a number of small revisions, and with difficulty persuaded herself not to go on writing. She would go to bed knowing exactly where she meant to take her story tomorrow. She would sleep with that knowledge, and even dream her fiction. Let her "unconscious" work on it, so in the morning it might take the pen from her hand (it happened sometimes) and seem to write itself.

The excitement of all this – it was such a long time since writing had come so fluently and seemed so good – made sleeping difficult. She took up a book and was reading in bed when she heard people running and shouting along the *quai*, and then the sirens sounding. She put out the light and went to the window, opening the shutters. Others in the building were doing the same. She could hear their talk, back and forth. As the sirens wailed, *doo-da-doo-da-doo-da*, the lights of Paris went out, a darkness sweeping away ahead of the incoming sky-ships like a giant shadow. The stars in a clear sky grew correspondingly brighter, and as her eyes adjusted, the people in the street and at the windows, who had seemed extinguished, came gradually back, all staring up where now a Zeppelin, a monster with silken grey fins briefly caught in the beams of two searchlights, sailed towards and high over them, silent at first, then audible, its motors drumming. A cloud with an engine! No one seemed to be running from it, as they were supposed to do, down into the cellars. They must all, she thought, be enchanted, as she was, by its size and its un-urgent command of the sky. Expecting bombs to fall, explosions, deaths, she stood there, waiting for them to start. None came and the great sky-whale sailed on and away into distance, replaced by the rush of fear that should have happened sooner.

Now conversations struck up in the darkness, window to window, window to street, and for a moment she felt a crazy love for France, the French, their language, their capital city.

As she settled into bed, turning on her side, drawing her legs up, pulling the blankets tight over her shoulder, it occurred to her that this was what the war, which in prospect had frightened her, was going to be: something very large, very terrible (who, after all, would want to float across the night sky hurling bombs down on innocent anonymous undifferentiated heads?) which would give her moments of terror – and then would sail on, leaving her untouched. Europe's "Moment of Destiny" would go on being uniforms in public places, bandaged limbs waved at her train, visits from her darling little brother; it would be Jack's anxieties and Lawrence's anguish, the arrival of "the wounded" at Charing Cross greeted by cheering crowds . . .

"The cheering crowds at Charing Cross." She said it over to herself, turning it into a chant, mere words, meaningless, full of sleep, or the promise of sleep. "The cheering crowds at Charing Cross, the cheering crowds at Charing Cross."

Her imagination returned to those dream-like characters she was creating in her new work, based on real people, family and friends in New Zealand, but who, as she imagined them, became separate from their originals in real life, became independent – aspects, perhaps, of herself – herself shared out and divided and made many, like the loaves and fishes . . .

"The loaves and fishes" she dreamed, smiling, and knew she was asleep.

Two months later she was still in Paris. The war had come nearer, had become more real to her, with "killed in action" lists appearing in the English papers, and with news that Australian and New Zealand forces had gone into action against the Turkish army in the Dardanelles. She was doing her best to keep it at arm's length. Leslie, still training near Oxford but soon to be at the Front, assured her he would be in no danger, and that it would all be over by Christmas.

It was spring. Lilac was everywhere, replacing the mimosa from the south that had earlier come into the markets. From her window she looked into, or down on, the trees of the Ile de la Cité, had seen the leaves *poussent* (as the concierge said) and grow, had watched the birds at work, building. She had made a brief return to London; but the consuming (perhaps extravagant – it didn't matter) love she now felt for Jack couldn't easily be sustained in a two-room flat where two writers, trying to stay focused on their separate work, broke in on one another's thoughts and moods. Maybe Jack could write his novel like that (she thought it no less awful now that she loved him better), and maybe later she would learn the trick herself; but for the moment she was best away; best alone. What she was writing was new for her; perhaps (she dared think) for anyone – and precarious. It had begun in Carco's apartment, and like a superstitious sailor she'd returned there. In this same chair, at this desk and window, with this view of Paris and its river still to be made out through and between the fresh green curtains spring was putting up, she would carry the work on until a first draft was complete.

But she was lonely. Invited to a party at Bea's apartment she went, hoping to meet new people. Pablo had been promised but didn't appear. Dedo lurched in, collapsed on one of the divans, talked incoherently, was taken aside by Bea, quarrelled with her and left.

"Too many drugs," Bea explained. "If I'd let him stay he would have taken off his clothes."

The others were neighbours, artists or poets, or friends of artists and poets. There was an art dealer, a Captaine Guillaume, very handsome and suave in his army uniform, who gave Katherine Turkish cigarettes and told her Beatrice (he pronounced it as in Italian) was cruel to Dedo and had no consideration for the effect she might have on his work. The poet Max Jacob, a tenant in the building, arrived with bags of shopping Bea had sent him to do for the party. He was small, bald, with dark eyes that seemed too large for the pince-nez he wore. "Where is God?" he asked Bea, unpacking the bags and standing on tiptoes to look over her shoulder into the room.

"He's coming, darling. Be patient."

"God is Picasso," Bea explained, aside to Katherine. "Max is in love with him."

"Is he . . ."

"*Tante*? Oh yes. *Très tante.*"

"And Picasso?"

"No. But he likes to be adored."

Soon Jacob was acting the clown, entertaining them all, reciting poems, his own and others'. One was about a rag-picker called Dostoevsky; another about Charlie Chaplin. He sang a song about a deeply sensitive lobster, and another with the refrain,

> *Ah quell' joie*
> *J'ai le téléphone!*
> *Ah quell' joie*
> *J'ai le téléphone chez-moi!*

He read Katherine's palm, predicting "a journey by sea and a storm of praise". Later, accepting at last that God was not coming, he was persuaded to do his imitation of the barefoot dancing girl, accompanying his extravagant pirouettes, swoops and dives with a humming high falsetto melody.

Bea played the piano and people danced. The music was, most of it, familiarly Viennese, waltzes and polkas, but with sudden variations into South American tangos and rumbas. A young woman standing beside Katherine where she sat listening and watching asked, "*Tu es mariée?*" It seemed to come out of nowhere, out of nothing. Yes, Katherine replied that she was. "*Et toi?*"

The woman replied without emphasis, "*Oui. Moi aussi.*"

There was a long silence before she said her name was Bert. Probably, Katherine thought, it was spelled Berthe; but Bert suited her better. She was dressed as a man, her beautiful face heavily powdered and made up in severe lines, her short thick blonde hair parted and slicked down. Her lipstick was black.

"Will you dance?" she asked.

Katherine waltzed. "It's because of the war," Bert explained. "One must." Katherine was not sure what was because of the war. Perhaps she meant the necessity of dancing. "*Tu veut dire qu'il faut danser?*" Katherine responded and got no reply. "*Faut danser à cause de la guerre?*" she repeated. Still nothing. Was her French suddenly unintelligible? Or was the concentration on the dance steps causing her partner's mind to short-circuit? Bert's intense serious stare – almost a glare – was too much. Katherine tried not to laugh, laughed, and Bert took offence. Bea stopped playing. "Why must you always be so superior, Katya? You see, you've made her cry."

Katherine apologised, to Bert, to Bea, to Bert again. "It's my head – and the war, of course. Wine and war. *Il faut rire.*"

She dropped into a chair. Bea resumed playing. Bert (or Berthe) sloped away to one side of the room and leaned against a wall, pouting at Katherine, unforgiving.

When the time came to leave Bea pressed her to stay. Katherine delayed, not wanting to upset her friend who seemed precarious. When the last of the guests had gone Katherine put on her coat.

"Stay," Bea said. And then, with intensity, "Please, Katya." It was out of character for her to plead.

Katherine explained. "Really, dearest, I must go. It's frightening out there after a certain hour. And there are the raids. They turn out the lights."

"Stay the night." She waved her glass at the other divan. Brandy sloshed on her dress. She made motions to wipe it away, and spilled more.

"I can't, Bea."

"Carco waiting is he?"

50

"Carco's at the Front."

"Your new lover, then."

"I don't have a lover. I have a notebook and a pen."

"*Merde*."

"I've made a resolution. My book's at a stage . . . I have to keep at it."

"Why are you so frantic, Katya?"

"What do you mean?"

"For fame."

Katherine asked, "Why aren't you?"

Bea was disconcerted. "Should I be?"

"Yes, foolish Virgin. *Yes!* And fame is *not* the point. Milton says 'Fame is the spur' but it's not. He says something else . . . How does it go? 'And that one talent which is death to hide / Lodged with me useless.' You have talent, Bea. I have it. We should use it. When I left London this time I said to Jack, 'I have to write this book or I'll die, and I can't write it here.'"

"Middle-tone bloody Murry," Bea mumbled, staring into her glass. A hard look had come into her face. "You're in a hurry to get your books written because you're afraid."

"I don't know what you mean."

"You know."

Now Katherine was disconcerted. Bea saw that she was, and laughed. "You think someone gave you a disease. You think you're going to go mad and die. Do a Maupassant. A Daudet. A Flaubert." She got up and staggered about the room, acting out, hamming up, what Katherine recognised as the last few moments of Ibsen's play, *Ghosts*, in which Mrs Alving watches her son Osvald going finally mad.

In a dead voice, "The sun, *the sun*." That was Bea being Osvald. Then she was Mrs Alving, shrieking, throwing herself about, tearing her hair: "I can't bear it. No, no, no. Yes! No. *No.*"

Then Osvald again: "The sun. The sun."

Katherine picked up her bag and headed for the door. Before it had slammed behind her she heard Bea shouting something about ovaries.

She blundered along the street, angry, tearful, uncertain where she was heading. What had she told Bea? There had been times when they were close, when she had thought of Bea only as her wicked, brilliant and beautiful older sister, and might have told her anything – secrets, intimate things. After the nightmare of Wörishofen and the miscarriage there had been an illness, an operation, hideous pain. Then strange symptoms, unpleasant things; and questions she didn't ask her doctors, embarrassed by the facts and apprehensive of the answers.

Of course she was afraid. At times the fear came right into her life, took up residence, disrupted her days and her nights and refused to go away; at others it withdrew, out of sight. But it was never not there; never gone absolutely.

She must not see Beatrice Hastings again. Never. Bea was two women, a clever angel and an envious devil. Alcohol was destroying the angel, and the devil was growing to fill the gap.

Katherine stopped on a corner, confused. A soldier came towards her and she turned away, not wanting her hesitation mistaken for something else.

"*Madame,*" he said, "*excusez-moi*, we met at the party of *notre collègue Ustings.* I thought . . . You are lost per'aps?"

It was the art dealer in officer's uniform – which he wore so well she'd thought of him as "dressed up". And yes she conceded, she was lost. She didn't tell him how much it amused her and lifted her spirits to hear Beatrice called "*notre collègue Ustings*".

"Then, *Madame,* you must let me call a *fiacre.*"

"*Merci, Monsieur.* You are very kind. *Très gentil.* But if I could just get my bearings, I can walk. L'île de la Cité – I thought it was straight up the Boulevard Saint-Michel."

"Ah, then you are facing the wrong way." He turned her about, pointing her in the right direction, and walked with her. He told her his name again, Paul Guillaume. They came to the river, crossed over and made their way to the Quai aux fleurs. At her street door she held out her hand to thank him and say goodnight. He took the hand. "But will you not invite me in?"

"For what purpose, Monsieur?"

He shrugged. "Shall we say . . . to look at the river?"

"Ah," she said. "The river. But we can see it from here. We're looking at it now."

"*Eh bien,*" he said. "Per'aps . . . to look at one another."

"You were waiting in the street for me?"

He spread his hands. "Is that so bad, Madame?"

"It's very flattering."

"No more than you deserve, Madame."

She explained that she had left at this hour, despite the protests of their colleague *Ustings*, because she needed a good night's sleep. She had work to do in the morning.

He assured her that making love helped one to sleep.

"Helps men," she said. "I've observed it many times. For women I think it often has the reverse effect. Hot milk and a little bread is much more effective."

Once again she thanked him and wished him goodnight. He kissed her hand and walked away, whistling. To press his case, even to show more than the mildest disappointment, would have been contrary to the code. He was a Frenchman, an officer and gentleman.

On the stairs she wished she'd asked whether his uniform had been supplied by the army or a fancy dress shop. The thought made her laugh. She was breathless and had to stop on the landing.

THREE

Late Summer 1915 – Leslie

LESLIE BEAUCHAMP, *COMMISSIONED OFFICER* BEAUCHAMP (SECOND lieutenant only, but you had to begin at the beginning) looked at himself one last time in the long mirror and then went to the window, considering. He was small, of course. That was true. He would have liked to be bigger, taller, stronger. But Napoleon (of whom he had recently read a biography, and who was often in his thoughts) had been short. Small stature, therefore, could not be seen as a barrier to military success. Still, Leslie would have been glad of longer legs, a stronger body (like his father's), a firmer face. The new moustache was fine and pale. It didn't stand out, but he felt it was an improvement; gave him something more like a look of authority; took away some of the resemblance to Katherine which everyone remarked on. Katie was lovely, but Leslie didn't want to be lovely; he wanted to be strong, handsome, manly, commanding.

There was no doubt he was fitter than he'd ever been, even in his days at Waitaki Boys' High, where the rugger-and-cold-showers routine had been designed to make men of them. During the eight weeks of the voyage from New Zealand he had walked the decks, eight to ten miles every day. And since his arrival in England and acceptance into the South Lancs Regiment, any ounces of fat remaining on his body had been replaced by muscle. Basic training, bayonet practice, rope-climbing, parade-ground drill, and above all the route marches with heavy pack along country roads and lanes – all this had given him superlative stamina.

Slowly the reflection of himself faded and was forgotten, replaced by the view beyond the window, the greenness of the London summer. He was not altogether new to London; had visited at seventeen with his family to see the coronation of King George. But the greenness of England's green, and its copiousness, still took him by surprise. It had been lovely in Oxford where he'd done his preliminary training as a bombing officer. After that had come Bournemouth, then Aldershot, and now a course on Clapham Common in south London, which was also a chance for him to stay with Katie and Jack Murry in St John's Wood.

Leslie went downstairs to the kitchen where Mrs Battle, the daily help, was making breakfast – porridge, bacon and eggs, fried bread. Mrs Battle, who "came with the house", "a fixture" included with the rent, arrived six mornings a week in time to make breakfast, and left after preparing lunch. Jack, who seemed afraid of displeasing her, left it to Katie to issue instructions, and took his revenge by referring to her when she wasn't about as "Mrs Bottle", "the Battleaxe" or "the Grim Retainer".

The kitchen was a long room, with windows at one end looking in the morning out on the cold shadow of the street, and at the other a bright conservatory in which vines grew up and across the inside of the glass, some out of pots, others that had found their way in from the garden through gaps under the glass. Already the full morning sun was coming in, causing the vines to give off their strange, not altogether pleasant, scents. Small green leaves and pink and yellow flowers had fallen in the night. They were scattered over the table, and Leslie brushed them to the floor so Mrs Battle, who cast him a tight smile of thanks, could get on with setting out the things she had brought to the table.

Jack Murry, Leslie now saw, was already in the room, standing by the street window, a book open, deep in his reading.

"Good morning, Murry," Leslie said in what he hoped was his officer's voice.

"Ah Beauchamp, you're here." Jack jerked to consciousness of the room, snapping his book shut. "And you see, as I said you would, you've brought us good weather."

"All my doing," Leslie acknowledged. "And what are we reading today?"

He heard his own father's voice and faintly patronising manner in the question, and winced at the imitation. But Murry heard only the question. "Still Dosty," he replied. Jack had a commission to write a book on Dostoevsky. "The longer you look the more mysterious and fascinating he becomes. You must try him."

Leslie nodded. "I must, yes." The name put him off. Dostoevsky. It suggested something challenging – and the books were very large. It was the kind of fare Katie would gobble up in a day. But that was Katie – and in Jack she'd found one of her kind. How the French soldier fitted in Leslie couldn't imagine and didn't ask. Katie had told him it had been "a wartime episode" and was over.

He went to the conservatory and looked out at the garden enclosed by a high brown-brick wall, part ivy-covered, and the tall, not altogether flourishing pear tree with a wooden seat underneath. Murry's plan was that they should play badminton there – he'd borrowed rackets and a net from friends. "That's as far as it will go," Katie had confided last evening as she and Leslie walked up and down the lawn, their arms around one another's waists, the ivy glittering under the moon and a breeze rustling in the pear tree. "With my dear Jack it's the thought that counts – alas!"

Afterwards, from his room at the top of the house – Katie's room in fact, but assigned to him when he visited – Leslie had lain awake thinking of her, not thinking so much as remembering, re-living her presence, and listening for the familiar sound of pears dropping, sliding down through the foliage and hitting the grass under the tree with a soft thud. They were not pears like the ones that had grown in their garden in New Zealand. These were London pears – like London people (or some of them) – that didn't seem quite to reach their full potential.

"A squirrel is on our seat," he told Katie as she came in.

She stood beside him at the glass, looking gravely out, her arm lightly brushing his. It was her way of repossessing him, by silent touch, or by a glance. He found it exciting. If there had been a girl in his life he would have liked her to be another Katie, fine and subtle and intelligent, one who would, without seeming to, take charge of him. That was how it was with their parents – the Mother, apparently so frail and indecisive, the Father such a Pa-man, so commanding and brusque, and yet the reality, when you knew how the family worked, entirely otherwise – she up on the bridge, steering the ship, he down in the engine room shovelling coal.

The squirrel twitched this way and that, as if electric shocks went through it. Between came moments of perfect, listening stillness. "He's dusting it off for us," she breathed.

"Shall I serve, M'm?" Mrs Battle asked.

"Please," Katie replied, moving away to make room for her, and steering Leslie with her. "I'm not used to being 'M'm'." She murmured this into his ear, a sort of tickling breath of sound that sent a ripple through his body. And then, "It won't last of course. Our fortunes are so rocky."

Their present affluence was because Jack had new work with the *Times Literary Supplement* – he was to be their reviewer of French books; and there was the commission to write the book on "Dosty". Thirty pounds for that – it would pay their rent for as many weeks. This much Leslie had been told; but he knew Katie's situation had improved also because their father had increased her allowance.

"I have the morning free," he reminded her.

"And I have every morning free, so there's no escape for you, Bogey."

They smiled at one another. They might walk up and down the lawn again; or stride out across Regent's Park, playing the "Do you remember" game. It was surprising, sometimes alarming, to discover how much was there, apparently forgotten but lying just below the surface. For Katie, he knew, it was more than a game. In Paris she'd been writing about their homeland, their family; and she'd read him, the other evening when she'd come to say goodnight to him, a fragment about Wellington, the wind, a girl's music lesson, a ship sailing out of the harbour which she said might be his ship, or hers. It was unfinished – something still being worked on. He'd found it vivid and exciting.

"Did I tell you?" Jack said as they sat down to their porridge, "the last tenant here was an opera singer. A tenor. He used to swallow a great many eggs. Raw. That's right isn't it, Mrs Battle?"

"'e did, sir," the Grim Retainer confirmed. "'e was a very nice gentleman. Very sensitive."

Katie laughed. "Well you must be glad of the change, Mrs

Battle." She left that hanging a moment before adding, "I mean of course that Mr Murry eats his eggs cooked."

They spoke of the latest news, inconclusively, because the news was inconclusive, as it always was. The war had lasted exactly a year and it was not going well for the Allies, especially since the Germans had begun using poison gas. The casualty lists were growing – so alarmingly Katie refused to look at them or to speak about them. Italy had come in at last against its old ally Germany. Little was said about the campaign in the Dardanelles – so little it seemed it must have failed. And now there was rejoicing in Berlin at the fall of Warsaw. In France the line was holding, more or less; there were even gains now and then, but always at a high cost, and never with an outcome that could be called decisive.

All this Leslie knew. There was no comfort in it. Yet he was keen to go, to experience it, to discover what it really meant. The worse the news seemed the more intense the fear, yes, but also the excitement. He had read in that life of Napoleon that an army going into battle, even against impossible odds, holds together because each man believes he will survive. Leslie knew that feeling. He believed he would survive.

"Tell me about these bombs," Jack said.

"No please don't." That was Katherine, but Jack wasn't put off. "You chuck them, do you?"

"Pull out the pin, hold the spring down with the thumb, throw with a round-arm motion . . ." He demonstrated.

"Like a bowler," Jack said.

"As you let it go the spring's released and that gives it ten seconds to get into the other chaps' space and blow him up before he can do anything about it."

"Does it blow him up?" Katherine asked.

"To bits, yes."

She winced and looked away into the garden.

Jack put down his knife and fork. "But look here, if these things are whizzing back and forth from one set of trenches to the other . . ."

"Not possible," said the young bombing officer. "Space between's too wide."

"So their use is limited."

"Yes. Night raids across no man's land. Attacks – when infantry go over the top. That kind of thing. This war's developed its own rules – a bit like chess."

"Perpetual stalemate isn't it?"

Leslie smiled. "So far, perhaps. That won't continue."

He said it in a voice that suggested he knew something that couldn't be divulged and that he mustn't be questioned about – and then looked down at his plate because it wasn't true. He knew scarcely more than they did by reading the papers. He caught Katherine's quick appraising glance. There was silence while they went on with their bacon and egg.

But then: "The round-arm throw . . ." Jack had stopped eating. "That seems a bit rum. I mean . . . I'm thinking of those cricketing chaps who can send a ball rocketing in from the boundary, straight into the keeper's gloves. Surely a conventional throw would send it further."

"Not permitted," Leslie said.

That interested Katherine. "Not permitted so you don't do it? Does no one explain?"

"When there's a rule in the army you don't break it and you don't question it." He said this with a kind of jaunty truculence. His loyalty to the army was strong.

"Ours not to reason why," Katherine said.

He changed tack. "If you think of a cricketer's bent elbow

throw," he said, "there's an element of *flick* in it. That's where it gets its pace. It travels further and faster, but that kind of throw would also shake up the mechanism rather violently. Your bomb might travel further and not go off. I've also heard it said they're unstable. Not in the manuals. But chaps say . . ."

"Unstable," Katherine repeated it. "Hell, Bogey."

"It just means you take extra care. And if you're told to stick to the stiff-arm throw, you stick to it. My job's to teach the lads how to use the wretched things safely."

"Safely for you and unsafely for the other fellow."

"Poor him," said Katherine.

That morning he walked with her to St John's Wood High Street. She wore a dark blue dress and matching beret, with dark red stockings given her, she said, by Frieda Lawrence. They took tea before walking to the churchyard where they sat among the gravestones.

"Do you remember . . ."

He was enchanted by her, in love with her, as he had been on that earlier visit, when she'd provided him with a means of escape from their mother's anxious vigilance by inviting him to stay with her, and then by giving him a latchkey so he could come and go at will making his own discovery of London as she had done at an even younger age. Much of her life had been concealed from her family, but she'd let him in on some of her secrets. There were lovers, dangers, triumphs and disasters. She was a writer, an artist, and had to live the free life, had to experience everything, had to know the world in order to write about it. He accepted this because she was Katie. She was special, the brilliant wayward ungovernable one who made her own rules.

In those days her flat in Gray's Inn Road had been "Japanese", with bamboo matting, paper lanterns, Utamaro prints, a stone statue of the Buddha, a bowl of water containing small bronze replicas of salamanders. She burned incense sticks and sometimes wore a kimono indoors. In her bedroom she'd worn nothing at all – the first naked adult female body Leslie had ever seen.

She'd taken him to the office of the journal she wrote for, *The New Age*, and introduced him there to Beatrice Hastings and to the editor, Mr Orage, who'd told him that everyone was talking about his sister's latest story, and that one day she would be famous. Leslie looked back on it as a time of excitement and self-discovery. Now, four years later, he'd come to London intending to stand further off from her, to be less the "little brother". But the old magic was working again. She'd taken possession of him. There was the army, and there was Katie. It left no room for anything else.

When they returned late in the morning from their session among the gravestones and climbed the steps to the front door of 5 Acacia Road he saw through the front window a man, gaunt-faced, ginger-haired and red-bearded, standing with his back to the window.

"Oh Lord," Katherine said. "It's Lawrence. Go and talk to him, Bogey, while I run upstairs. Tell him I'll be there in a moment."

Lawrence was pacing the room. Leslie knew he was there to talk about the literary journal which he and Katie and Jack had been planning. Katie had talked of putting her new Wellington story into it – the one about the wind, and the brother and sister. Lawrence intended to expound ideas, his latest thinking on men and women and society. Jack would write the critical notices.

Lawrence stopped pacing as Leslie came in. His clothes were rumpled and too big for him. His sandy-red hair, cut short, looked unbrushed, but perhaps was only difficult to manage. The beard,

63

startlingly red, jutted. His silent stare was uncharming, almost impolite, but neutral and strong, as if its point was not to make an impression but to gain one. Leslie announced himself, going forward. "I'm Katherine's brother. Leslie Beauchamp. You're Lawrence."

Lawrence shook the hand held out to him. His eyes remained on Leslie with a look that scarcely softened. It was the uniform, Leslie decided. He'd heard something of Lawrence's view of the war. He didn't like the military.

"I'm afraid I haven't read any of your novels yet."

He felt at once that this was not what he should have said, but he blundered bravely on. "I certainly mean to. Katie and Jack of course . . ."

He'd been going to say that they had said wonderful things about Lawrence's novels, and so they had. But he was checked by the recollection that the most recent conversation he'd heard on the subject had been about a novel called *The Rainbow* which they'd read in proof. It was to be published any day now, and neither of them liked it.

Still Lawrence stared, unsmiling. "Aye, well, there's plenty of time for that," he said. He nodded. "You're not unlike your sister. There's a resemblance." And he turned away, walking to the end of the room to look out over the garden.

"It's looking unsettled," Leslie said. Lawrence turned towards him again, with a puzzled, faintly irritable, expression.

"The weather," Leslie explained.

"Oh the weather," Lawrence said. "I don't consider it." And he turned his back again.

"Lawrence. Did I keep you waiting?" The novelist turned to look at Katherine. There was something amused in his keen eyes, as if he'd picked up in her voice a signal that she was in a mood to mock if he gave her the least opportunity.

64

"I had your brother's company," he said.

"But did he have yours?"

"Oh come on, Katherine, none of that," he said, smiling now. "We have work to do."

Two nights later, the eve of Leslie's departure for France, they had a special meal, just the three of them, he and Katie and Jack – not, they warned him, "haute cuisine", just good plain English fare: soup, meat and two veg and a pudding. Katie and Jack cooked it together, and it was served with two bottles of a claret Mr Orage had given her on a week when there'd been nothing in the kitty with which to pay for her contribution. At the table they sang a round she taught them, *Dona nobis pacem*, and only after they'd been through it two or three times to get it right, reflected that it was a prayer for peace, and were moved. So they made a joke of it and Jack quoted lines of a poem by Ezra Pound in which a French troubadour complains that the south "stinks peace", and prays for war.

> Hell grant soon we hear again the swords clash!
> Hell blot black for always the thought of Peace.

But that didn't suit their mood. Katie said Pound should stick to tennis, which he played rather well, and leave poetry to those who could write it. But then she contradicted herself, remembering a poem of his she'd read in the magazine he edited, the *Egoist*. Some of the lines had stayed in her head:

> Dark eyed
> O woman of my dreams
> There is none like thee among the dancers,
> None with swift feet.

I have not found thee in the tents,
In the broken darkness.
I have not found thee at the well-head
Among the women with pitchers.

Her voice was beautiful. Leslie remembered it from childhood, how well she read, how she could add life to words on a page. "Go on," he urged. But that was all she could remember.

Jack, watching in his dreamy thoughtful way, said, "It's a pity you don't have a girl, Beauchamp. You should have a soldier's send-off."

Leslie asked what that meant, and then felt his face redden when they looked at one another and smiled. "Oh I see. Well you don't know that I won't, do you?"

They acknowledged it was true. "Do you have secrets?" Katherine asked.

They talked about what they would do after the war, made fantasies about it, pretended their future would be together, the three of them on a little farm somewhere in Oxfordshire or Somerset, with a farmhouse that was spacious and dry but thatched, perhaps a mill house with a stream running past the door. At last they stacked their dishes for Mrs Battle to wash in the morning, and Jack retired to bed, while brother and sister did one last turn up and down the garden.

"I know I'll come back from this war," Leslie told her. "I have a kind of certainty about it."

"I know it too," she said – and he could tell that she meant it, believed it with a confidence as unshakeable as his own.

"It's not that I fear death, although I'm sure I wouldn't like any of the ways of getting there. I might be wounded of course – I'm prepared for that. I can stand quite a lot of pain – dentists and so on. But I'm ambitious, you see, Katie. I want to go on afterwards and do great things."

"And you will, Bogey. I know you will. And so will I. We'll do them, both of us, together or apart, and when we're old we'll look back on this moment."

"Promise?"

"Darling boy, I promise."

"I love you, Katie."

She shook her head, squeezing her eyes tight shut. "I can't speak, darling."

Later, when he was already in bed, his light out, he heard her climbing the stairs. Her voice came to him in the darkness. "Let me lie down on your bed, Bogey, like I used to when you were really my little brother."

He had only a sheet over him, and she lay beside him, her head close to his, and was silent for so long he thought she'd gone to sleep. He could smell her perfume and, faintly, the scent of her skin and hair. He remembered that only weeks ago he'd written to her that he felt for her as "no other living soul" could, and that the relation between their bodies and minds was "one of the most beautiful works of God" – and then had worried that she might think this extravagant.

He was dreaming now – that her hands were on him, and her mouth. They were in a wood in which the predominant colours, like the illustrations from some picture book of their childhood, were swirls of purple, dark blues and reds. She was bending over him, whispering, kissing him.

Early in October, aided by a sergeant, he was giving instruction in the use of grenades to a platoon of men who were being prepared for a quick forward assault that would be limited to "straightening the line", but would be intense, using everything close-quarters called for, including the bayonet. They were in a wooded area, a mile or two back from the line. The occasional artillery shell had shredded the tops of some of the trees, and others had been cut down or had branches removed by men shoring up second- and third-line trenches against the expected onset of autumn rains; but this part of the wood was largely intact, unspoiled. Birds could be heard singing evening and morning. Not far away, over pastures and fields of corn, Leslie had heard a skylark singing during a bombardment. There were yellow flowers around the trenches farthest from the line. In the wood the leaves were still green, but dry, brittle, with here and there signs of a fading towards yellow.

This was Ploegsteert Wood, which the troops had renamed Plugstreet, not far from Armentières but on the Belgian side of the border. A few of the farmhouses round about were still occupied by tenacious souls who had hung on, had seen the German army stopped just short of swamping them, and who couldn't now let themselves believe it would ever move again except back in the direction from which it came. The wives gave milk and sometimes eggs and fruit to the troops when they could spare them. In the village nearby a baker's shop was still baking and had lately begun to sell watery beer. One house, damaged in a bombardment and roughly repaired, operated as a brothel. In the railway station a train had stopped, engulfed by the fighting, and remained, carriages bullet-holed and shell-damaged, weeds growing up around its rusting wheels. Ahead and behind, sleepers had been torn up from the tracks to support the sides of trenches. For some part of each day the stationmaster could be seen in the signal box, oiling levers and pulling at them, polishing brass, keeping things ready for a resumption of services; and his wife, whose profitable sideline was the doing of extra laundry for officers, swept the little waiting room every morning and the platform every evening.

Leslie was comfortably billeted in a barn, but he and his sergeant had spent the previous night on watch in no man's land, something everyone took a turn at. Faces blackened, and taking a groundsheet each, they'd crawled and belly-slithered out, over the top and under the wire. Halfway between the opposing lines they had found a hollow and lain down to watch and listen for any German incursion. The challenge was to stay alert, and much of the night passed in kicking one another awake. They could hear Germans talking to one another, deep guttural sounds, homely, distinctly human, from the opposing trenches. When a German flare went up they'd seen they were lying only a few yards from a corpse, one of their own, and only recently dead. He'd been shot through the head and lay on his back, arms and legs spread, like a bather enjoying the brief brilliant sunshine of the flare. The light faded and the dark closed over him. His summers were over. Leslie had tried to think of something, "a few words" to say in his head by way of acknowledgement and farewell, and could only think of "Bad luck, old chap" and "Goodnight".

Before the earliest pre-dawn light was coming into the sky beyond the German positions, they'd slithered their way back into the fire trench for cocoa and a few hours' real rest.

As Leslie was beginning his grenade instruction the German guns started up. They were right on time, "shooting by the clock", as their habit had been in recent days. Some answering fire came back from the British guns, almost casual, like an acknowledgement – "Your message received and returned herewith" – a dull boom, a whining scream overhead and the explosion of the shell landing in the distance.

Leslie had been through his routine many times – storage and carrying of grenades, how to detach one quickly for use, the pin, the firm clamp of the thumb, the wide stiff-arm throw. The need for care, practice, rote, habit. He was demonstrating in slow motion . . .

He was lying on the dry ground staring up at the sky. He could hear nothing but a buzzing shriek, intolerably loud, like a mechanical saw close to his ear. He was aware of himself as if it was another person, another's body. The body was damaged in some way. Beyond repair perhaps. The thought came to him like that; and then the further thought that his mind was still working, so perhaps things were not so bad. He knew he was groaning, couldn't stop himself, but couldn't hear the groans. Heads came in sight looking down at him, worried faces, and then were withdrawn. He tried to move the arm that had held the grenade, could not, and thought possibly it was no longer there. He felt no pain. What he felt was not numbness either; it was a kind of rapid vibration within himself. It was as if he longed for pain but could feel nothing that was appropriate, nothing that was not horrible, terrifying.

He thought he might be dead, and then thought, No, not dead. Dying.

Now there was fear – fear of death, of what might lie beyond. He remembered there were ways of dealing with this. He began to say, to repeat, "God forgive me for all I have done. God forgive me for all I have done. God forgive me . . ."

Though he could not hear the words he could feel them in his throat and mouth. On his tongue. There was blood there too.

The words – or the blood? – choked him. He found it hard to breathe. He was losing something – losing everything. He needed to breathe. His friend and fellow-officer Jamie Hibbert was there, crouching over him. He was speaking but Leslie could not hear him; could hear nothing but that continuous grinding buzz.

"I can't breathe," he said. "Lift my head, Jamie."

He didn't hear his own voice but Jamie must have heard it because his head was lifted. He saw better now the men, standing back. That was horror in their eyes. He recognised it. He must look bad. Wrecked. And yes, dying, certainly. Over and beyond their heads he saw leaves, and blue sky. He saw a black dot rising and falling in the blue that must have been the lark. Though he could not hear it, he tried to fix on it, as a test, and to take his mind off this lack of breath.

It became two dots, then four . . .

FOUR

Autumn 1915 – Jack

KATHERINE HAS JUST RECEIVED THE TELEGRAM. SHE HAS RUSHED out of the house looking for a taxi to take her to the Bank of New Zealand where she can talk to Mr Kay who sent the news on to her.

Bewildered, apprehensive, Jack has gone at once to write in his journal. He asks what will happen now? He reports that Katherine's face was white as she showed him the message. There were no tears. She said, her voice hard, unmusical, not her own, "It's not true. Can't be. He wasn't the kind to die."

Jack is afraid. He depends on her. Will she hold up against this blow? He should be sad for Leslie but at this moment the death is not real to him. Not yet. But perhaps never. He has reproached himself for this already – that at the deaths of men who were his contemporaries and friends he has felt only sorry for himself, and a kind of generalised, abstract pity for England, for Europe, for civilisation.

Why did they not expect it? There are so many deaths now, casualty lists growing longer, with surges over on to extra pages when there is an offensive – by the enemy, or against, it makes no difference. Yes the possibility was there, but abstract, not seriously considered, certainly not spoken about.

Jack sees again Katherine's white face and dark wide-spaced

eyes as she stared at him, looking for something, he didn't know what and neither did she – anything that might alter or diminish the hard fact of it. "Deeply regret to inform you . . ." She read the date of the death, 7 October, and asked which day that was. He thought it must have been Tuesday. She said, "The day I bought the South Lancs badge." That was the badge of Leslie's regiment, also called the Prince of Wales' Volunteers. Bought to be worn for luck.

"That means he was dead when we got his letter." And still no tears, nothing, only an awful uncomprehending blankness and disbelief.

Jack's mind jumps to particulars. They have people coming to dinner this evening. Gordon and Beatrice, Anne, their Russian friend Kot. That must be called off, surely. And how is it to be done at such short notice? Too late for the post.

Jack scribbles in his journal, talking to himself on the page.

The dinner party went ahead. There was, she insisted, to be no mention of Leslie; no hint that he was dead and that they were grieving. It was to be like *Alcestis*, in which Admetus conceals the fact of his wife's death.

He wanted to tell her they were not in a Greek tragedy, but said nothing, simply acquiesced in what seemed a madness.

Preparing the meal with Mrs Battle's help Katherine was grim, silent, dry-eyed. When she had to speak to him it was as if she were suppressing anger. She put on the embroidered "peasant" dress Kot had given her. The guests arrived and she was lively, charming, frantic, and he thought perhaps they could detect the falseness, or at least recognise that there was something wild and strange about her behaviour. Leslie was not mentioned.

During the next days Jack was anxious, wanting to talk to

her about it but afraid to break the silence which her coldness signalled must be maintained. If there could have been a funeral, that would have helped, but there could be none, nothing. Leslie was already underground, his "terribly injured" body rolled or wrapped in a blanket. Buried where it had happened, in "a little wood", and when it had happened – or that same evening, his fellow-officers present. No time for anything else. On with the war!

On her desk, in the room that had been Leslie's on his visits, two telegrams lay side by side. One was Leslie's farewell: OFF AT LAST THE GOODBYE WOULD HAVE BEEN TOO AWFUL AU REVOIR LESLIE. The other, Mr Kay's, sent from the Lombard Street Post Office and delivered from St John's Wood: DEEPLY REGRET INFORM YOU LESLIE KILLED 7TH COME AND SEE ME KAY. How long she sat at her desk with these in front of her, helpless, frozen, dry-eyed, Jack wasn't sure, but he suspected many hours at a time.

He felt she should weep, should melt, break down – that this must happen, and that he was failing her because he couldn't help her towards it. She was too strong for him; too strong for her own good, as obdurate in grief as in everything. It made him recognise his own weakness, and feel that she recognised and probably despised him for it.

An invitation came in the post to dine with the St John Hutchinsons at Hammersmith. "Of course we won't accept," he said.

She stared at him, her face pale, her eyes huge and dark. "What are you talking about? You think everything has to come to a stop because someone is blown to bits?"

"Are we not to tell them?"

"No. Not a word." He frowned, appealing silently for reason.

74

"I'm not going to bask in sympathy," she said. "Other people do that. I won't."

She wrote a note saying they would be delighted to come. Jack in his corner re-heard that phrase, "*blown to bits*", with the peculiar angry emphasis she'd given it. How could they go on like this?

But next day she told him she couldn't stand living at Acacia Road. Not a moment longer. She had already spoken to Kot. He and his friends would take over the house.

Jack felt the weight of this in his shoulders and back, a further burden. He said he would look for another house.

"Not in England," she said. "France. We'll go south. They say the war's hardly touched it. We've never been to the Mediterranean. It'll be warm there, and beautiful."

This was the longest statement she had made for several days and he tried to take heart from it. "'Oh for a beaker full of the warm South,'" he quoted.

"Yes," she said, "if you like," – and turned away.

Somehow the plans were made, the tickets bought. A telegram was sent to the St John Hutchinsons. The Murrys could not, after all, come to dinner. They were "leaving England suddenly". And they left.

It should have been exciting; and for Jack there were moments when it was. But the grimness continued. It was as if they had Leslie's body in their luggage. It travelled with them, across the Channel on the night ferry, and on the long train journey south. She spoke to Jack about practical things and was otherwise silent. There were times when he wanted to shout at her, "*I* didn't kill your brother. It was the Germans. It was the war. It was that stupid bomb."

But he said nothing, afraid that in some way he *was* responsible;

or at least culpable. Why had this young man, this loved brother, come from the other side of the world to fight in England's war, and he, Englishman Jack Murry, not been there at his side? Was that what she was thinking?

During the first part of their train journey, as the day dawned, he tried to make conversation, to engage her interest in the countryside, asking was she warm and comfortable, arranging the travelling rug over her knees and feet. At Amiens he found a wagon on the platform and bought her (wincing at the extravagance) ham and rolls, oranges, and even a bottle of white wine. She was civil, ate and drank a little, but didn't want to talk nor to read. As it grew lighter, and it seemed nothing he might think to say could interest her, he took out a book and read. But soon there came across to him, by means of that silent, subterranean communication which is a condition of being a couple, that he was being insensitive, neglecting her.

Inwardly he rebelled. He tried to go on reading but the meaning of the words wouldn't stick in his mind. He read each sentence, and re-read it, and found he could not fight against her silent reproach. She was behaving absurdly; being (he thought) a woman. But he supposed she might say with equal justice, or injustice, that he was being a man. If that were so, neither he nor she could help it.

He knew it was his job to rise above the obstacles, not to rail at her, not to shout or protest, but with calm and sympathy and reason to take charge. He knew what was required and that he couldn't do it. If he tried it would go wrong, he would lose control, there would be a row, unforgivable things would be said. Silence was the best he could do – a silence matching hers. They made a grim pair.

There was a terrible moment, mid-morning, when he had

drifted off to sleep in the warmth of the compartment and was suddenly woken. She had him by the shoulders, gripping tightly, shaking him. Her eyes were staring and her face full of alarm.

"I'm sorry," he stuttered, behaving like a soldier who has fallen asleep on sentry duty.

"His cap," she was saying. "Bogey's cap."

It took a few moments to understand that she was talking about one of her brother's uniform caps. Leslie had given it to her as a memento and now she'd remembered she hadn't packed it. Thought of losing it was making her panic. Patiently Jack made her think back, remember where she'd left it. She thought in a drawer in the attic room at Acacia Road.

"We'll write to Kot," he said. "He'll find it and keep it for you."

She stared into his eyes, then unlocked her fingers from his upper arms and settled back in her seat. Yes, that was what they must do. "I'm sorry," she said flatly. "I startled you."

So the iron hours clanked by through pasture, woodland and vineyards, past farmyards and villages, along highways and through the ragged edges of towns and cities. As the long day wore on a change was taking place, not between the couple in the train compartment but out there in the world – one he recognised, before he was quite conscious of its elements, as the first taste of that "beaker full of the warm South" that he hoped was to be the cure for her grief, or perhaps its release. Rain that had been falling at Boulogne had given way to a misty dampness, then cloudy light, and at last to full sunshine. There were orange roofs and yellow houses, vineyards alternating now with smoky grey-green olive groves. As they trundled through the edges of towns he began to see tables set out of doors and on balconies, people sitting eating meals, drinking wine. The colours were

77

becoming lighter, brighter, more various. And then, at last, there was feathery mimosa, there were oranges and palms, and there was the sea, a bluer sea than he'd ever seen before.

"The Côte d'Azure," he said, and she smiled and nodded, and the light for a moment came back into her eyes.

Marseilles was noisy, with trams along the seafront, and full of soldiers – French, North African, Indian, British. Jack and Katherine were woken early by the clatter of horses and mules – white mules wearing red tasselled fringes over their brows. Gun carriages trundled over cobbles in the street below their hotel. There were stamping boots and officers shouting orders. It was a big busy blowsy indifferent city, tough and grasping, and every time he bought anything she told him he'd been cheated. He suspected it was true but would have preferred not to hear it from her.

She fell ill there, lay in bed, feverish, telling him she could see the flowers in the wallpaper, a kind of extravagant lily of the designer's fantasy, coming out and bowing to her. He wasn't sure that it was a true illness. It might, he thought, have been her soul's way of expressing the grief she would not give words to. But the hotel keeper's wife had no doubt. "Marseilles fever" she called it, prescribing (and supplying for a small charge) hot milk and orange-flower water, with little shots of brandy.

They decided they would move a few miles east, away from the bustle of Marseilles to Cassis at the mouth of the Rhône. They took the train along the coast, only a short journey, and as they went, even in such brief time, a mistral blew up, hurling branches about, throwing up clouds of dust, churning the sea's blue into a sludgy orange. At the station they told a cabman to take them to a hotel – any hotel that would give them shelter from the wind – and by luck were delivered to one called the

Firano, where they were offered a room more spacious than either had seen or heard of in a French hotel. For two days they listened and watched as the wind whistled, banged shutters, tossed palms and plane trees about. They felt like prisoners. Jack read guidebooks in the hope of better things to come.

The foothills of the Massif de la Sainte Baume rose sharply behind the town, covered in bright green pines. As the weather grew calmer they went walking and found wild flowers and scented shrubs among the rocks. Katherine sat on their hotel balcony listening to the sea. "It makes me think of New Zealand," she told him, her voice flat, uninflected, as if she could feel the pain but wouldn't yield to it.

He was growing weary of her. Grief was natural, but he had expected that he and she would be sad together, and closer. Instead there was this continuing anger, and he was finding it intolerable.

On the second day after the storm they were in their room, he reading on the bed, she writing at a small table. He had written the day before to Kot, and now she was writing to him. She got up and left the room. He knew she'd gone downstairs for coffee. Smarting from the sense of yet another silent rebuke – why had she not invited him to come with her? – he got up from his chair and read as much as was visible of what she'd written. His eye raced over sentences about pines and rosemary and a tall flower with pink bells, until it was arrested by this: "Jack has read to me what he wrote to you. Don't believe the conjugal 'we'."

He read it again, turned away, and stared out at the palm tree beyond the window. The denial and the disloyalty disturbed him; but there was something else. He had *not* read to her what he had written to Kot. So she had read it herself.

There had long been an understanding between them – part

of the separateness, the independence, she insisted must be maintained – that they did not read one another's letters or diaries. But there had been an occasion before she ran off to be with Francis Carco when she'd chastised him for something said about her to a friend and recorded in his journal. This transgression of his, disloyalty she called it, had even been made to do service as partial excuse for her running away.

She had claimed that this was the only time she had ever broken their rule – but why should her first and only look have revealed something she didn't like when almost everything he wrote about her was either neutral or flattering? It was possible of course, but unlikely.

From that moment he suspected – more than suspected, held in some closed compartment of his mind as a certainty – that the rule existed only for him. He was not to invade her private space while she allowed herself the liberty of crossing into his.

In these days since her brother's death the fact that she had been a closed door to him had made him want as never before to read what she wrote – yet still he was restrained by a sense of propriety. Only once, while they were still in Marseilles, he had read one of her letters. It was the one to Kot asking him to look for Leslie's uniform cap. She'd written an account of Leslie's death, based on a letter from an officer friend, Jamie Hibbert. She told how Leslie had said, "God forgive me for all I have done." Then, she went on, he had spoken his dying words: "Lift my head, Katie, I can't breathe."

But Leslie had *not* named her. He had asked his friend to lift his head – that was all. The "Katie" was invention.

The effect of this on Jack was something like embarrassment – and guilt at an intrusion into her private world. Now he was invading it again; but this time what he felt was something nearer to anger. If her privacy was only so she could be disloyal to him and escape reproach, why should he respect it? Why should he not read her letters? And why not also some of the copious entries she was making in the notebook she always carried with her?

He waited his chance. It came two mornings later. She'd seen a skirt in a shop window and decided she would go back and try it on. He knew she wouldn't want him with her. She'd told him once, joking but also serious, that she found him an inhibitor to inspired shopping. "You're a bargain-hunter, darling," she'd said. "I'm interested in style."

There were no jokes this time. Just the fact was enough. She was going to look again at that skirt. "You won't want to come," she told him, and he agreed. He wouldn't.

What he found in the notebook disturbed him. Most of it was addressed to Leslie, a sort of on-going love letter in daily instalments, recalling New Zealand and their remembering of it together at Acacia Road, telling him that she would write of their childhood as she'd promised, and then would follow him in death. Apart from this task, she told him, she was already dead. "Nobody knows how often I am with you . . . I will never be away from you again. You know I can never be Jack's lover again. You have me. You are in my flesh as well as in my soul. I will give Jack my 'surplus' love but to you I hold and to you I give my deepest love. Jack is no more than anybody might be."

Did she mean it about dying, he wondered, and decided yes and no. She was not going to kill herself. Someone on the brink of suicide doesn't interest herself in new skirts. But in some sense she felt her life was over, or that it ought to be. She loved no one but a dead man, and so felt dead within herself. As for the rest of it – it was hysterical. Whether it meant anything or nothing, little

81

or much, there was no way of knowing. He felt he wanted to avert his eyes. He *had* invaded her privacy, and he regretted it.

Next morning after breakfast they walked in silence. The waves lapped gently at the sea wall. The sun shone and the sea that had been churned up and opaque during the storm was once again clear, concealing nothing. White pebbles, chips of marble, old broken tiles still with traditional patterns as if preserved from Roman times, could be seen bending and stretching under the brightly moving water. They clambered down on to brown shiny rocks at the far end of the bay and walked on, holding on to one another for balance. At last they stopped to look away into the distance where sea-blue became sky-blue, a division less and less well-defined as the day warmed and the heat blurred it.

It took Jack courage – or he felt it did – to speak the forbidden name, but at last he came to it: "Darling, why do we never talk about Leslie?"

She shook her head. "No, please. I don't want to."

He persisted. "Leslie's dead and we're alive. It's a sad and terrible fact, but it *is* a fact and you have to come to terms with it, Tig. We've got to get on with the business of living."

"No." She put one hand to her eyes, half turning away from him, waving the other behind her as if to keep off an attacking dog.

"Yes," he said. "We must."

"*We* don't have to do anything. What *you* have to do is your business."

He adopted a reasoning, caressing tone. "I know how you're feeling at this moment . . ."

But she turned towards him, eyes cold. "You know nothing about feelings – mine or anyone's."

He bridled. "You're the one who lacks feeling. You have none for me."

"Is that your complaint? That I'm neglecting you?"

"I think you're behaving extravagantly."

"You expect me to behave normally when my only brother . . ."

He interrupted her. "No, no, no. Of course I don't. But we can't go on like this. We'll go mad."

"I'm mad already. I don't have to *go* mad."

He was losing his grip on himself. He heard the bitterness in his own voice as he said, "You ask too much."

"I ask nothing from you, Jack. Nothing. I don't need you."

"Then I should go, should I?"

"Yes, if you want to."

"Katie . . ."

"Don't call me that. That's not your name for me."

"Oh for heaven's sake! Tig, then. Listen to me. It's Leslie who died. I think you should let him have that all to himself. It's his, not yours."

She stared at him, checked.

"Stop appropriating his death."

He could see the reproach she wanted to deliver caught up and impeded by the recognition of what he had said – the hard truth of it. And then, as if there was no way out of a trap, like a child denied something she wanted very much, she began to weep. The tears streamed. She reached out to steady herself and he helped her as she sank down to sit on an outcrop of stone. She sobbed. She bent forward over her knees. Her whole body shook.

He had expected this. Sooner or later it had to come. And he'd thought that when it did, *then* he would feel a more complete sympathy for her, the kind of pity anyone who lost a dearly loved son or brother in this horrible war deserved. He'd been sure that at this moment his love for her, which had seemed frozen, would surge out to comfort her. But it wasn't happening. Not at all. It was anger he was feeling, anger and jealousy. As her grief was released, so too was his rage. He wanted to beat her.

"Are you going to carry a dead man with you for the rest of your life?" He heard his own voice, cold and harsh. The sound only made him angrier. It was the voice of a man who had right on his side. Was that himself, Jack Murry, confident he'd been wronged? He began to shout: "Carco was bad enough, but at least he wasn't a corpse."

She looked up at him, an expression of astonishment recognisable through the wet shine of the tears: "Carco?"

"Your French soldier-boy. Have you forgotten him? Your cocksure would-be novelist. Your grubby little *amour*?"

She sobbed one more time, like a gasp for breath, looking down at her knees, swallowing and widening her eyes as if gathering her thoughts and her strength. Her inner storm had passed, or was passing. "At least," she said, almost casually, "Francis Carco is fighting for his country."

"Oh thank you for that! A white feather. My first – and it comes from my wife."

"I'm not your wife, Jack. Had you forgotten?" She brushed her skirt and stood up. "And is Carco a would-be novelist? His novel was published – something you have yet to achieve."

He absorbed that.

"You were bored by Leslie."

"That's nonsense."

"You don't care if he's dead. Why should you? He was not

84

clever, not literary, not D. H. Lawrence. He hadn't read Dostoevsky. He was nothing to you."

"For heaven's sake, Tig, stop this. You know what Lawrence would tell you. Stop wallowing in it."

"What does it matter what Lawrence would say? He doesn't like the war because it's going on without him. What right have all these foolish young fellows to die and take the world's attention away from *him*?"

But these were only words. They didn't any longer come like flaming swords. The fire had gone out of both of them. Soon they were walking in silence. He felt shame. Did she? Possibly, but he couldn't be sure.

That evening, over dinner in the hotel, they talked. The air had cleared. They were not close, not intimate, but frank, calm, almost honest, like two old friends who led, or were about to lead, separate lives.

He admitted that on this journey he'd been lonely as never before with her, and she said it wasn't surprising. In her mind she'd been with Leslie every moment. Everything had been referred to her dead brother. In her imagination she'd been showing him a part of France he hadn't seen and would never see. It was a way of dealing with her grief. It would pass, she supposed, but meanwhile there was no reason why Jack should have to suffer it.

He said he would have suffered it gladly if only she hadn't behaved towards him as if he'd been an interloper, and to blame.

She said she was sorry. She said he must go back to London. Lawrence needed him. And there was the magazine to think of.

"You won't come with me?"

"I can't face it. Not London. Not yet."

"But soon."

For a moment she looked uncertain. "I suppose so. Yes."

He reached out and held her hand across the table, and felt tears. "Then we'll be together," he said. "Properly."

She smiled. "Yes, properly, Jaggle."

That night they made love. It was the first time since Leslie had left.

In the few days that remained they moved from Cassis, along the coast to Bandol, to the Hôtel Beau Rivage. It was at the western end of the little town, and from their window, which looked south, they could hear the sea lapping at night against the sea wall and sounding, *hish hish*, up the gravelly beach. There were walks along the seafront, or over a headland to another bay where the water was dark blue inshore with a white silky fringe; or they could go inland on a road that climbed beyond shops and villas, through small farms and into hills and woodland. They had begun to enjoy one another's company, to love one another again. She was almost the old Katherine – the person who noticed so much and could be so funny about what she saw. His own habit was to walk along locked, usually unhappily, in his thoughts, unable to escape. He'd grown accustomed to think of her as his rescuer, the one who could "take him out of himself".

So he felt regret at the decision they'd made. But he wavered and didn't say so, because London, and the thought of Lawrence, tugged at him. And there was also the sense of release, of adventure, at the prospect of being alone.

FIVE

Winter 1915 – Fred Goodyear

HIS PACK OVER HIS SHOULDER, CORPORAL FREDERICK GOODYEAR made his way through an alley from Southampton Row into Queen Square, and down into Devonshire Street. It hadn't changed, a slum pretty much, running down to Theobald's Road and Holborn, with its three pubs, poky shops, pawnbroker and goldsmiths' workshops, and its pallid cheeky urchins playing marbles in the gutters.

Before the war they used to call out to one another, "'ere's another poetry geezer, Bill. Cor, look at 'im." They knew at a glance which of the people going along the street were heading for the Poetry Bookshop, and it was always good for a bit of cheek. Today they were not respectful exactly, but the uniform made a difference. One grimy ragged bandy-legged boy with a catapult hanging out of his back pocket gave Fred a smart ironic salute. "Mornin', major," he said.

"Morning, private," Freddie barked, acting the part. "At ease, lad."

But the lad didn't laugh. His smile froze and turned to a frown. Maybe the geezer was a major *really*. Or maybe he was poking borax. That was the trouble with toffs from outside the area – you didn't know where you were with them.

Fred stopped by the single gas lamp under the big-lettered

sign, THE POETRY BOOKSHOP, and did a quick survey of books displayed in the window. *Georgian Poetry* II, of course, the one that contained Rupert Brooke's "The Soldier"; and Brooke's *Collected Poems* – both selling in thousands since his death and Mr Churchill's statement in the House. There was the last issue of Harold Monro's periodical, *Poetry and Drama*, also a little book by someone called F. S. Flint, and a new book of just eight poems by W. B. Yeats. Fred had done a detour, on his way here, up to Woburn Buildings to linger outside the house where Yeats lived when he was in London, hoping he might catch a glimpse of him entering or leaving or standing at a window.

On one occasion Fred had seen Yeats, here at the Bookshop, giving a reading in the little auditorium, once a goldsmith's workshop, up a steep stairway at the back. There had been hessian curtains dyed dark blue, a tall oak candlestick on either side of the stage, and on the reader's table a green-shaded oil lamp casting over the poet's floppy-haired sleepily beautiful face an appropriately Irish tinge. As for the poems – "The Stolen Child", "The Man who dreamed of Faeryland", "The Lake Isle of Innisfree" and the rest – they were intoned in a voice so lugubriously rich and strange a part of Fred's mind and imagination had sailed away with them to "faeryland", while another part, English and sharp and mocking, had wanted to call in the voice of one of those street urchins, "Wake up, Yeatsy, there's a war on."

On another occasion he'd heard a reading of modern poetry given by Harold Monro's assistant, Alida Klementaski. She'd included poems by Monro himself, and some by James Joyce, one by D. H. Lawrence, and two or three by a strange mannish little woman whose work the Bookshop promoted, Charlotte Mew. And Fred had been there when Monro had opened a new season with his own reading of Shelley's "Hymn to Intellectual Beauty".

The relation between Monro and his assistant fascinated Fred. Miss Klementaski was so beautiful, efficient, passionate, and so utterly devoted, yet Monro, though grateful, seemed to hold her at arm's length. It was a mystery. Why did some men seem to get the woman they didn't deserve, while others . . .

Through the glass now he could see the tall sallow-faced figure of Monro tidying his shelves.

As Fred went in Monro turned from the shelves with the encouraging look of half-recognition, half-acknowledgement he kept for customers he couldn't name but knew he'd seen in the shop before. Jack and Katherine had published one of his poems in *Rhythm*, "Overheard on a Salt Marsh", about a goblin who wants a fairy's glass beads and is refused. Fred had been in and out of the Bookshop often but had never introduced himself.

The floor-to-ceiling shelves, the table on which books were laid out for display, the ladder for out-of-reach volumes, the settle on which you could read undisturbed by any pressure to buy – all were of heavy handsome wood. There was a fireplace and a coal fire burning with even a cat stretched out in front of it. Around the room, hanging from shelves and draped over the table, were Rhyme Sheets, each containing a single poem, some by Blake or Shelley or Keats, others by modern poets. Printed in black and white, but some painted over by hand in bright colours, they were priced at "A penny plain, twopence coloured". Everything was quiet except for the muffled beat of the goldsmiths' hammers from next door and the occasional shouts of the urchins.

Fred browsed. He was to meet Jack here and dump his kitbag in his friend's room just along the street before going with him to meet D. H. Lawrence. Jack had tried to get a room here at the Bookshop – one of the two attic rooms Monro kept for poets at three shillings and sixpence a week – but both were occupied. So he'd had to settle for an inferior room at five shillings above the pottery shop three doors along.

The two had found themselves together last evening for supper at the Gordon Campbells' – Fred over from France on a five-day leave, Jack back from a brief sortie with Katherine to Marseilles and Bandol. It had been a disappointment for Fred: he'd been shown in, had seen Jack already in a comfortable chair, holding forth, glass in hand, and his heart had leaped up at the prospect of seeing Katherine too – only to be told she was still in France, still trying to recover from the shock of her brother's death.

Fred had been in love with Katherine and had put a lot of time and effort into getting over it. That had been his project. His mission. Since joining up and being assigned to a meteorological unit, which had given him many months of quiet contemplation and boredom rather than the anticipated life of action and danger, he'd concluded that he was still in love with her; that even his year in Bombay, which had been meant to work a final cure, had not made much difference.

Fred and Jack had been undergraduates together at Oxford, literary lads, members of the Brasenose College Pater Society – Fred's invention – where poetry was read and written and talked about. Jack had started his literary magazine, *Rhythm*, and Fred had written a manifesto for it. Fred had also had a piece accepted by *The New Age*, where he began to notice very clever sketches and satirical pieces by someone who sometimes signed herself Katherine Mansfield, and was sometimes (he believed) recognisable under other noms de plume. He'd thought of writing to her, care of the magazine, to tell her how much he admired her style, but had decided (a mistake, and only the first) that she was probably a successful middle-aged writer who would be uninterested in his praise. But he mentioned her name to Jack who, enterprising as always, wrote at once inviting her to offer something for *Rhythm*. She sent a short story, Jack published it, met her, and reported that she was their age – in her early twenties – and entirely approachable.

One evening at the end of the university year the three met in Leicester Square. The introductions were awkward at first. Fred blushed and stammered and laughed too overtly at her jokes. But they bought her a meal at the Dieppe, where you could dine for one shilling and threepence, and she liked them well enough to spend the evening with them.

He and Jack were scruffy undergraduates, Katherine all style and sophistication. She wore a black dress and dark velvet jacket, but with touches of white and scarlet. She was small, neat, shapely. Her dark sleek hair was brushed close to her head and in a fringe over her broad pale forehead. Her voice was low and musical, with a clear trace of colonial vowels. Her face was constantly alert, poised on the edge of laughter. Most often she made them laugh without laughing herself; but the laugh was there – in the voice, in the keen eyes and at the edges of the mouth. Every story she told, each reminiscence or fragment of gossip, had a shape to it, a funny and wicked edge of satire, sometimes of malice. Fred found her refreshing, exciting. The rules of polite conversation didn't quite apply. Wit ruled the roost; no piety was respected.

This was the woman of his dreams. He knew she saw that he caught every least crumb of her wit; that he could be almost as quick as she; that when Jack was still lumbering with ought and should, he was laughing and thinking of a quick rejoinder. There was between them what Fred thought of as Recognition, each alert to the other's alertness. The excitement was intellectual and it was sexual.

It was a fine spring evening with a big moon hanging over Piccadilly, and they walked around and around the Circus, arm in arm, not wanting it to end. Jack told them he might soon have to return home and live with his parents because he couldn't afford the ten shillings a week rent on his London room. Fred, who was at that time living with his father, intending to return to Oxford when the autumn term started, insisted that Jack must not give up the room. He went on about it, and Katherine agreed. It was no good living with parents. If Jack intended to leave Oxford, as he was talking of doing, then he must find a way of remaining independent.

It was then that Katherine made her offer. She had a flat in which there was a spare bedroom. Jack could rent it from her for seven shillings and sixpence a week, which would include his breakfast.

Many times since Fred had played over that conversation and the way it *might* have gone. Had he known her circumstances and foreseen what was coming, he could have talked about his own needs, not Jack's. She could as easily have made the offer to him. He might have found himself, for that summer anyway, living under the same roof with her – as Jack had done – sharing kitchen and living room, taking turns to use the bath, talking until 2 a.m., shaking hands to say goodnight. They would have got to know one another slowly, easily, inevitably. His habitual shyness would have been an obstacle, just as Jack's had been. And she would have overcome it, as she had for Jack, by asking at last, "Why don't you make me your mistress?"

Thereafter Jack and Katherine were a couple. At times Fred was drawn by Katherine's magnetic force. Mostly he stayed clear.

There had been a time when he'd gone with them to Paris, trailing around behind them, happy to be so close to her, unhappy not to be closer. He'd flirted with her friend Beatrice Hastings; gone with a French prostitute; got drunk, often, but not drunk enough to declare himself. Between him and Katherine the accord, the Recognition, continued; but Fred's shyness meant she would have had to make the first move, recognise his faint desperate signals and act on them. While Jack remained in the picture that was not going to happen. A bolder, braver man would have challenged, played the competitor in love, but not Fred Goodyear.

And they were not able to pay him much attention. They'd left London partly to escape creditors, and to live an impractical dream of being "young writers in Paris". It hadn't worked out. There was nothing for them to live on and they had no choice but to return to London. Saying goodbye, Fred gave Katherine his copy of the book he valued most at that time, *The Oxford Book of English Verse*. He inscribed and dated it, and she kissed his cheek and squeezed his hand and his upper arm and said she would treasure it always.

Fred stayed on in Paris writing a novel about a young poet in love with a brilliant young woman attached to a man who was neither her intellectual equal nor . . . And so on. The novel resolved nothing and came to nothing.

Later he'd spent a weekend with them at their cottage in the Buckinghamshire countryside. He arrived full of strategies, plans for how to get her alone, how to make the conversation take certain paths, determined that this time his courage wouldn't fail. But Rupert Brooke had turned up uninvited, had been welcomed and urged to stay. They tramped the moors chanting poems, singing, shouting the choruses of songs Fred wrote and taught them. They had a lovely time together, the one young woman and the three young men. But Katherine was like every woman, fascinated by Rupert's good looks, saying behind his back that he was not her kind of man, but admitting she couldn't take her eyes off him. It was not an occasion for declarations by the lesser mortal Fred considered himself to be.

It was on that weekend she'd told him, as he lingered behind the other two to catch a moment alone with her, that she felt as if he and she were friends for life. It seemed to him, as he brooded on it afterwards, that this statement, exciting at the moment it was made, was probably her way of telling him they would never be *more* than friends.

He'd gone away from them after that – right away, to India.

Fred was reading Rupert's poems, picked up from the display table, when Jack's hand gripped his shoulder. "Isn't it strange that he's dead?"

"'If I should die, think only this of me,'" Fred intoned. "'That there's some corner of a foreign field / That is for ever England.' Yes, dead and famous. The new young Keats. One would never have guessed."

"It's hard to comprehend. Katherine dreams about him."

"That must be a busy street."

"I'm not sure the poems deserve it. The fame, I mean. Do they?"

"Well, they're good of course, but perhaps not *that* good. It's the handsome face isn't it? And the war. The war-sentiment. 'Now, God be thanked Who has matched us with His hour.'"

"Lawrence remembers him in a deckchair in pyjamas at Grantchester. He says when he hears that poem he imagines it spoken by a public schoolboy in striped pyjamas."

"You know he died of a mosquito bite that turned septic?"

Jack knew, and smiled too. And then they stood a moment, uneasy at having been amused. Death was death, after all. But there had always been something so "favoured of the gods" about Rupert, so public, if he was going to die in uniform it should have been heroically – leading a charge, or last man defending an outpost. Death by mosquito bite was one of those bad taste jokes the gods went in for, especially in wartime.

"Well, he was nice," Jack said, "and it's sad."

Freddy said, "I never hear the line about 'laughter learned of friends' without thinking of our weekend at Runcton Cottage."

"We did a lot of laughing," Jack said; and then, the shadow of it seeming to sweep over him: "Oh God, this war – what's it doing to us all?"

They spent the afternoon with Lawrence, first walking on Hampstead Heath. His latest novel, *The Rainbow*, had been declared obscene by the Magistrates' Court, all copies ordered to be destroyed. His publishers hadn't argued in its defence. Cravenly, they'd pleaded guilty, destroyed the books, and even asked Lawrence to return his advance, which would leave him, he said, with just a hundred pounds in the bank. He saw it as part of the war madness – the malice that was in the air. "They know I have a German wife. That's enough to condemn my books."

By the pond on Spaniards Road a group of wounded soldiers were out in their hospital blue with red neck-scarves, some bundled up under blankets in wheelchairs, others on crutches. Four one-legged amputees tried to play football, using one crutch to whack the ball, or swinging briefly on two crutches to kick with the surviving leg. They were cheerful lads, shouting, laughing at their own ineptness, falling over and having to be helped up by nurses. Some in wheelchairs watched and cheered; others seemed crushed by what had happened to them, or in pain, or too cold in the wintry sunlight to enjoy what was going on.

The scene upset Lawrence. He seethed and clamped his jaws together and had to contain his rage. These wrecked men represented the war he hated; but it was as if he hated them too, for letting themselves be seen, for surviving, for impinging on his consciousness.

"They should be screaming at us," he said, "'Look what you've done to me!'"

Later, as they climbed Parliament Hill, he was calm again: "The old world's gone. The England one knew. The human world. It's smashing itself to bits. We're going to destroy ourselves completely. Or if we don't, the angels and demons will do it for us, because it's clear now that *we* are Creation's mistake."

He stopped under a tree to catch his breath, making short fast panting clouds like a small steam train in the cold air. "Sometimes it can seem infinitely sad, the thought that the whole enterprise has to end. But then one thinks of the woods and the fields and the roadside flowers without us, without human interference, and it's rather lovely. Last evening I saw a fox on the Heath. He stood up straight, looking over the grass at me, ears up. You know the way the ears seem to point and spread, as if they don't belong on that small head."

Lawrence's two hands became momentarily the fox's ears. "I suppose he couldn't see me as well as I could see him, but he was listening and sniffing the wind. I thought, Well, Sir Fox, your descendants are going to inherit all this. Mine will have blown themselves to bits with their cleverness. I did him a little bow and it made me cheerful again – as if one were leaving the world in good hands."

Fred felt the moment of the fox, and Lawrence's kinship with it, as if it had happened to himself. But it was Jack who responded. "The personal life is what matters now," he said, "while the world's going insane."

It was meant to please Lawrence, but it didn't, not at all. "You're wrong," he said. And to Fred: "You can count on Murry to be wrong. Have you noticed? He'll never let you down. Wrong. Always wrong." And then to Jack again: "I can't tell you how bored I am by the personal life – Cambridge introspection, Oxford self-analysis, varsity men inspecting their own entrails."

Jack met his eye. "What's your colony about, Lorenzo, if it's not about the personal life? Why else are you proposing it?"

Fred had heard about the colony. If it happened it was to be in Florida, or possibly California – some place where a small group of like-minded artists and intellectuals could withdraw to live and work together.

"It's about the *im*personal life," Lawrence said. "It's got to be something better than a collection of lost souls feeling sorry for themselves. If the axe is coming down on your neck, Jack, *submit*! If you can't submit, then have a good rage about it. It's your down-in-the-mouth pose I can't stand; your *doloroso*."

Jack was going to walk on but Lawrence took hold of him, a hand on each shoulder, pulling him around so they faced one another. His expression had softened. "You're a dog, Jack, but you're a good dog and your master loves you."

"Woof," Jack said, and they both laughed.

Later, back at the house, while Frieda made tea, Lawrence asked how Katherine was doing, and reproached Jack for abandoning her in Bandol.

"I thought you needed me," Jack said.

97

"She needs you more. I had a letter from her. She's unhappy."

"About her brother. Of course she is."

"But not just about the brother," Lawrence persisted. "There's been a small black cloud over Katherine for a long time – even the Katherine who knows how to make us all laugh."

Frieda, bringing the teapot to the table, put a hand on her husband's shoulder. "Lorenzo is God, Jack. You must listen to him."

"Shut your mouth, woman," Lawrence said; but he was laughing.

That evening Fred took Jack to a restaurant in Charlotte Street. They talked about the war, the numbers being hurled into it with no counting of cost and no end in sight.

"I tried to sign up at first," Jack said. "I'm not sure what was driving me. Probably thinking it was a modest skirmish to save poor little Belgium from the German jackboot. And the word 'adventure' kept being bandied about – remember?"

"Yes – and 'over by Christmas'."

"Fortunately I didn't get in straight away. There was time to recover my senses – and now I'm not quite in the 'fit for active service' class. But one's made to feel every kind of cad . . ."

"Be a cad," Fred advised. "There are worse things than a white feather. Boredom for example."

He said he was thinking of going for an officer training course. It would make a change. "Once I have my commission – if I decide to go for it, and if I get it – I'll be pitched right into the real stuff."

Jack was alarmed. "Don't do it. You're in uniform. You're doing a job someone has to do. You're beyond reproach . . ."

"Oh I don't care about reproaches."

"Listen to me." Jack was insistent. "I've been reading statistics for subaltern survival. Why would you take the risk? What's the point?"

"I think death's the point." Reading the expression on his friend's face, Fred intoned, "'Now more than ever seems it rich to die, / To cease upon the midnight with no pain . . . ' Have you never felt that? 'With no pain' seems unlikely, however. I imagine there might be quite a lot of it."

Jack was shaking his head. "This is madness."

"Don't be alarmed, Jack. No doubt good sense and my mother will prevail."

When they came out there were eddies of cold mist, like smoke around the gas lamps which, though turned down low in case of a raid, seemed to cast a pale expanding orange balloon of light. As they headed back towards Russell Square the sirens sounded, and then, from down by the river, there was the crash of bombs, anti-aircraft fire, searchlights sweeping the sky. They heard a drumming overhead that was probably another Zeppelin's engines, but nothing fell on them or round about, and the stalking beams caught nothing except furry-grey cloud and the black gulfs between. Frieda had told them that one clear night she and Lawrence had seen a Zeppelin from up on Parliament Hill – quite clear it had been, like a huge floating cigar – and the awful thought had come to her that up there, flying it and hurling down deadly explosives, might be one of her cousins, or one of the boys she'd played with at school; and then the anti-aircraft guns had started up and she'd been afraid it might be hit.

By the time they were back at Devonshire Street the excitement was over. They lit candles, climbed to Jack's attic room and made up the fire to keep them warm through the night. There was nowhere to wash, but Jack said "the hag" would bring hot water in the morning. He was planning to find a better room somewhere in Hampstead, to be nearer to Lawrence. Fred curled up on the floor on pillows and under blankets. "Are you and Katherine . . ." he began.

Jack creaked over to the side of his narrow bed. "Are we what?"

Fred had lurched into the question because it was always in his mind. Now he had to finish it. "Well," he said, sitting up. "One shouldn't ask – but are you two still . . . *together*?"

"Together? Yes of course."

"I mean – a couple."

Jack laughed. "You mean are we still in love."

"I suppose I do. Are you?"

"More than ever," Jack said.

"Lawrence seemed to think . . ."

"Oh Lawrence. He listens too much to Frieda."

"He'd had a letter . . ."

"Katherine was unhappy so she wrote. It's true we had a bad patch when her brother was killed. She had to have someone to blame, I think, and I was to hand . . . But that's over."

Fred nodded, and lay down again. He thought it was probably true, but he wasn't sure. It still seemed strange that Jack was here in London and not with her in France.

Jack leaned over. "Here. Read this."

Fred propped himself on one elbow and held his candle above the sheets of paper Jack passed down to him. He read, "My darling, The 'comfortable one' brought me your letter this morning on my breakfast tray. I read it and kissed it."

He recognised the writing. "It's from her."

"Came yesterday."

"I shouldn't be reading this."

"Read it. No harm done."

Guiltily, Fred skimmed and skipped, looking for signs, for

"evidence", for anything at all. He'd expected at the very least a tone of misery, of grief, but it wasn't like that. The letter was affectionate, and there was an undertone of mockery in it, especially about money. She'd bought biscuits and oranges and "entered them in my Account Book". It had been "wicked and awfully sweet" of Jack to send her five francs. (*Five?*) She'd had a "chaste repast", and "your serviette, my precious, was still there – I got awfully sentimental over it".

Fred glanced down at the bottom of the third page and read, "That is all, my darling heart. Here's your toothpick that you left, and you also forgot your face rag. But I won't send. You can buy one (a wash glove) for 4pence three farthings anywhere."

Fred could see her keen eyes and alert face; could hear her voice – the same voice she'd used in so many of her pieces for *The New Age*. Did Jack hear it? Could he read *tone*? Fred doubted it, and felt almost cheerful until he turned to the next page and read the end: "You know I love you. I love you simply tremendously. I put my arms around you and kiss you – Tig."

Fred handed the letter up to Jack and fell back among pillows that smelled of dampness. In the silence that followed he felt depressed, defeated. He spent a few moments hating Jack, a few more hating Katherine, and more than a few hating himself. "She's wasted on you, Jack," he said at last.

"I know," Jack replied. "Aren't I lucky!"

SIX

Winter–Spring 1916 – Katherine

THEY ARE IN FRANCE, IN BANDOL, IN MUCH BETTER SHAPE, AND in love.

They are Mansfield and Murry, Katherine and Jack, Wig and Tig; they are the Two Tigers. Both are working; or, more precisely, it appears to each that the other is working. Every day he goes to his desk, upstairs, and she to her table, down. There is constantly the scratch of scribbled drafts and the clack of later ones. Jack (with her conversational assistance) is writing his thirty pounds' worth of book 'on Dosty. It is moving, developing, growing. Katherine is not writing exactly, but readying herself, preparing her mind, thinking about it, writing in her journal, keeping up appearances.

She is still grieving, but it has somehow been transformed, made over from the negative to something very nearly positive – something, if not to be enjoyed, at least not to be damaged by and rendered helpless. Writing has become the promise to her dead brother and there is now in her a confidence, very nearly a sense of certainty, that it will be kept.

It is 21 January, 1916 and she has just written in her notebook that the people she wrote about in the past no longer interest her, no longer seem close or real. The threads that bound her to them were false and are all cut away.

She looks up at the photograph of Leslie above her desk, stares into his eyes until it seems there is a momentary flicker, a living response. She knows what he wants of her – that she should write recollections of their own country. In the past she has avoided New Zealand; rejected it. Since Leslie's death the memories, the sense of places and people, have filled her consciousness. There is a "sacred debt" to be paid because of Leslie; and the idea of it no longer goes against the grain of her ambitions.

She reads what she has written in her notebook, and goes on, "Oh, I want for one moment to make our undiscovered country leap into the eyes of the old world. It must be mysterious as though floating – it must take the breath. It must be 'one of those islands' . . . I shall tell everything, even of how the laundry basket creaked at '75' – but all must be told with a sense of mystery, a radiance, an afterglow because you, my little sun of it, are set. You have dropped over the dazzling brim of the world. Now I must play my part."

She looks up from writing those words, looks out into the garden where Madame Allègre's cat is stalking something, stalking nothing, just for practice, and recognises that she is happy. The wrenching pain of the weeks immediately after Leslie's death is gone. The grief is still there, the regret, the pity, the sense of waste for him, of anguish for her parents, of loss for herself. The love is still there. But life has begun to reassert itself. She no longer wants to die. She no longer feels she owes Leslie a death. What she owes him, and can perhaps provide, is a life.

And Jack is no longer shut out. She has, but for occasional Sunday night lapses, stopped crying with sadness for Leslie. She has not stopped crying with happiness for Jack. It's because he came back to her from London; chose to come back; missed her and couldn't stay away . . .

She has turned away from her desk and, still seated, is looking down at the floor, concentrating. An ant – one of the large black variety that sometimes nip if you sit, or rest an arm or a leg, in their path – is struggling across the tiles with a crumb of the sticky sweet *tarte aux pommes* she and Jack had with their coffee last evening. It catches her attention, distracting her from her thoughts. She bends over it, watches, follows.

The crumb is half the ant's size. She imagines herself carrying a piece of sticky tart twice as large as her head; almost as big as her own torso. The ant staggers. Now and then the weight of the piece causes him (she thinks of it as him) to topple forward, back legs and tail-end in the air. Just beyond the French doors that are open to the garden he comes to a deep narrow groove cut into the stone. He must have passed this obstacle coming in, but returning with the trophy will be a challenge. He gets down – more or less falls tart-first into it – but now is trapped there, unable to climb out. It seems he must either give up the tart or remain there – perhaps eat it himself. He will do neither. The tart is for the nest, for the family or the tribe. Think of the cheers he will receive, the honours, the paragraphs in ant history! Again and again he attempts to climb out, fails, won't give up.

Katherine drops her handkerchief into and across the gap making a ladder and a bridge. He is suspicious at first, undecided – then goes for it, up and over. Now he has crossed the white stone terrace and is making his way down the three concrete steps into the garden. Katherine follows. At the edge of each step he must go down vertically, and then, briefly, upside down, because the steps have a lip. That, it seems, is no trouble; then down vertically again. He has reached the path now, goes a yard or two past the steps down to the little cellar, and turns left into grass under the flowering almond. But for him the grass is a jungle. Sticks, fallen leaves, small stones, have to be got over or gone under or around. Obstacles everywhere. Sometimes he climbs backwards, dragging the tart, then turns again and heads forward.

But there is not one clear overall direction. Katherine is down on her knees now, watching. He is having trouble finding the entrance to his nest, which she thinks should be a small hole in the ground. A feeler wavers out on either side. Perhaps the fragrant tart is confusing his sense of smell (does he have one?) or blocking his view, so he is missing markers along the way. A huge circuit, ten minutes or more of this frightful toil, and covering not even three yards, brings him back only to the path again, almost where he left it. But home is somewhere in that jungle. He pushes back into it.

"Tig darling, are you working?" That's Jack calling down the stairs.

She clambers back to her feet, darts indoors and sits at her table in the *salle à manger*, pulling her notebook into position. "Yes, darling. More or less. Did you want something?"

"What time is it? I was wondering . . ."

That's hunger setting in. She feels it too. Ravenous. They are living on a shoestring, lunch their main meal of the day, and the rule is they work until midday. She calls up the stairs, "A piece?"

"Oh yes, please. I know it only makes it worse . . ."

"And a date or a fig?"

"A date — yes, d'you think?"

"Just one," she says and goes to the kitchen.

Five minutes later she is back in the garden, chewing very slowly on the piece she has broken for herself from their baguette. Upstairs, Jack is chewing on his, spilling crumbs over his notes. She bends forward, hovers over the grass/jungle searching for her valiant friend; doesn't find him; thinks (contrary to thoughts earlier in the day about the kind of fiction she wants to write): Stories should have an end. Did he get there? Did he find his way home?

She goes in and sits at her table.

When she wrote, from the Hôtel Beau Rivage in Bandol, her disillusioned letter to Lawrence in London, and Lawrence told Jack she was unhappy and that it was all his fault (something she hadn't intended – it was a Sunday evening and she'd been spilling ink and tears together) she'd thought: That's done it. It was the end for her and Jack. Infidelity was one thing; but this was disloyalty and Jack would hold it against her.

But he'd taken it like a man, as he always did from Lawrence, and seemed to bear her no grudge.

Then came the news that while she would be spending Christmas alone in Bandol (it was her own doing – she couldn't complain) he was to spend it at Garsington Manor with Ottoline Morrell and her troupe of Bloomsbury writers and artists. Katherine had thought then: Now the end has *really* come. He would find new friends there, new stimulus, new entertainment. He would remember all the bad things she'd done to him; her hysteria, her waywardness. He would *kiss* someone. It would be like a door opening, an escape hatch . . .

Her hotel room looked south over the water. The sea glittered and the little sailing boats came and went. The palms shone in the morning light, and in the evening the bats flickered between them, silent against the deepening velvet sky. To take her mind off distant things there was the morning market in the town square, the cafés along the seafront, *The Times* and the French newspapers with their reports from the Front. There was an elderly Englishman who courted her with an embrocation for her "rheumatiz". There was her writing; her plans for writing. And there were letters to and from Jack – written every day, his in London, hers in Bandol, but received erratically and creating an on-going drama, absurd but real, full of torment and exaltation. There was a war on, she knew that, and could laugh at herself; but not even war could excuse lateness in the postal service. These were love letters, after all, and this was France. Death had to go on – but so did life!

More than once she dreamed that her brother was sitting with her, or lying beside her, and she was holding his hand. She woke, lying with her eyes closed, hearing the quiet *hish hish* of the waves on the gravelly beach below her window, knowing he was there, feeling the warmth and weight of his hand in hers. And then, as she woke more fully and opened her eyes to the greenish light coming through the shutters, she found that her arms were apart, on either side of her body; and her right hand was still where it had been, but empty now. It was not her own hand she had been holding, but now Leslie's was gone.

Slowly it seemed that she was catching up with the fact of his death; that she could look at it, say it over, learn it. Leslie was gone but not gone. He was there with her. The hand she held had the substantiality of real things.

And slowly, in her thoughts and feelings and imaginings, Jack was readmitted into the circle: they were three, or would be three, she and her dead brother and her living lover: they would make together a single small world, beautiful and self-sufficient.

Those were the days when she changed the pattern of her walks – not along the seafront and around the bays to Sanary (the long walk, from which she returned by train); or out on to the harbour bar with the sea on either side where a handsome

French officer with a silky moustache had propositioned her; or to the café by the fountain in front of the strange square little church with the heavy brown doors; or over the headland to Bandol's other bay. Almost always now it was the road inland she took, at first just to enjoy the feeling of being in the countryside – the olive groves, the small household farmlets with their friendly goats, pigs and rabbits, their ducks and scrawny hysterical half-dressed chooks; and then, further on, flower farms; and finally the herby scrubland and the pine woods with their sad and beautiful scents, especially after rain.

But as the road wound up towards the foothills it took her – before the little town of Bandol was entirely left behind and the farms and countryside had quite declared themselves – past a straggle of free-standing villas, often very small, with tiny gardens, sometimes fenced, sometimes walled. She dragged her feet going past this one and that, stopped altogether for another, turned back and looked in, said "Bonjour 'sieur, 'dame" to the owners catching a bit of winter sun on their garden seat, and let herself imagine they were herself and Jack, two writers, "*écrivains anglais*", who had come south for warmer weather and to escape the oppressive odour of death that the war was bringing to London.

Sometimes there was a villa signposted *à louer* – to rent. One of these in particular took her eye, called her back, captivated her. Its name, Villa Pauline, was represented in curly letters on the gatepost. It stood up pink in the sun among the foothills that rose directly behind the town, with a view of the sea – very small, hardly more than two rooms upstairs and two down, with a small enclosed garden in which she could see an almond tree, bushes of lavender and rosemary, geraniums like splashes of red paint, a round stone table, and steps down to what must have been the cellar. It was owned by a M. and Mme Allègre who occupied the larger villa next door. And *Oui, bien sûr*, the some-what elegant Mme Allègre confirmed, it was available and the rent (an exact figure wasn't named) would be modest. If Mme Murry should care to take it for a fixed time, three months for example, or six, renewable, the rent would be correspondingly reduced.

Mme Murry explained that she was not in a position to take it herself. All would depend on Monsieur, who was in London.

Mme Allègre understood and would hope to hear from her when Monsieur had spoken.

Meanwhile the villa stood empty, and its *à louer* sign, on which a dream depended, remained, passed and noted most afternoons by the "sad young Englishwoman" (as she'd heard herself described) on her lonely walk towards the hills. Of course she mentioned – casually – in her letters to Jack that there were villas for rent. She expected no response and there was none.

There were still times when she reproached him because letters didn't come – and then they came, shaming her into making new rules for herself. "Courage, Katherine," she said on bad days, looking at herself in the mirror, determined she would not again become the sack of gloom and despondency she had been, a dead weight Jack had had to cart about on his shoul-ders, and which she didn't blame him for dropping and running from. If he should want to come back to her, that would be wonderful; but she wouldn't ask, wouldn't badger or cajole. Only she allowed herself to say sometimes how much she missed him, and tell him the things about him she missed especially – his whistling, for example, so horribly out of tune it made her love him like a small boy.

And then had occurred a sudden, terrible, panicky confusion of hope and fear – letters crossing, cancelling one another out, telegrams meant to clarify that only added to the misunderstandings. He couldn't live without her ... She wanted him, but not unless ... He would come, but no point if she didn't intend to ... She should/would take the villa, not take it, only take it if ... She loved him whether he came or not ... He wanted/did not want ... He was *coming* although ...

She took the villa even before the matter was settled. To celebrate, she bought roses and violets in extravagant quantities and put *new relief nibs* in the crusty old pens at the post office ...

And then he was there, really, little Jack with his beautiful dark eyes and thinning curls, his moody charm and intellectual intensity, his bow legs and rolling, lurching gait. He was there in Bandol, in her arms. They were together. They were in love.

They rose at six every morning, lit the charcoal fire in the kitchen that had been made ready the night before, ate a French breakfast of bread and jam and *café au lait*, after which Katherine, or sometimes she and Jack together, took the short-cut she'd discovered through a field white with jonquils and past a grey-green olive grove, down into the town, to the market, with their *filet* for the day's food – the price of every item noted in a little book and added to the total of spending for the week. Then it was back to work – he upstairs, she down – which began at 8.30 and continued, past the dreadful hunger hour of eleven, until it was time to begin preparing lunch at twelve – often (too often) an omelette, because usually by the end of the week the budget wouldn't stretch to include a chop or a chicken breast.

Afternoons were given over to the siesta, newspapers, and long walks always carrying an old baggy satchel with oranges and their favourite honey biscuits. Into the satchel on the way home went pine cones and wood for their fire. In the evenings they sat on either side of a table in their kitchen, knees banging together, still warmed by the fire-heated stove on which their supper had been prepared, playing chess, writing comic poems on an agreed theme, exchanging ideas, especially about Dostoevsky whose novels she was re-reading so she could help him with his book. There was also Shakespeare, read aloud to one another, working their way through *Antony and Cleopatra*, *As You Like It*, the *Henry IV* plays, *Twelfth Night*, *Troilus and Cressida*.

She loved Jack and yet still sometimes she was unkind, even cruel to him. It was easy to do, difficult sometimes to resist. She resented it that he seemed so effortlessly well while her own young body that had once seemed invincible was still unaccountably subject to pain, as if she'd been Caliban tweaked and tormented by the spells of Prospero. This was not Jack's fault, but she could make him suffer for it as if it was.

One night, almost asleep, she turned to him in bed, wanting him, thinking he was only lightly asleep and that she would wake him – and saw in the moon-filtered half-dark that it was her brother lying beside her, naked, young and beautiful, as he had lain beside her in the upstairs room at Acacia Road. There was no wound on him but she knew he was dead. The shock of it froze all feeling. It was like a judgment, God's accusing finger. She couldn't look a second time – knew it was Leslie's body she'd been going to take in her arms. Eyes tight shut she slid out of bed, out of her dream, and padded downstairs and out on to the white stone terrace beneath the flowering almond that seemed to cast a blue shadow in the moonlight. She looked up at the pale stars and called his name – his pet name: "Bogey", that had also become Jack's pet name. The stars didn't respond; nor did anything come from the darknesses between. That afternoon she'd written a poem about him in which he had offered her poisoned berries saying, "These are my body. Sister, take and eat." She'd dreamed it the night before, and made a poem of it, not – or not until now – connecting it with the hand she'd held in bed while Jack was in London.

The war went remorselessly on. They read *The Times* (a day late) the *Radical*, and Paris papers too when they had a few sous to spare. And there was always talk in the marketplace – someone whose friend or relation had news of what was happening at the Front. Since the New Year it seemed the Germans had been putting themselves into position to attack the fortress town of Verdun, and now it was beginning. Perhaps they thought it a weak spot, and perhaps it was. Soon everyone seemed to know about it – the immense German artillery bombardments which the defending army was having to endure. These were the same guns that had destroyed the Belgian forts, now ranged, it was said, along an eight-mile front, with Verdun, in a loop of the River Meuse, at its centre. It began to seem that here more than anywhere French honour was at stake and the cost in lives was going to be terrible.

One morning French soldiers marched through the town. Katherine was surprised that although there were some very young men – hardly more than boys – there were many more who looked to be in their thirties or even forties. They marched casually, talking as they went, without bravado, seeming neither happy nor sad to be in uniform, just toughly resigned to the fact and to their fate. They wore heavy greatcoats which (how French, she thought, how practical!) were buttoned back on either side to allow their marching legs to swing freely. Two leather straps crossed diagonally on their breasts and another went around the midriff with ammunition pouches attached. Each wore a peaked cap of soft wool and carried his rifle and a small kitbag over his shoulder.

The sight of them, the uniforms, the warm woollen smell of them as they swung by, reminded her (with more than a twinge of regret) of her affair with Carco. She felt she could have picked one of these men out of the battalion and gone away with him somewhere private and talked, and they would have understood one another. He would know how to conduct himself with her, and she with him. They would be at ease. It was part fantasy, she knew, but she believed it. Life kept presenting itself to her in that way – a parade of possibilities, continually declined, and marching away from her.

Later on the soldiers lounged about in the marketplace, exchanging chat with the locals. There were questions about Verdun. Yes, an officer acknowledged, they could expect to be sent there. It would be hell. Fritz was hurling everything he had at the fortifications, as determined to break through as France was to hold the line. One would not go into that zone expecting to return. One would count the days and hope – that was all.

As she and Jack walked back to the Villa Pauline they were silent until she said, "When we had our quarrel . . ." She stopped and began again. "When I had my hysterical outburst . . ."

He looked at her, puzzled.

"Before you went back to London, Jack."

"About Leslie? You wept, Tig, and I got angry . . ."

"There was something you said . . . About Carco. About my going to him . . ."

"I don't remember."

"A grubby little affair."

"Ah."

"It wasn't grubby, Jack."

"No, I don't suppose it was." And then, after a minute's silence: "I was jealous."

"I know. Of course. And I'm sorry I hurt you." She grabbed his arm and pushed up close. "Truly sorry, Boge."

He didn't look at her. His eyes were focused up ahead where the villa seemed to be watching them over its wall. "Not of Carco," he said. "Of Leslie."

That came as a shock. She absorbed it, wished she'd said nothing. The impulse had come from seeing those French soldiers, and the thought of Carco as one of them. She hadn't been thinking of Leslie.

They walked on in silence.

It was about this time that she found among her papers the story she'd been writing in Paris and had called "The Aloe". She'd known it was there and that it was based on her childhood in Wellington before the birth of her brother.

She began reading, idly, indifferent, associating it with "the time of Carco", which she'd put behind her, and thinking in any case, as she always did with her own work, that what belonged to the past was best left there. But the writing took hold. The characters were vivid, real. This was better than anything else she'd written. And wasn't it what she'd promised Leslie she would do, and had gone on promising to his ghost? The keeping of the promise had begun even before it had been made! It was all there, done, or waiting to be done – the people, the relationships, the "special prose" she'd promised herself, the wandering ghost-consciousness that saw through the eyes, and spoke in the voice, first of one character, then another, a third . . . It was the life of a family, seen as only the child sees, but with an adult understanding; stored with all the meticulous detail of childhood memory, the store seemingly unlocked by the kind of shock foreign places and new love can deliver. So the Carco adventure had done its work after all!

She wanted to take it up at once, get on with it, write more about Linda, the stylish sensitive mother – a shining star, but why so cold? Much more about her. And about the young unmarried aunt she'd called Beryl, looking for romance, wanting (but not quite facing it) sex, and troubled by the sense that there were two selves – a false and a true, and that it was the false one she was becoming . . . . And the absurd generous loving unsubtle energetic bull of a Pa-man she'd called Stanley Burnell! How had she managed it? How had she set aside her old grudges against her father? There was room for more of Stanley. Then there was the servant girl, Alice, tormented by Beryl . . . And Pat the handyman chopping off the duck's head when the little boy cousins were there with their dog . . . She knew exactly where she would go next, and next after that – how she would go about it. And might it not, this section of it, end with the birth of the little brother?

She sat that morning exulting over what she'd found and dreaming of what she would do with it. But not a word was written. The next day, which began full of urgency and promise, was no more productive. That evening she wrote in her note-book, addressing Leslie again, "The thought of you *spiritually* is not enough. I want you by me."

The day that followed brought just words and sketches on odd scraps of paper – screwed up and thrown away – and anger with herself. The memory of her brother, which had seemed such an incentive to work, now seemed to stand in the way. In her notebook she wrote: "My head is full of only one thing. I can't begin writing or even thinking because all my thoughts revolve around *le seul sujet*. It is a real vice *avec moi au présent*. I keep thinking round and round it, beating up and down it, and still it stays in my head and won't let me be."

Most of a week went by. It was like one of those dreams of a crisis (she had them often) in which some action was needed *at once*, and the limbs, heavy and dead, simply would not, could not, move.

And then, one morning, she found herself writing, already halfway into a sentence before any decision had been taken. She'd remembered how, when she was ill in the hotel in Marseilles, the flowers in the wallpaper had seemed to open and move in the breeze, and now she was writing about Linda's physical weakness and how it affected the way she saw the world around her.

There were no more hesitations, no longer any pretence: she was writing really and truly. That day and in the days that followed it went almost effortlessly. Even the hour of eleven passed unnoticed, and at midday it was Jack who had to call down that the time had come for them to stop working and make lunch.

Letters came from Lawrence, full of his old warmth, his old charm. He and Frieda had decided to put London behind them and live in Cornwall, at least until he was able to leave England altogether to set up his colony somewhere warm and away from the land of his birth that had hurt him so badly. He'd had Katherine and Jack's news and was glad they were happy together. That was the right way – "a nucleus of love between a man and a woman, and let the world look after itself . . . One should be in love and be happy – no more."

He said "no more", but he didn't mean it, because he went on, "Except that if there are friends who will help the happiness on, *tant mieux*. Let us be happy together."

It was Lawrence's old dream of a group, a community, himself as leader of course. Katherine recognised it at once. They'd tried it before and it hadn't worked. Now he was wanting it again, though it came only as a hint. She knew it would tug at Jack, who missed England in a way she did not. The home she missed was elsewhere, far away, and she was inured to homesickness as he would never be. It was just another of the aches that came and went, and for which there was no embrocation. You sat it out and it passed, slipped below the threshold of feeling like a bad goblin, with the promise that it would be back.

"We should think about it," Jack said.

It was an afternoon in February and they were sitting in their kitchen, close to the fire. Cold rain was falling on the garden. There would be no walk today. What could she say? If it had been a day with sun on the sea and a warm breeze in the olives, she might have asked how they could leave all this for cold stony Cornwall. But she knew too that, irrespective of climate, idylls had to come to an end. She fought a feeling of disappointment that Jack should not want to hang on to what they'd made together in this place; but it mattered less now, because her own work was going well, and she felt she could take it with her. While that was so she could be "good" (as she thought of it); less clinging, less demanding. If Jack wanted to answer Lawrence's call, well – let it happen. Still, she said nothing.

"Soon we won't have a choice," Jack said.

She knew what he meant. There was legislation before the British Parliament to conscript all unmarried men into the services. She and Jack were not married, and could not be until there was a divorce from Bowden. It would mean non-combatant duties for him, but it was true he couldn't avoid it by lurking in the south of France – not without being classed as a deserter.

"When we *really* don't have a choice," she said, "that will be the moment to make our move.'

He said it didn't do any harm to look ahead.

"Something is harmed," she said. And then, seeing him frown, she agreed they could send some kind of signal to Lawrence. She would do it herself, if that was what he wanted.

So a message went, not quite a commitment, but positive. Lawrence was pleased. His reply took it for granted that "perhaps" meant "certainly". He wrote (and though Katherine thought it nonsense, she was touched), "I've waited for you two for two years now and am far more constant to you than ever you are to me – or ever will be." Their "destiny", he insisted, was "beyond choice. And in this destiny we are together."

Now, with a sense that it might be coming to an end, the idyll seemed more than ever perfect. Day after day "The Aloe" ran on ahead of her, and the ghost of her brother, appeased, retired smiling into the silver frame around his photograph and vanished from their bed. The sun shone on their walks, the Mediterranean disclosed its best blue, and the terracotta town showed off against it. The food seemed to get better, the *haricots verts* cheaper and more plentiful, the *magret de canard* fatter and more tender, the local wine more palatable – and they were more reckless in buying all of these things. The draft of Jack's book on Dosty was finished, only revisions and corrections remaining.

Lawrence wrote again. He had found a cottage at Zennor for himself and Frieda, just two rooms and only five pounds for a year's rent; and there was a larger one beside it for Jack and Katherine at sixteen pounds. Theirs had a little tower – "Katharine's tower" he called it, misspelling her name as he always did. She would work there on her novel, with a view over sloping fields to the Atlantic. "Henceforward," he wrote, "let us take each other on trust . . . We are so few and the world is so many, it is absurd that we are scattered. Let us be really happy and industrious together."

Frieda wrote too, to Katherine. The granite walls of the cottages were very thick and "*quite* dry". Lawrence had made buttercup-yellow curtains with green blobs. The food in that part of Cornwall was plentiful and cheap – thick cream, fat chickens. Lawrence, she said, had had a bad time, and some of the wonder of the world had gone for him. "But we will get it again for all that! We will be jolly."

"Much love to you both," she concluded. "I am looking forward so very much to your triumphant arrival!"

Jack was restless now. Katherine could see how these appeals to "*Blutbrüderschaft*", as Lawrence called it, stirred something in him that needed to be satisfied. And she was herself tempted, curious, wondering whether after all it might not be as Lawrence wanted it to be – a unity of mind and purpose among the four of them, producing (why should it not?) fiction and criticism that would match the colours of the post-war world. "We count you two our only two *tried* friends," Lawrence wrote, "real and permanent and truly blood kin. I know we shall be happy this summer: *so* happy."

"Courage, Katherine," she told herself once again. The whole of her life since the age of fifteen had been built on the premise that it was best to dare, to take risks. But as the iron gate closed on the Villa Pauline and she handed the keys to Mme Allègre and kissed her goodbye and said she hoped one day they would be back, the tears seemed to come from somewhere deep and unfathomable.

.SEVEN

Spring 1916 – Frieda Lawrence

FRIEDA IS LAUGHING. WHEN HE ISN'T MAKING HER RAGE, OR weep, Lawrence can still make her laugh; can make her love him again, sometimes, with the sort of reckless love that led her to run away with him leaving an outraged husband, three weeping children, and respectability destroyed for ever.

He is jolly because gorse is flaming along the clifftops, primroses and bluebells and foxgloves are everywhere, lambs are frisking and bouncing below their windows, the blackthorn is in bud in Chapel Hollow and celandine is out along the walking paths. The morning sun, clearing the hill behind the cottages, appears and disappears through breaks in cloud like a face moving from window to window, casting, on fields and ocean, beams of that strange Cornish light Lawrence says makes him think of Blake's "bow of burning gold".

They have more or less settled in at Higher Tregerthen cottages and are preparing for the arrival – the advent, Lorenzo calls it – of the Murrys. Frieda has been washing sheets at the spring that runs out of the hill, and has thrown them over the hedge along the path from the road. They will dry and bleach there, hooked by twigs and thorns against gusts that come from the sea; and this has set Lawrence singing something remembered from his student days at Nottingham -

The white sheet bleaching on the hedge,
   With hey! the sweet birds, O how they sing!
Doth set my pugging tooth on edge;
   For a quart of ale is a dish for a king.

But now he's got on to the subject of the war and he's telling her that it doesn't matter, is best forgotten; that (responding to her snort of surprise and disbelief) no, it does *not* matter, not to him, not any more. He's had enough of raging and caring and swearing and complaining. He won't any longer let it make him angry. Young men are dying needlessly in numbers that take one's breath away? Very well, that's the fact, and facts have to be accepted. If the young have decided to share the madness of the old and die with enthusiasm, why should he complain? Let them go to hell in their thousands, in their hundreds of thousands, whole battalions at a time if that's their wish. Europe is sick. Europe has chosen its purge. So be it.

She knows this isn't a mood that will last but, expressed without too much of the usual bitterness, it's welcome. Spring has come, his winter sicknesses are passing, and Frieda can see it, as so often before, the life welling up in him. He turns to her with his slightly crooked grin and says, in the accent that makes her think he must be quoting something heard in childhood: "Why should I howl if grandfather is pushed over a cliff? Goodbye, grandfather, now it's my turn."

"Only it's not grandfather that's going over," she says. "And it ought to be."

Lorenzo is happy because the Murrys are coming. It's definite, they will arrive quite soon. He still talks as if it doesn't matter whether they come or not; tells her that Murry is a broken reed; that Katherine will never flower while she remains tied to him; that they can't be relied on. But that is bluff. In every letter to friends over the past weeks, Frieda has noticed, he mentioned them – that they're coming, *when* they're coming, that they will be living in the cottage next door, that the four of them will form a community, that they are going to be productive and happy together. He wants them to come, but he has taken out an emotional insurance against disappointment.

Frieda is pleased too, and more likely to remain pleased, she thinks, than Lorenzo, whose moods, since the suppression of his novel, have taken more frequent and terrible plunges. If he gave way to grief it mightn't be so bad; but his pride forbids that. It must be rage, always rage. This is a strength she admires – that he won't be cowed; but it's something she has learned also to fear.

They have come to Cornwall to escape from the world – or (as he puts it when he tries to focus his mind on everything they've turned their backs on) from the Café Royal. He has erased that literary waterhole from all respect and consideration as surely as if it had been demolished by bombs from a Zeppelin. Here in Cornwall, he feels, or wants to feel, there is no more "society" – just themselves and the stone cottages; the farming folk and their crops and livestock; the fields, cliffs and ocean; the wildflowers; the foxes and the seabirds.

But lately it has been hinted (in the guise of a kindly warning from neighbours) that because she's foreign they might be watched, questioned, reported on, especially if anyone overhears them speaking German. It's something that could destroy once again everything they are making of their lives. With his usual courage Lorenzo has pushed it aside. But it lies in wait, a trap, a poison.

Frieda hopes the company of the Murrys will keep him

cheerful. He has started a new novel. Damn the world, he says, it will carry right on from the one that's been banned.

She hopes the cottage they've chosen, only a few steps from their own, will suit the Murrys. They've assured Katherine it's dry, but that isn't quite true. These cottages are never perfectly dry. The walls are thick granite and the beamed ceilings are low, making it easy to heat the little rooms; but the gaps between the stones are filled only by packed earth, with a bit of mortar smeared on the outside – "like butter smeared on bread", Lorenzo says. And the slate roofs need repairs. In winter, when gales howl off the Atlantic, there's no keeping out the weather. Even in summer there are times when it looks in uninvited and without warning.

But will they and the Murrys last together until next winter? Lorenzo is so volatile, Murry so lacking in ballast, and Katherine so inward, so much a law unto herself, it seems unlikely. Lawrence, when he isn't saying Of course they won't come, allows himself to dream they might be together for years, a community, a nucleus of faith and hope that could move to America when the time is right. Frieda has learned it's best to live from one day to the next.

She knows too that having the Murrys there will mean a degree of exposure. Life with Lawrence can be rough, turbulent, robust – and it has been so much worse since the banning of his book. He admits to trembling at the slightest upset, and has asked her to be mild with him when the Murrys are here. (She will try!) It's why, though he wants them, he pretends indifference and speaks disparagingly. She understands that; and she can see the weaknesses he complains of in Jack. But she's susceptible to Jack's charm. As for Katherine – Frieda loves her like a sister.

"Katherine's exquisite," she tells Lawrence.

"Yes, well . . ." He doesn't argue.

"And clever, Lorenzo. She makes you laugh."

It's true, she does. He acknowledges that too. "There are lots of laughs with Katherine. So why is she always so untrusting?"

"She feels unsafe. You should understand that."

Yesterday in St Ives, completing the furnishing of their cottage, replacing some necessary things that haven't been sent from Hampstead, they bought a green-painted wardrobe with a full-length mirror, a chest of drawers, a bedstead – second-hand things, and only two pounds four shillings for the lot. They were delivered by cart early this morning and (with help from their neighbour, farmer Hocking) hauled upstairs through movable floorboards. Lawrence is triumphant and goes on to her about the chiselled workmanship around the mirror, the dovetailing, the spaciousness and solidity of the drawers which will only need a little easing with sandpaper and a candle. They represent, he tells her, a golden time before mass production destroyed pride in crafts.

"Please don't make them preach at me," Frieda says, interrupting him, "or I might stop liking them."

"Well, the green paint is nice," he says, smiling.

The planks are back in place and now, while she's washing the linen, Lawrence is putting down coco-matting on the floors up there. He has put their best (their only) spread over the bed, and hung their clothes in the wardrobe. He enjoys home-making and does it better than any man she has known.

Downstairs, on a wall he last week painted in the pink – almost magenta – colour of the foxgloves, he hangs an embroidery Lady Ottoline has done for them on a sketch by Duncan Grant. It is of a tree with bright flowers, moths and birds, and under its branches the lion and the lamb, neither looking happy about it but seeming aware of their mythical obligation to lie down together. Frieda, who often tells Lawrence he is fawning and ridiculous in his dealings with Ottoline, mocked the thing when it was delivered. Now, seeing it on the wall, brightening the little stone parlour, she's silent. She is not going to admit that she likes it, but she does.

That afternoon they made their way to Zennor through spacious sloping fields divided by stone walls, broad at the base and in some places as tall as a man, that must have been there hundreds of years, added to as more and more stones and boulders had been pulled from the pasture. Almost completely overgrown with bracken, heather and wildflowers, they appeared from a distance – from the hill behind the cottages – like enormous hedgerows, a darker green than the green of the pastures. Those walls were serviceable, but intractable. They couldn't be changed. They made a landscape that seemed ancient, eternal, as if God had ordained it thus on the fifth or sixth day of Creation.

Walking paths crossed at odd angles and went through gaps left in the walls where deep ditches had been dug and narrow stepping stones put in place – so the farmer and his family passed while cows and sheep were held to their allotted fold. That, Lorenzo told her, was what marked the difference here between man and beast. Man could pass through the stone walls, his live-stock could not.

As they walked through cow pasture the animals stopped grazing and came crowding towards the human pair, curious, sniffing, and then blowing out, a kind of snorting rejection and backing away to let them pass.

Zennor was a granite village of one pub, the Tinner's Arms,

a church, and fewer than a dozen houses and cottages, all sitting high above the ocean, but overlooked in turn by the hill the cottages of Higher Tregerthen were tucked against. Lawrence and Frieda sat in the pub parlour and drank a glass of scrumpy, and then walked on through fields as far as the cliff edge. Far – very far – below, the big sea, flecked white with foam and with the hover and swoop of gulls, rolled in, breaking on rocks and surging into crevices and caves. It was the coast and seascape of smugglers' tales, tales of storm and shipwreck. A steep path zig-zagged its way down, following the gully formed by a fast-running stream.

"We'll go down there, Murry and I," Lawrence said. "He'll like that."

Remembering the warnings they'd had, and feeling cheerful and defiant, he began to sing a German folk song. Frieda joined in with the refrain. Nobody heard. Their song was taken up and swallowed whole by the immense land- and seascape. Away to their left the sun was going down, turning the slate-grey of the western sea into burnished silver. They turned for home, taking the road this time, and then the lane that led down from the hill to the cottages.

A month later and the "community" of four was holding. There were good times and not so good, but it was holding. It was like the Cornish weather: some days the sun shone, the land was green, the sea blue and the wildflowers extravagant; others, fog rolled in from the Atlantic, rain fell in sheets, there was neither sky nor sea and no colour except grey.

There had been some awkwardness at first, getting used to one another again, but working together – making the Murrys' cottage ready, painting, buying furniture for it in St Ives – had helped. And Lawrence was writing again – that, Frieda knew, gave him an underlying contentment and made peace possible. He said that while *The Rainbow* couldn't be published this one, its sequel, couldn't either; but it was the novel he'd wanted to write and now he was writing it – and he seemed able to go to it at any time, morning or evening, or to leave it aside for a day or days and come back to it, and still it went ahead, effortlessly.

But he was unpredictable, becoming less restrained, less considerate, as they grew more used to being together; often irritable, easily aroused.

Alone with Frieda one morning, after a night of fierce debate, Katherine said, "I can't argue with him. I can't stand the noise. He's so loud and so angry. So I stop and then he tells me I'm sulking."

"I don't stand for his nonsense," Frieda said.

"I want to tell him that everything's not sex. Or sex is not everything."

"Sex is everything when it's not right," Frieda said.

"You mean between you and Lorenzo? Is something wrong?"

"No. It's all right. But he has his theories, you see. He has more theories than . . ." She stopped; but Katherine's eyes were fixed on her, wanting her to go on. "He thinks that if sex is right you should . . . I've forgotten what the polite word is. You should *arrive* . . ."

"Climax?"

"Yes. You should climax together."

"And you don't?"

Frieda shrugged. "Which climax?"

"You mean you have . . ."

"More than one? Yes. Don't you?"

Katherine didn't answer. Then she said, "I don't always have one."

Frieda nodded. "You see. These men have theories, but they don't *know*. That's what makes me angry with Lorenzo. He has to know everything, and I'm supposed to know nothing. And there are things I can't say because how am I supposed to have learned *that*? I've learned them with other men, that's how I know, but I can't tell him. There'd be an inquisition. Which man? When? How? Did I enjoy it? He'd beat me."

The two men had gone off with their rucksacks on one of their expeditions. They'd left early, full of jokes and good humour despite the previous night's argument, taking a thermos flask and sandwiches. "But have you noticed," Katherine said, "they go off full of beans and when they come back they often seem glum."

"It's Lorenzo," Frieda said. "You can see him charming Jack, wooing him like a girl. And Jack swoons and goes off with him, goes off with the great writer, the great D. H. Lawrence . . ." She shook her head. "It makes me sick."

"It's his brotherhood of the blood idea."

"Yes. And nothing will come of it. Not with Jack."

"Jack wants to please," Katherine said, "but I don't think he knows what he has to do."

"And I don't think Lawrence knows either."

They sat in silence for a time, until Frieda took it up again: "Lorenzo's always so full of hope. The *idea* of something takes hold, and then the disappointment is huge. And next thing he'll be saying *now* he's learned his lesson, *now* he knows how to live alone. *Alone!* As if I don't exist. He's never alone."

But when the two men came in they were not glum. They were excited, agitated, full of talk. They brought newspapers with the latest reports from Dublin. In the past ten days they'd all been reading about an uprising there by Irish Republicans. After a week of war in the streets the British army had them beaten, and now – this was the news the men brought from St Ives – three of the leaders had been tried by a military court, sentenced to summary execution and shot. Others would follow.

While Frieda made tea Lawrence worked himself into a rage about it – not against the British military who, he said, were fools and beyond contempt, but against the fools of Irishmen who had given the English the satisfaction of shooting them. Sacrificed themselves for nothing. These revolutionaries were worthless windbags.

"Shamrock Irishmen," he said, "with nothing in their heads but incense, stout and bad poetry. And now they want to be tragic heroes. There's a real war going on, a huge historical drama they want no part in, and they turn on a toy war of their own and expect people to be interested."

"But you are interested," Frieda said, putting down cups for them all and a plate of small cakes.

He cast her a black glance and said nothing.

"Shooting people," Katherine said. "Putting them up against a wall and just . . . *shooting* them. I can't bear to think about it."

"The only known cure for the common cold," Lawrence said. He pulled the door open and walked into the lane. When he came back he had an armload of wood. He was humming an Irish ballad, then singing the words. It might have been mocking, or commemorative. He sang it with an Irish accent.

"Down by the salley gardens my love and I did meet;
She passed the salley gardens with little snow-white feet.
She bid me take love easy, as the leaves grow on the tree;
But I, being young and foolish, with her would not agree."

Soon they were drinking their tea and talking again about the rebellion. Lawrence was calmer, more reasonable, but still the schoolmasterly way he held forth, and the serious face Jack turned to him, irritated Frieda.

Lawrence mentioned Shelley. He thought he remembered that Shelley had gone to Ireland for a time and had propagated ideas of revolution. Republican ideas.

Frieda interrupted him. She knew Shelley was one of his literary heroes. "Shelley was just another tedious English preacher."

Lawrence stared at her, all three did, as if she'd sung a wrong note – deliberately. That didn't displease her, and she went recklessly on with another. "Really," she said, "his skylark thing is just a lot of footle."

Katherine laughed. "*Footle*. What an excellent word."

Lawrence turned on Frieda. "His skylark thing. So you know Shelley wrote about a skylark. Congratulations. What else can you tell us about English literature?"

"I could tell you about another false prophet," she said, stirring herself up, challenging. "Another preacher to impressionable young women and weak-minded men. Another little English God almighty who thinks he should be able to rule the waves and couldn't even command a dog. I live with him."

Lawrence hurled himself out of his chair and stood over her, pointing to the door, shouting. "Then stop living with him. Get out of his house and stop blighting his life."

She faced him. There was something reckless in her that could never resist these confrontations, even liked them. "His house? Why is it his house? He doesn't own it. If someone has to go it should be you, Lorenzo. *You* get out."

As she spoke she saw the Murrys getting up to leave. "We'll get the supper ready," Katherine said, bent forward, nodding her head like a bird and scuttling towards the door. "Come over in twenty minutes."

Lawrence was leaning over the table now, both fists on the cloth, staring down at its blue and white checks, moving his head slowly from side to side. The veins stood out on his forehead. Frieda felt a twinge of pity for him; but something stronger was in control. "You're a conceited fool," she said, "and I've had enough of you." She turned away and climbed the stairs to their bedroom.

She stood at the window looking out over the landscape, so green it seemed unreal. Beyond the clifftops and away to the left the sun spread itself over a great sweep of ocean in alternating bands of mercury and pewter.

She lay down on the bed and for a few minutes fell into a light sleep. She was woken by the sound of him stamping out and slamming the door. He was going to the Murrys without her. Very well. Let him go. She wouldn't follow. She'd wait until they called her. Jack could come and beg before she would stir from the bed.

But time went by and no one came. No one shouted from the other cottage to say that supper was ready. What had he told them? That she wasn't hungry? That she was regretting her outburst? That she was repentant?

The thought of it propelled her out of bed. She rushed downstairs and out into the garden. It was getting dark now, the Murrys' door was wide open to the early summer evening, they had lit their lantern, and she could see the three sitting at the table, eating. She wanted to rush in and ask what he'd said about her and deny it, but pride prevented it. She folded her arms and stalked up and down the little lawn, furious, knowing they must see her there.

They stopped eating. She could see them in the lamplight, all three peering out at the white figure as it passed and re-passed their door. She felt her marching foot slide and sink into the soft soil of Lawrence's beetroot bed. Well, what did she care about his precious garden? She would grind her heel in it.

The silence was broken by a roar from Lawrence – "I'll kill you, you bitch. I'll cut your throat" – and the clatter of his chair falling to the floor as he sprang up from the table. He came running towards her, his fist raised, and struck at her, hitting her forearm hard as she raised it to defend herself. She ducked to get past but he grabbed at her by the hair. She shrieked and covered her face as his blows rained down on her head and shoulders, arms and back. They were flailing blows that mostly glanced off, but they hurt. Still she managed to shout at him so the Murrys would hear, "That's right, Lorenzo, show your little Judas what kind of a Jesus you are."

The blows stopped a moment. She straightened quickly from her defensive crouch, pushing him off balance, and got past, running into the Murrys' kitchen where Katherine and Jack sat, both quite still, their faces rigid with a kind of wincing blank-ness and distaste. Lawrence came after her, shouting, pursuing her around the table and getting close enough to strike further blows. One hit her ear, another sank into her midriff, a third struck her in the middle of the back between the shoulder blades. She cried to Jack to do something, to help her, but he sat, head bowed as if in prayer, and didn't move.

Suddenly it stopped. Lawrence was standing, his arms dropped to his side, panting, exhausted, looking as if the effort had destroyed him. His knees gave way, he wobbled and sank into a chair, his chest heaving, the breath rasping in his throat like a death rattle. The normal colour was draining from his face. She thought he

132

might die. Good, she thought. Let him. Oh yes please, God, let him die. *Make* him.

She was still sobbing, half-blind with tears, partly winded from a punch to the solar plexus. Apart from the pain she felt nothing but triumph. She'd known this feeling before – often. She didn't quite understand it. It had to do with not letting him defeat her, but it was more than that. It was the thought that one day he might kill her – and the pleasure of that thought. Then she would have defeated him.

The three sat at the table, Lawrence heaving, almost retching, with the effort to breathe, the Murrys seeming not to breathe at all. Frieda, too, sank into a chair. Katherine passed her a hand-kerchief. Many minutes later her sobbing and sniffing were under control. Lawrence was still panting, but less dangerously.

Katherine, eyes still down, murmured to Frieda, "Will you have some supper?"

Frieda didn't reply. She wouldn't. Why should she? She noticed the ticking of a clock. Jack's fingers drummed briefly on the table top.

Katherine stood up, slowly, not creating the least disturbance, and began to clear plates. Lawrence turned sideways, leaned forward, biting his nails and staring at the floor. He sighed, an enormous gulping shuddering sigh like an infant at the end of a tantrum, and cast his eyes around the table. He did have the face of a Christ on the cross, Frieda thought, and again there was a faint stirring of pity for him.

And then he breathed deeply, and spoke. He asked Jack, "If you could have Flaubert or Balzac to visit, which would it be?"

Jack looked across at Frieda – a quick, nervous glance – and then at Katherine. "Well I . . ." he said. "I think, yes, I'm sure. Balzac. It would have to be Balzac."

"We haven't enough coffee," Katherine said.

Jack said there was coffee in the cupboard. "Yes," Katherine said. "But not enough for Balzac."

The Christ face managed a smile. "Ah yes. It killed him. Twenty or thirty cups a day, black."

"I thought it was gangrene," Jack said.

"Coffee first, then gangrene," Katherine said. "Gangrene was the cup of grace."

"I would like some coffee," Frieda said. She was careful to sound tentative.

"If you promise not to die," Katherine said. She offered supper again. "It's only macaroni cheese."

"Oh but I like macaroni cheese," Frieda said. And then, "D'you remember, Lorenzo . . ."

There was a macaroni cheese they'd had once in Hampstead – very rich, very good. There must have been cream in it. Maybe eggs as well. Could there have been eggs? Anyway, extravagant.

And yes, he remembered. He'd told Katherine and Jack about it while they were eating.

"This is just macaroni," Katherine said. "And cheese." Her voice was full of repressed laughter now. Frieda could hear it even without looking. She was bubbling with it.

Frieda ate with relish. She was always hungry after a skirmish. Her bruises ached.

That night Lawrence climbed into bed with her, silent, subdued, rueful. He wrapped himself tight around her – arms, legs, his face in the crook of her shoulder. She was used to this. They were silent a long time, holding on to one another, she rubbing her hands through his dry, unyielding hair. She was remembering occasions and places with the Murrys – the four of them in their best clothes when she and Lorenzo married;

134

doing charades at Cholesbury and acting in the play Katherine had invented there; Jack and Katherine making faces at one another on top of a London bus; and perched on their luggage, riding down the lane on the cart that brought them to Higher Tregerthen from the Tinner's Arms. She thought of their walks together along "the rim of the Atlantic", all the way to St Ives, singing ballads and rounds, joking, arguing, stopping to play the "stone game" the Murrys had invented in Bandol, in which a stone was placed at the edge of the cliff and the players took turns to throw smaller stones at it until someone – the winner – knocked it over the edge. And Katherine's excitement when the Murrys were first settling in – at the bluebells; at the patterns of cloud shadow racing over the grass she described as "silky"; at the lovely movement of light in the lower room when she sat on the "tower" stairs; and at the clear strange sound of voices heard at night from the upper room. And telling them, when she and Lorenzo sat among the foxgloves at the front of the cottage, that they looked like happy prisoners in a camp of Red Indians. Katherine was like Lorenzo: she noticed so much, took such pleasure in it, and made you see what was she saw.

Frieda shed a few tears. He felt them on his face. "Are you weeping?"

"The Murrys won't stay," she said.

"They didn't say so."

"No. But I know them. They'll go."

"Why should they?"

"They'll find a reason."

"You mean because of our fight."

"Because of our *fights*, Lorenzo."

He grunted, pushed back from her as if staring at her in the dark. "She'll write to Kot about us."

"And to Ottoline probably."

"She'll tell them I beat you."

"Kot will say I deserve it. Katherine thinks so too, I'm sure. I overheard her talking to Jack about me yesterday. She called me the German pudding."

"Better a German pudding than a British celery stick."

"She's not a celery stick, Lorenzo. When she takes her clothes off to wash she's lovely. Exquisite." Another lapse towards sleep, and then, "But they'll go. I can feel it."

"They used to put up with us."

"We weren't so bad then. And they were younger."

"Are we worse?"

"Yes."

He was silent, absorbing this. "Well, so be it."

"I'll miss her."

"I won't miss Jack."

"Yes you will, Lorenzo."

"Let's wait and see. If they go, they go."

"What about your novel?"

"My novel doesn't need the Murrys."

"Aren't they in it?"

"Katherine's there; and there's something of Jack. But I don't need them under my feet."

They dozed until he stirred and said, "I'm sorry I hurt you."

"I provoked you."

"Are you damaged?"

"Bruised. Sore. And my ear – I think you scratched it with your nail."

"I'll bring you breakfast in bed in the morning, shall I?"

"That would be nice."

"D'you regret . . ."

"Regret?"

"Us. Everything. The whole . . ." He was lost for a word. Finally he murmured, "experiment?"

"The whole adventure?" she suggested. "The whole disaster? Often, yes. But not always. Not now. What about you, Lorenzo?"

He kissed her. "I was thinking of trimming you a hat. Something new and extravagant for the summer."

It was some days before the Murrys announced they might soon be leaving; and some weeks before they left. It was the wrong coast for Katherine, they explained. She couldn't cope with the damp, the rain, the mists that rolled in from the Atlantic. The Lawrences didn't argue, didn't point out that the days were getting warmer and that often now the sun shone on a sea that glowed with the blue-green of peacock feathers. They knew the real issue was peace and quiet, something they couldn't offer, had never been able to achieve even in better times.

The Murrys had found a cottage at Mylor on the south coast, a river inlet close to Falmouth. The weather would be milder there; drier, more suitable. They asked if Lawrence and Frieda would like to move with them, but it was a politeness.

Lawrence said they should visit one another – often, since they would all still be in Cornwall. He said he'd grown attached to the wild north coast. The magpies and foxes would miss him if he went, and the gulls would have one more thing to complain about. He was writing his new novel. He felt he should stick where he was and get on with it.

When the day arrived he helped Jack tie down on the farmer's cart the luggage and the few pieces of furniture they were sending over to Mylor. Katherine had gone already, by train from St Ives, and would be waiting in Falmouth. When the cart had gone they walked with Jack as he wheeled his bike to the top of the lane. The two men shook hands in the shadow of granite boulders, a formal farewell, with some feeling of resentment on either side. Jack kissed Frieda, hugged her hard, waved one last time, and wobbled away.

Frieda wiped away her tears. Lorenzo's face had set into an expression stonily neutral. As they walked back down the lane to the cottages the landscape seemed to Frieda suddenly empty, unfriendly. And then, making the best of things as she'd learned to do, she said, "Didn't the Murrys take their cottage for a year?"

"A year, that's right." She could tell by the lift in his voice that he'd guessed what she meant.

She said, "You've had so little space for working, Lorenzo. We can spread ourselves a little. You can write in Katherine's tower."

He smiled, picked a blue flower from the wayside, and stuck it into her unruly golden hair.

EIGHT

Summer 1916 – Katherine

KATHERINE IS SITTING AT HER DESK. SHE HAS IN FRONT OF HER the draft of "THE Aloe" completed in Bandol. It seems so good she doesn't know how she did it. It needs shaping and tidying, but she can't bring herself to do more than read it – and not read it all, right through. Glancingly, a bit here and a bit there. She has to pull the sheets out from under the kitten, Wilkins, who has curled up and gone to sleep on her desk.

Her desk is turned to face the wall so she won't be distracted; but she doesn't have to swivel far to look at the scene out there – Jack at this moment working in the kitchen garden that slopes down to the water; and in a dinghy tied to the jetty, Fred Goodyear, sprawled on his back, eyes closed against the glare, the puttees and boots of one leg hanging over the side, heel just touching the water, his tunic wide open and his belt undone. The inlet itself is pale and tranquil. On the far side the land slopes up, grassland dotted with sheep, cow pasture, small orchards, patches of copse and clusters of trees. With windows open she can hear water lapping, birds in the orchard trees, the distant bleating of sheep. Mylor is hardly more than twenty-five miles from Zennor but it seems half a world away and reminds her, achingly, of places she has known in New Zealand.

The garden has been neglected by the previous tenant but

Jack is working at it. In the past week, before Fred arrived, he has also been writing reviews of French books for the *Times Literary Supplement*. To make himself better equipped for that he has bought a pile of second-hand books, including a number of classics of French literature he feels he should know, or know better, and rowed them up the estuary from Falmouth, together with two second-hand chairs. His industry is a constant reproach to her. He seems only to need to think of a project, and then to begin it and work at it, and complete it. Simple! She, by contrast, has ideas, brilliant they sometimes seem. Each one as it comes to her, usually in the form of a story, she follows through in her head, finding the tone, the narrative sequence and strategy, the right words and phrases. She laughs at her own wit, admires her own devices. She goes over and over it, often in the night when she can't sleep. Gradually the urgency goes out of it, as if the task has been completed. Now it looks like a fish caught an hour ago and well dead. The colours are still there, but the brilliance, the shine, the living gloss are gone.

Her mood has been dark in recent weeks. She knows she should take pleasure in Jack's industry but feels it only as a reminder of her own failings. Even his having rowed the books down to Mylor Bridge irritates. He has always talked of wanting to own a sailboat with a centreboard – something dreamed of as a boy, until now impossible; and here at last they are living at the waterside, a calm inlet, and he refuses to buy one offered for sale by a neighbour, because, he says, they can't afford it. He has hired the dinghy instead.

It's one of those pinched petit-bourgeois things about Jack that make her want to walk away and never see him again.

She tells him, "You should be more like Lawrence."

"D'you mean like Lawrence, or like you?"

"I mean you should please yourself for once."

"I see. Like you."

So the reproach is turned back on her, and an argument develops.

At close quarters she'd feared Lawrence's violence. Now she was finding she missed his vividness – and missed Frieda's company too, the company of another woman. At Higher Tregerthen she hadn't often been alone with Lorenzo, but occasionally they'd gone for walks together while he gave her lessons in local lore, history, botany. He was a natural teacher. He took her through the fields telling her the names of plants and flowers she didn't remember having seen in New Zealand – cow parsley, campion, yarrow, scabious, love-in-a-mist, vetch; and pointing out examples of others that were not unfamiliar, but different, or hidden – primrose, violet and bluebell, foxglove, wild fuchsia, hydrangea, and a kind of wild oat springing up among the bracken. He showed her where to watch for an adder that came out sometimes and lay sunning itself. He took her partway along the footpath route that went over the hill and across the moors to Penzance. He led her up to a place, above the cottages and beyond the road to St Ives, where a fox pair could sometimes be seen lying among rocks while their two cubs played and practised fighting.

Lawrence's charm, when he gave her his full attention, was compelling, and there was never anything sexual in it. There were a few men she'd met – even one or two she didn't like – whose sexual presence was so strong it seemed almost to assault without a word spoken or the least physical contact. For her, Lorenzo had no such presence. But when his angry, messianic ego was set aside he could be the most amiable of men. She could love him, and feel loved. Nothing was demanded except attention, which she gave willingly and for which she was well rewarded.

Leaving Bandol had broken a spell between her and Jack, and Lawrence seemed to know that it had. On more than one of their walks he urged her, for the sake of her writing, to learn to be alone. "Forget about being in love," he said.

"I want to be in love."

"Yes, and children want sweets. But they grow up."

"Aren't you in love with Frieda?"

"I'm married to Frieda."

"And that's enough?"

He smiled. "More than enough."

She supposed he meant what he said, and even that it contained a kind of wisdom. But he was also telling her that there was something wrong with the love between her and Jack, and that she couldn't depend on it, or build on it. He repeated that she had to learn to be alone. Once she'd learned that, then she would know how to live with a man without clamouring and demanding and suffering disappointments.

She listened in silence, remembering Frieda saying that Lawrence always persuaded himself he was surviving alone when in fact he was depending on her. But she believed he was right. Her relationship with Jack was something *made up*, like a story. For three and more years she'd worked at it as at nothing else. There were times when she loved him with her full power to love; but looking back she saw that this had mostly been when they were apart, loving one another by letter; or when, as in Bandol, they'd been alone and her control of their lives had been very nearly total. She'd loved Jack, and she supposed would love him again, but only when he lived by her script; and it was at those times she had to suppress a feeling that he was behaving falsely in order to please her. That falseness was the price of her love, and its destroyer.

She asked herself the hard question: whether this was so of every man in her life, and would go on being so until she found some way to reform and discipline her emotions. She was uncertain what a truthful answer might be. But she believed, felt she had no choice except to believe, that there *could* be a man, if only she could find him, who would fill the role she cast Jack in, not because it was demanded of him but because it was in his nature. Her perfect man! She could mock herself for entertaining such an idea. She could tell herself it was a delusion, worthy of servant girls who had little knowledge and no hope of better. Self-mockery had its effect, but it couldn't entirely dislodge the dream. She longed for the freedoms she'd once had – youth, money, health – to go in search of love, as a man might go into Africa or across the Antarctic ice in search of adventure. Pointless enterprises perhaps, and she'd lost the courage it took to undertake them; but the restless – and reckless – spirit craved them none the less.

Lawrence was not the only promoter of her restlessness. In Bandol she'd received a "strictly confidential" letter from Fred Goodyear addressing her as "Dearest Darling K.M.," describing himself as "a lonely soldier", and telling her how much he regretted that they had never been to bed together. "All the time I have known you, you have been fixed up with Murry and that's been final as far as I was concerned, though it has made things very awkward between us." He was under a great strain in the army, he told her, and might at any moment break down, do something silly and get a term of imprisonment. But he'd applied for a commission, and expected that if he got it, it would put an end to his present problems. Meanwhile, he concluded, "I think everything everywhere is bunkum".

This had come at a time when her whole horizon was filled by Jack and by her work, and she'd dealt with it by not taking it entirely seriously, writing a reply meant to entertain him, relieve the boredom of his days as a non-fighting soldier, and asking him to write again when everything was "not *too* bunkum".

By the time his next letter came they were in Zennor. It was sober, analytical. He described himself as disillusioned to the point where life now presented itself as a huge practical joke. Her own character, he said, was more serious. As a writer she had important decisions to make, and could yet take a right path or a wrong one. The letter seemed to her so serious, so unlike anything anyone had ever said to her about herself and her writing, it had given her a great craving to see and talk to the man who had written it.

And now Fred was with them; had arrived unannounced at their door, having somehow found his way from the station at Falmouth, on leave before going on his officer training course. He was handsome, strongly built, brown-haired, still pink-cheeked and inclined to blush, but manly – the soldier-poet and self-declared cynic who didn't think cynicism good enough for *her* because he believed in her future as a writer. And bearing gifts of chocolates, perfume, French wine.

He'd been with them a few days, and they'd talked, walked, eaten and talked again, late into the night. He'd become familiar, close, the old friend with whom they'd had their first experience of Paris.

One day they took the ferry from Falmouth to St Mawes, hired a fisherman's boat, and went across to a lighthouse on a headland under which was a little beach, with deep orange-yellow grainy sand and grey rocks, where they lay in the sun looking up at the pines and the blue sky. When he got his commission, Fred told them, he would be posted, almost certainly, to the Somme. "You've read about the new offensive? They're dying in such numbers, there isn't ground to put them in. I should feel terrified – and I suppose that will come. But it's strange – what I feel at the moment is an immense curiosity."

He said his life since leaving Brasenose had been for the most part tedious and unsatisfactory and he didn't feel any strong urge, or find any good reason, to cling to it. "I'm not talking about suicide," he assured them. "It's really just a matter of co-operating with whatever my fate happens to be. Not fighting it. Keep my eyes open, watch what happens – and no regrets."

She and Fred left Jack sleeping on the sand and clambered over the rocks to a secluded place where he kissed her, something he'd never done before, or not in that way, so much (she thought) as if he meant business. She disengaged gently, not wanting to seem to mind. They sat, backs to the rock, soaking up the sun. She said, "I was grateful for your last letter, Freddie. You told me something about myself."

He nodded, looking down at his legs spread on the rocks and making a big khaki V. "If you felt like that when you read it then you knew it already. But that's good. That's how it should be."

"You reminded me . . . I'm arrogant."

"Not arrogant. No. It's just that . . ." He hesitated, thinking how to explain his idea of her. "When I first knew you, you made such prodigious demands on life. On everything and everyone. You tended to be impatient with people who couldn't match you. There was a bit of contempt and it got into the writing."

"It's true." She took his hand. "I scored off people in my writing. I still do."

"Listen, Katya." He sat up straight and turned to look at her. He was like a schoolmaster, determined to be understood. "What I said, or what I meant to say, was that there's that clever satiric side of your character and your writing. I admire it. I enjoy it. I marvel at it. Everybody does. But there's also the person who feels union with created things."

She smiled. It was the part of the letter that had given her hope and she remembered it well. He'd spoken of "a republic of scents and grasses and dews and café mirrors". She was, he'd said, at one with that external world; and he'd asked why she shouldn't see humankind as just "another phase of Nature". When she achieved that, she would move forward as a writer.

"It's happening," she told him. "There's a change in my work. It's since my brother died and I've started writing about my own people . . ." She grasped his hand in both of hers. "We have to be allies in this, Freddie. I need you, and maybe you could get something from me. Something in return. Your poetry . . ."

He shook his head. "My poetry is entertainment. My muse is a budgie in a rhyming cage. If I had half your talent, I wouldn't be going to war. I'd be going into hiding."

No, she couldn't accept that. She was emphatic. "If I can write, so can you. I've seen what you wrote for Jack. And other things. You haven't written all those poems and essays without hoping to find readers. If you insist on believing in me, you have to let me believe in you."

He smiled and she could see that, of course, he did want to believe in himself. "Well, maybe . . ."

She kissed him, lightly on the cheek, and then properly, on the mouth. "Come. Jack will be wondering what we're doing. But we have a pact, don't we?"

He scrambled to his feet. "What will this do to my courage,

Mansfield? I'm supposed to be a man who doesn't care whether he lives or dies."

"Change your plan, darling."

"New orders?"

"New orders. Scrap the old ones and start again."

The next night was to be his last with them. She was full of good cheer and hope for the future. She prepared a stew of shin of beef. It was cheap, which meant she could buy enough to offer hungry men big portions; and if it was cooked well, long and slow, with the right vegetables and herbs, it could be tender and tasty. Jack's leeks, onions, carrots and new potatoes went into it, with some of Lawrence's herbs. "It should have been shin of Thomas Hardy," she said. "But the butcher hadn't read him."

"Or organ of Morgan Forster," Fred suggested.

"Oh we don't do organs here," she said, in the accent of the butcher. "Not while there's a war on."

After the stew came raspberries and cream. The raspberries had been brought that afternoon – carried in a rhubarb leaf – by May, the daily help. May had also had a hand in preparing the stew.

The men talked about Nietzsche. Jack spoke with an intensity that was familiar to Katherine. He radiated an enthusiasm that suggested knowledge beyond knowledge. She could see that it worked at first on Fred who then began to resist, to disagree, faintly to mock.

To Katherine it was as if the men were speaking about two different Nietzsches, Jack's a gentle suffering humanist who threw his arms around the neck of a horse when he saw it being maltreated in the streets of Turin, Fred's a half-mad dancer among the stars who believed in the *Ubermensch*.

"But it's true he was kind to animals," Fred said. "There's a story that he saw a dog with its paw caught in something. He released it, washed the wound, bandaged it with his handkerchief and sent it on its way. Next day the dog found him on his usual walk. It was carrying the handkerchief in its mouth, washed and ironed."

Katherine said a dog that could wash and iron a handkerchief should have bandaged its own paw. "I favour philosophers whose names I can spell," she said, "and for the moment I can't think of any."

Fred said, "I don't believe you can't spell Kant."

"I can," she said, "but I won't."

She drank very little. Fred didn't hold back, and Jack kept pace with him but was out of practice. Since they'd left Bandol there had been no alcohol except an occasional glass of cider at the Tinner's Arms. As the wine went down Jack's speech became slower, more strained, as if English were a foreign language he understood and spoke well only by paying it careful attention.

Fred talked about India, how he'd hated his countrymen and the way they treated the people there. "It can't last," he said. "One day the Indians will get up a revolt and throw us all out."

As he talked Katherine's mind plucked and kept impressions – the colours of cottons and silks, the smell of vegetable curries, the elegant spaces of courtyards and verandahs, the beating of monsoon rains, the thickness and blackness of women's oiled hair, the dry brown dusty landscapes, and (a particular memory for him) the sun going down beyond the Towers of Silence, a sunset that had been, he said, the colour he imagined the famous pink terraces in New Zealand must have been.

"How do you know about the pink terraces?" Katherine asked.

"How else than from you, my darling?"

"I told you about them?"

"Vividly. You said you'd walked on them. Climbed them, I think."

"I must have made it up. They were destroyed – covered by a volcanic eruption a few years before I was born."

There was a burst of Fred's snorting, boyish laugh. "You were always such a liar, Mansfield. How do you deal with it, Jack?"

Jack didn't smile. "She tells the truth when it suits her."

"Lying," she said, "is my profession. I'm a fiction writer."

They played a game they'd played on that first evening together when they met in Leicester Square, each choosing a favourite place to go to in imagination. She chose Day's Bay on the eastern side of Wellington harbour, where her family had taken their holidays when she was a child. As she described it she saw it in the hot middle of a summer's day, the deserted beach, small waves flapping lazily over one another, bathing suits hanging on verandah rails, the store owned by a very large Mrs Stubbs – and everywhere thick dark green bush pressing in on the little settlement. She would write about it one day. This was where she might next take the family she'd created in writing "The Aloe".

Jack chose somewhere he'd never been – sat himself at a café table in a little town somewhere in Spain, listening to guitar music, watching the passing crowds. But then he changed his mind. His Englishness asserted itself. He wanted to be in a farmhouse in Sussex, knocking about in his own garden, rolling the lawn. Yes, that especially. The idea of rolling the lawn pleased him no end . . .

For Fred it was going to be somewhere in Scandinavia – in Norway, Sweden, the further north the better. He thought Katherine should go there – first in summer, to experience the long days and magic nights; later, maybe when the war was over, she should go in winter, which was more dramatic and even more beautiful.

She was excited by this. She wanted to say that one day she and Fred would go there together.

When it came time to go to bed Jack stood, blinking and rocking on his feet. "We must be up in good time for Fred's . . ." The word he wanted wouldn't come.

"Breakfast?" Katherine supplied. "Departure? Train?"

Jack's smile was grim. "You see how fortunate I am?" he said to Freddie. "When I lack a word, my friend supplies three." He made his erratic way to the bathroom.

Fred and Katherine looked at one another. His eyes were glittering, intense. She asked, in a voice she herself could scarcely hear, "What are the towers of silence?"

"That's where the Parsees put the bodies of their dead."

"Why?"

"To be eaten by the vultures."

"Ah. How practical."

"A sort of home economics."

"The towers of silence," she repeated. "That's a poem in three words."

"Four."

"I'm sorry. Four. You can't expect me to count as well."

"As well as what?"

"As well as you."

He laughed. "You are very beautiful," he said.

She closed her eyes. "And you are very kind."

Jack came out of the bathroom, hesitated, then lurched sideways into their bedroom and closed the door. "You next, soldier," she said. "I'll smoke one last cigarette."

She went to the window and opened it wide. There were a

150

very few weak lights shining on the other side of the water, and a clear skyful of reflected stars. She smoked, hearing behind her the sounds of Jack, then Fred, stumbling about, getting ready for bed. She wondered whether she too, like Fred, should resolve to co-operate with her destiny, and if she did, what that might mean. Was it life and death for her too, or was her feeling that it might be just another example of her tendency to exaggerate?

When all was quiet she turned out the last of the lights and went to Fred's door. She could see his outline on the bed in the darkness, lying on his back, very still, hands behind his head.

"Fred." She said his name quietly, hardly more than a whisper.

"Oh, hullo, Mansfield." It was a boyish half-whisper. His breath was thick. He must have been close to sleep. "Come in." She could just make him out as he pulled himself up and patted the side of the bed for her to sit down.

She asked was he comfortable and he said he was. "It's a crazy old bed," she said, but he assured her that after his army bunk, it was very cosy.

She said, "I want you to live, Freddie. I know you think you don't care if you die, but you have to. I care, and so you must too. You have to survive.'

He took her hand and squeezed – so hard it hurt. "I'll do my best." She thought she could see tears.

She said, "You know that Jack and I are going our separate ways." It had crept over her in the past few weeks that this was true, but it was the first time it had been said. Yet she was sure Jack knew it as well as she did.

"Hell, Katya." Fred ruffled his hair. It was a dry sound. "Should I say I'm sorry to hear it?"

"Say nothing. Just note it. Keep it in mind when you're feeling reckless."

He put a hand to the back of her head, drew her towards him and kissed her. "When this is over, will you come with me to Scandinavia?"

"I will."

"Promise?"

"I promise."

He wanted her to lie down with him but all at once she remembered her last night with Leslie, and checked herself. If she kissed him again it would be too late; there would be no turning back.

"Not now," she said. "Not with Jack in the next room."

She wanted, superstitiously, to do the right thing, the thing that would protect his life – but what was that? She didn't know, couldn't be sure. Very gently he was pulling her towards him.

She was full of fear and then, as he kissed her again, fear was forgotten.

NINE

Late Summer 1916 –
Dora Carrington

CARRINGTON DIDN'T SEE HOW IT BEGAN – KATHERINE
Mansfield's singing. They'd all been taking tea together in the
Red Room at Garsington, Ottoline Morrell's country house.
Ottoline, her considerable height augmented by built-up shoes,
her face mauve-tinted around the eyes and rouged at the cheeks,
wearing a dress of embroidered green velvet, had just joined her
guests around the table. The conversation, or the part Carrington
heard, was about the war, the new battle – eighty miles of
mayhem and slaughter the newspapers were calling it – developing on the Somme; and then of the anti-war lecture tour
Bertrand Russell had embarked on – his bravery, his willingness
to accept hatred and contempt and to risk physical attacks and
even a prison sentence. Already fined for speaking out, he'd been
denied a passport so had to cancel a visit to America; and now
it was said he was to be sacked from his lectureship at Cambridge.
Bertie Russell was a hero at Garsington among the pacifists and
conscientious objectors. Lady Ottoline was his mistress – or had
been, and they were still close; and her husband, Philip Morrell,
who must surely have known about the affair, seemed to be his
friend. Bertie remained cheerful. "These are fierce times," was
all he'd said about his trial; and he'd asked how anyone could

talk about *his* courage when perfectly ordinary men off the streets of Great Britain were being asked to climb out of trenches and slog forward through mud and shell-holes in the face of machine-gun and rifle fire, seeing their fellows falling all about them. Twenty thousand, it was said, had died on the first day of the new battle.

A separate conversation must have started up at the other end of the table – something about music, Clive Bell holding forth, Dorothy Brett angling her ear-trumpet; and then there was the sound of a guitar and a voice, quiet and low, singing an Elizabethan ballad. Everyone fell silent, listening.

Katherine stopped. "Sorry," she said. "I was just explaining to Mr Bell . . . Illustrating . . ."

But they wanted more, insisted. The war was set aside. She began again, finished the ballad, sang another, this time Shakespeare's song about the wind and the rain that ends *Twelfth Night,* and there were demands for a third. She sang a sentimental Victorian song, "Scarlet Ribbons", half mocking, but seriously enough to bring a tear to Ottoline's eye. "My nurse sang it to me when I was very little," Ottoline murmured. "I used to wish I could be poor – it seemed so romantic." Clive Bell gave Katherine the first line of another, she picked out a chord or two, and in a moment he and she were singing it together:

> "This life is wea-ry
> A tear, a sigh.
> A love that changes
> And then *goodbye*.
> This life is wea-ry
> Hope comes to die . . ."

Her voice was like honey. Ottoline with her big head and orange hair bobbing in time, fiddling with the silver cross and pearls at her throat, beamed around at them all, blinking and smiling. It pleased her when something like this happened, something unscheduled, spontaneous and beautiful. That was what Garsington was meant for, a haven for fine minds and true artists, for love, poetry and song; for all that was good and original in thought and feeling. That's what she liked to say – to intone, to boom out – whenever the chance arose, and it was written now on her face.

Carrington hadn't been pleased, or at least had felt uneasy, when Ottoline had told her that Katherine Mansfield was to share her room. Katherine would be here for the weekend, Ottoline said; possibly longer, until Tuesday or Wednesday. That would be all right wouldn't it?

What could she say but "Yes, of course, perfectly all right"? She was there as a guest, as they all were. Everybody who was anybody wanted to come to Garsington. It was a grand house with many rooms, and Ottoline was a great welcomer. She packed them in, especially at weekends.

That had been this morning after breakfast. Katherine would arrive at Wheatley by the mid-morning train, and already the pony-cart had been sent to collect her from the station.

Carrington was interested, curious, half pleased but uncertain. It might be all right. There was no doubt Katherine could charm: she'd charmed Ottoline, and had been invited to her ladyship's room, after lunch, for "a little talk". Men loved her. Lytton Strachey conceded she was clever, though he'd said her face was "a Japanese mask". Bertie Russell had lately shown signs of twitching at the mention of her name. Even Gertler had forgotten his obsession with Carrington for a few days after acting in a play with her last year at Cholesbury, but his interest hadn't lasted.

Katherine had a reputation for being mysterious, secretive, sometimes black-humoured, often sharp-tongued, ironic, even malicious. Nothing unusual about that either; not at Garsington, where everyone was more or less brilliant and most were competitive. It was just that the thought of sharing a room with her had seemed too close too soon. It had made Carrington nervous. This singing, however, was something new, another aspect of Katherine's character. It softened her image. Perhaps after all they would get on.

Katherine had stopped singing and was tuning a string. Lytton turned to young Aldous Huxley, sitting beside him fiddling with his cup, and murmured something. Carrington didn't catch what it was but Aldous half hiccoughed, half snorted a laugh, then blushed and suppressed it. This was bad. Carrington adored Lytton. But he could be cruel, silly and destructive.

Katherine stopped tuning the imperfect string. The pale mask of a face, capable of such expressiveness and subtlety, went blank. She put the guitar down on the floor behind her chair. "Enough," she said.

"No, no," Ottoline stared wild-eyed around the table like a person appealing to a crowd for support. "Never enough." Her voice was unduly loud, absurdly rich, extravagantly aristocratic, somewhere between a croon and a boom.

The faces along the table smiled at Katherine, agreeing with Ottoline. "Please," they said. "Another one." "It was beautiful." "You have *such* a lovely voice." Aldous, trying to repair his part in the interruption, said, "If music be the food of love, play on."

They'd been enjoying her singing, but that was no longer the point. The young woman, the newcomer among the house guests, had been stung by the old wasp.

"Really and truly," Katherine said. "No more. I think Mr Strachey wants to say something about the war." She looked at him across the table. The mask was animated again, but with a gleam of steel in it. "Don't you, Mr Strachey?"

"The war?" What had he said to Aldous? Something clever and funny at her expense. It had shaken her for a moment but she'd recovered. Aldous was still blushing. Lytton was cornered. "No," he assured her, "I've nothing to say."

"Oh," Katherine picked up her cup and sipped; "I was sure you'd say *something*."

It wasn't clear how she'd done it, because it was not easy to ruffle Lytton; but somehow, quite delicately, she'd got the better of him. Carrington felt it, and thought everyone did.

That evening after dinner she and Katherine talked in their room. She explained that she was called Carrington partly because she didn't like her given name, Dora; but also because that was the convention among the women of her year at the Slade. The men came mostly from public schools, calling themselves Brown and Black . . .

"And Pinkerton-Green," Katherine said.

"That kind of thing, yes. So I was Carrington. And Dorothy Brett was Brett."

"Then you must call me Mansfield."

"Oh good-oh, then. *Mansfield*. Yes." She thought about it. "I like it. It suits you."

"So why is young Mr Huxley called Aldous? And Mr Strachey. He's Lytton, isn't he? Why isn't he Strachey?"

"And Russell's Bertie. It's almost a reversal, isn't it? The girls are chaps and the chaps are girls."

As their talk went on Carrington felt herself becoming eager, animated. It was partly because Katherine asked personal questions, and seemed more interested in the answers than in talking about herself. But the voice too was part of it – low and expressive, with a neutral accent in which, now and then, you could catch a colonial vowel or diphthong. One tended to forget about hearing. Being a painter, you thought it was all in the face, in appearances, and in what a person said. You forgot you were *hearing* the personality as well. Carrington had often thought how awful it would be to be Aldous with his impaired sight. But how awful to be Brett with her defective hearing and that trumpet thing! Not to hear Katherine would be not to "see" her properly either.

She asked what had happened during the after-lunch audience with Ottoline.

Katherine's smile was rueful. "It was dreadful. One of those occasions when someone frightfully, but *frightfully*, intense, stares into your eyes and says, 'Tell me about yourself, my dear. Tell me *everything*. I want us to be friends, to know one another, *really*, *deeply*.'"

As Katherine spoke Carrington heard Ottoline's whinnying speech. It was near-perfect mimicry.

Katherine went on: "My mind goes blank when that happens. I become inarticulate. I told her a bit about my childhood in New Zealand. That was all right I think. But then she asked about my feelings for Jack Murry. You know how she does it – the *feeling* question begging for a *feeling* response. I said, 'Oh Murry's a little mole hung out on a string to dry.' It just popped out. So then I had to laugh it off. Make it sound like a silly joke. 'I don't mean that of course. Murry the mole. Ha ha. Of course not!' But that left a gap, you see. A silence. I had to say something about us."

She stopped. Carrington urged her on. "And you said . . . ?"

"I made something up on the spur of the moment – something totally stupid. I told her Jack and I once took a very expensive house in the country, with servants, a gardener, the whole caboodle. We attended the local church, ordered supplies on tick at the village shops. The local folk, tradespeople and so on, treated us as gentry. And then, I said, after we'd enjoyed this life for a few weeks, we ran away without paying the rent or the wages or the bills – because of course we had no money."

There was a silence. "Would you believe that?" Katherine asked.

Carrington thought about it. "I might have a moment or two of doubt. But then I'd think, Why would anyone make it up?" After another silence she asked, "Why did you?"

"God knows. It was a story I once thought of writing." Katherine frowned. "I do wish I hadn't."

"Did she seem disbelieving?"

"Not really. Just surprised. Astonished, I suppose . . ."

"As you would be. Well . . ." She patted Katherine's arm. "I shouldn't worry about it. She'll think it very romantic and forget the details."

They talked about Mark Gertler. Katherine knew of his obsession with Carrington. Everyone did. He talked about it so much, appealed to so many. He and Carrington had loved one another since being students together at the Slade. As painters each admired the other's work. They exchanged ideas and encouraged one another. It was a meeting of minds, but of hearts too, and all their friends expected them to be married. But she wouldn't go to bed with him; didn't want to, couldn't face it. Everyone was on to her about it, reproaching her for old-fashioned Victorian puritanism, for cruelty, for stubbornness.

"I know he complains far and wide," Carrington said. "I

expect one morning to read a letter in *The Times*. Or a news item, 'Artist denied sex. "Shocking" says Bishop.' I'm sure you've heard about it."

Katherine acknowledged that she had.

"Last week," Carrington said, "I had Ottoline walking me up and down the garden and around the asparagus beds for half an hour, lecturing me. About virginity, and 'poor darling Mark', and Marvell's 'To his coy mistress'. Do you know it? It's all about getting on with it now because soon you'll be dead." She quoted some lines:

> "Then worms shall try
> That long-preserv'd virginity
> And your quaint honour turn to dust
> And into ashes all my lust."

"Ottoline made such a to-do about my still being a virgin at the age of twenty-three." Carrington stopped a moment, looking at Katherine. "What age were you?"

"When I lost my virginity? Oh I don't think I had one. God forgot it when he put me together. Left it out." After a moment she said, "Seventeen."

"Seventeen when you lost it?"

"I didn't lose it. I gifted it to the nation."

Carrington gave a brisk little nod. "Impressive, Mansfield."

Katherine shrugged. "It wasn't difficult. I just lay there and counted the stars. But you . . ." She looked at Carrington. "It's not a *duty*, for heaven's sake."

"Philip Morrell seems to think it is. I've had him telling me he's *disappointed* to hear I'm still denying Mark. Told me a depressing story about his brother committing suicide – the point being, I suppose, that I might be driving Mark down the same road. I wanted to say, 'Pipsi, you should save your silly speeches for the House of Commons,' but I didn't have the balls . . ."

She broke off to look again at Katherine's face. "D'you mind that word, Mansfield?"

"Balls? No, certainly not. It's a perfectly good monosyllable. I haven't a word to say against balls. But if you don't want them in your life . . ."

"No, and I don't, you see. Or rather, I wish I had some of my own. That's the real point. I wish . . . I do wish I'd been a boy."

"Well, why don't you pretend?"

Carrington was struck that Katherine should say this. "I do. So that doesn't seem strange to you?"

"Not at all. I often pretend I'm a mother."

"Truly?"

"I give myself an imaginary child. I give it a name. I care for it."

Katherine's face was so kind, so comprehending, Carrington found herself saying, "Mansfield, would you mind very much . . . Pretending, you know?"

'That you're a chap? I'm doing it already. You're a chap."

Carrington laughed. "Am I? Are you sure?"

"Absolutely certain. You're a chap, and I'm a mother."

"Oh yes you are. I've seen your little girl . . ."

"Boy," Katherine corrected. "She was a girl last week, but this week she's a boy."

"I say, isn't it nice that it can change."

They had moved to the window and were standing side by side. Carrington pushed it wide. There was a moon shining on the cypresses and the ilex, and on the patterns of formal flower gardens and yew hedges. The sound of a piano and thumping feet and loud voices came out from the open windows below. Carrington said, "They're dancing. Let's go down into the garden. I like to look in at them through the windows."

Katherine put a shawl around her shoulders and followed down the stairs, out on to the gravel forecourt and around to the side of the house where they could look in and see the lights shining on the red panels and gilt trimmings of the Red Room, the heads bouncing, bobbing and jerking in time to music from the piano, Aldous towering over them all, Ottoline not far beneath, her hennaed hair coming loose from its clips and flying about to left and right. They must have rolled back the Persian rugs, so their shoes were clattering and thumping on floors of polished wood. The night scent of stock came from the garden. They watched for a while, then Carrington took Katherine's hand and led her down the terrace steps to the ancient monastery fish ponds that served as a swimming pool. The statues around its edges gleamed in the pale light.

"I haven't told anyone yet," Carrington said. "There's been so much fuss about *not* doing it, it seems embarrassing. But it's time I told someone. Gertler and I — we've *done* it."

"Good for you!"

"It's because I've fallen in love."

"But everyone says you two have been in love . . . for ever."

"Oh not with Mark. I love Mark. I'll always love him. But I'm not *in love* with him. I'm in love with Lytton."

"You're in love with Lytton and so you've 'done it' with Gertler?"

"Yes. D'you understand that?"

Katherine poked at the gravel with the toe of her shoe. "Yes, I suppose I do. You mean it matters less . . ."

"Exactly."

"But I thought Lytton wasn't . . . Didn't . . ."

"You mean he's a bugger. Yes. He does it with boys."

"So you want to be a boy for Lytton?"

"No. Yes, but not so he can *roger* me, you know. I just want to serve him. I want to be his slave. I want him to walk over me."

"Why?"

Carrington knew what she meant. Why limp, preposterous, waspish, unmanly Lytton? They would all think that – even Lytton. She thought it herself, but it wasn't what she felt.

"Why *not* Lytton? I'm in love with him. I can't help it, I just am. Why shouldn't I be?"

"Of course." Katherine nodded slowly, retreating. "Why shouldn't you be? It's just that, at first, and quite superficially, one thinks a nice young lad like you . . . But you're quite right."

Carrington laughed, won over. They strolled on for a while, until Katherine stopped and asked, "Did you enjoy it with Gertler?"

Carrington reflected. "It's quite a business, isn't it? That thing stuck into you – it takes you by surprise the first time. I've made it clear I wouldn't like it too often."

"How often would be too often?"

"I've said he can do it three times a month. Once a week for three weeks and a week off for . . . You know. My monthly thing. What do you call yours?"

"Aunt Martha."

"Yes, well, a week off for Aunt Martha."

"What do you call 'doing it'? Do you have a name for that?"

"We call it sugar."

Katherine laughed. "Three spoons a month. It's not a lot."

163

"Not enough for Mark, no. He'd be banging away at me every night and the following morning as well if I let him. But it must be better than nothing."

"I'm not sure."

"You think it might just whet his appetite?"

"Yes. And you're in love with Lytton. He won't like that."

Carrington sighed. "One can only do one's best."

They came to a garden bench and sat down. The big moon swam and shivered on the surface of the pool as a momentary breeze caused the leaves to stir in their sleep. Carrington said, "What a funny place this is. Such brilliant people saying such silly things. Last night we were all admiring the night sky and Duncan Grant said we should take a vote on whether the moon was a virgin or a harlot."

"How did it come out?"

"We never got to the vote. It turned into an argument about where the question comes from. Mr Grant said it was in Oscar Wilde's *Salome*. Aldous said no, in *Salome* the moon's referred to as a dead woman, and a mad woman and a drunken woman, but never as a virgin or a harlot. Of course Aldous knows everything like that, but Ottoline sent Philip indoors to get a copy of the play, just to make sure. The conversation turned to something else. I don't think Philip came back."

"Which would you have voted for?"

"Virgin or harlot? I think I'd have abstained. Or . . . varlet, perhaps."

Katherine took her hand. "Shouldn't a strong young varlet like you be at the Front? I should be sending you a white feather."

Carrington laughed, shaking her hair hard, electric and bushy around her ears and over her eyes. She squeezed Katherine's hand. "If I had those necessary bits, you know – balls – and the other thing . . ."

"Cock. Phallus. John Thomas," Katherine intoned. "Pork sword. Willy."

"Yes, well, if I had one – I'd be there. *It* would be there."

"You'd make a very handsome soldier."

"It's not because I'm patriotic, or any of that. I think the war's obscene. Bertie's right. Bertie's a hero. And I admire Mr Bell and the conscientious objectors. And Ottoline and Pipsi for giving them work here, and speaking up for them and protecting them. But if I were called up, I wouldn't hesitate. I'd go. My brother's there. I feel so scared for him. I love my brother."

"Mine's there and he's dead." Katherine said.

Carrington had heard of the brother's death and forgotten. "I'm sorry," she said. She put an arm around Katherine's shoulder. "You loved him didn't you?"

"Oh yes, I did. Too much. He was such a lovely, eager boy."

There were two small tears catching the moonlight on the smooth creamy cheeks. Carrington dared to touch them lightly away. "I'm so sorry, Mansfield."

Later, when they were lying in the dark in their separate beds Carrington said, "If you're tired of Mylor, and not getting on with Murry, why don't you come and live with me and Brett in London. We're taking Maynard Keynes's house in Gower Street. We'll be sharing the rent. It would help to have a third party."

Katherine was so long silent Carrington thought she must be asleep. But then she answered: "I'm not sure Jack and I are ready to live apart. It's in the air but it's not really settled between us."

"Both of you, then."

"It's a nice idea. What about Brett – would she . . ."

"Brett likes you, Mansfield." Carrington gave the idea time to settle, and then: "Will you do it? We'd have fun."

In the half-light she saw Katherine turn on her back, putting her hands under her head and staring up at the ceiling. "I'd like to," she said. "I'll talk to Jack."

TEN

Autumn–Winter 1916 – Katherine

KATHERINE AND JACK HAVE BEEN SOME WEEKS AT 3 GOWER STREET, though Jack is gone much of the day and often late into the evening, working at the War Office. Since he can't, aged twenty-seven and unmarried, continue as the self-employed literary man, and must contribute to the war effort, he has offered himself to Military Intelligence (MI7) as someone competent in German, able to work as a translator. In fact he knows next to no German. He's learning it as he goes along and it's a difficult, slow, exhausting business. His eyes hurt, his head aches, his back pains him, he feels dried out, mentally spent. He comes home crushed, goes to bed, rises early and trudges off into the London crowds. Katherine admires his ability to bring the deception off – his competence, his industry. She pities him. How heavily the shackles of this war fall on the men, whether or not they're fit to be soldiers! But her feelings for him are distant, objective and (she knows quite well) unfair. For example when she thinks about the evening with Freddie she can't quite forgive Jack his enthusiasm for the idea of rolling a Sussex lawn. Rolling it! It seems so English. Rolling *in* it would have suited better her idea of a good time.

Has she stopped loving him? She asks herself this sometimes and the truthful answer, she thinks, is No she has not. But it's as if the extraordinary love she has felt for him at times has been put into storage, reserved for the future perhaps, for that unimaginable time called "after the war". Meanwhile they are both free. That's the agreement – the understanding – or she thinks it is. Which means he's free to work and she to play, and she wishes – half wishes – he would reproach her. But he does nothing of the kind; says only that his life is hard, that he's very tired, and that German is a beast of a language if you have to learn it in adult life.

Katherine and Jack have the ground floor; Brett, officially Maynard Keynes's tenant, has the first, and Carrington the attics. In the basement lives Keynes's housekeeper, Miss Chapman, who comes with the house and is known to them all as Chappers. Chappers is unobtrusive, sinisterly so, and considered to be more a spy than a servant. Carrington and Brett are at work on their separate floors, both finishing portraits begun at Garsington, one doing Lytton, the other Ottoline. Carrington complains that Brett, daughter of a peer and used to a household of servants, is untidy – even dirty. Brett has similar grumbles about Carrington. They complain, not to one another, but to Katherine who, manifestly clean and tidy, is able to agree with both. Her own habit of constant picking up and tidying away, however, doesn't altogether please her, since she sees it – along with straightening pictures on the wall, talking to Chappers on the stairs, running to the front door to see if the postman has been, and going out for cigarettes – as another of the ways her inner, uncooperative self finds to avoid getting on with the job. The post is her obsession – has always been. She wants – needs – letters from home, from Frieda, from Ottoline; but most especially from Freddie Good-year who has so far only managed scraps telling her the officer training course is very tough, exhausting, leaving them not a moment to themselves, and that he misses her constantly.

Carrington also grumbles, but ruefully, good humouredly, that Katherine snares all the visitors before they get beyond the ground floor. Ottoline, Aldous, Bertie Russell, Lytton, even Lawrence on a visit to London – they all get drawn into her web and sometimes go no further. "They find you interesting," Carrington says. "I don't blame them. You are. But Lytton . . ."

Katherine knows what she means. Carrington will forgive her the others – she can have them, keep them – but not Lytton. "I don't snare him," she says. "He comes uninvited and he's hard to shift."

"Don't make it worse," Carrington says.

"He does it to make you jealous," Katherine says, making it better; but she doesn't entirely believe that. She and Lytton can strike sparks off one another, and enjoy doing it. "Next time," she promises, "I won't let him past my door. I'll tell him I'm in the middle of the sentence of the century."

"Oh darling, *would* you? But don't say it so interestingly or he's sure to force his way in. Just say 'I'm sorry, Mr Strachey, I've a bad cold.' That should work. Say it in a low flat voice, and hold a handkerchief over your mouth, will you? *Could* you?"

Katherine promises.

Brett, though hampered by her deafness, has a special role in the house as Ottoline's informant. She takes note of everything that goes on, does her best to pick up the gist of conversations, asks bold frank questions when she's in doubt, and reports by daily letter to Garsington. Katherine doesn't mind this too much; nor, she thinks, does Carrington, since Brett, in turn, either tells them what Ottoline writes to her or leaves the letters lying about. Brett is like the switchboard girl on a party line. She is a conduit for things that shouldn't be said but need to be known. It means that misunderstandings among them, and between Gower Street and Garsington, are less likely.

In his lacklustre way Jack appears to be doing his best to flirt with Brett. He sometimes goes up there in the evenings. Carrington tells Katherine he left a poem on Brett's pillow and Brett is in a spin about it. This seems to Katherine foolish, pathetic. She can't believe he finds Brett intellectually stimulating or sexually exciting. But then, how can she be sure? What men find attractive, or consider worth exploring under a blanket, is often deeply puzzling. Brett is like a big schoolgirl, and perhaps that appeals to Jack.

Katherine doesn't mind – or thinks she doesn't. She knows at the very least that she has no right to mind. But, "You'd better be careful," she tells him, "or you'll find yourself compromised, and honour-bound to make an honest ear-trumpet of her."

Jack's smile isn't amused. It's as if he thinks he deserves credit, not mockery, for doing his duty at home as well as at the office. "Brett's deafness isn't a joke," he tells her.

This is a time when the obscure and frightening aches that sometimes rack Katherine's body have retreated, faded, are so nearly not there she feels her spirits lift, her courage returning. Perhaps her secret anxieties have been groundless. Perhaps she will live for ever! She feels well and adventurous. She has begun writing again. And Bertrand Russell is courting her. There's no doubt of this, and though some part of her mind thinks it inconvenient, she's not altogether displeased.

Bertie is unlike any man she has known before. She has heard Lytton say that he's the most important modern philosopher. But the talk is that just before the war his pre-eminence was being challenged by one of his students, a young Austrian Jew called Wittgenstein.

"When I didn't understand Wittgenstein," Bertie tells her, "I always had a feeling it was my fault, and that he was right. He criticised my most recent work in a way I didn't know how to deal with. I began to think my time as a real philosopher might be over."

They are in a little sunken garden he has taken her to — a private place belonging to a friend's house not far from Russell Square — sitting in outdoor chairs at a picnic table on a lawn under trees.

"But it wasn't, of course," Katherine says.

He looks uncertain. "I suppose I'll go back to it. What I'm writing just now is the man in the street's notion of philosophy. I turn as clear an eye as I can on problems of personal behaviour and social organisation. I offer wisdom . . . what I hope is wisdom."

Katherine is puzzled. "I must be the man in the street."

"Thank God for him. He might have to be my bread and butter."

"But before that — while you were still what you call a *real* philosopher — what kind of thing did you do? Lytton said it was mostly mathematics."

"Logic and mathematics. The logic of maths." He frowns. Clearly it's difficult to explain. "Problems about the nature of proof, for example. How can something we know to be so — like that one plus one equals two — how can it be proved?"

"Is that difficult?"

"Extraordinarily. You can demonstrate it over and over again. Every time you take one bean and add another, you have two beans. But how can you *prove* that it will be so every time and for ever?"

"Tell me."

"I couldn't. I could only show you on a few pages of mathematics. And you wouldn't understand them."

She considers before delivering her verdict. "I think I might find it very hard not to see that as a great waste of time and energy."

He nods. "I understand that. You wouldn't be alone, of course."

"I'd be the man in the street?" She stares at him with a comical frown. "*Blast!*"

Bertie laughs with her. A moment later he takes it up again. "The work I'm doing right now – it's second best. For lack of anything better."

"There's no pain?" Katherine asks, and then is distracted by the thought that she has spoken like a doctor to a patient with an obscure complaint.

"There's a certain regret . . ." He's tentative, but then emphatic: "Yes, of course there is. But there's no choice. With mathematics and logic you do your best work while you're young and the brain's uncluttered. It's the same as for an athlete. When you can't do it, you might as well stop."

"You mean once you've won the gold medal you don't want the silver."

He laughs. It's a noisy, rather ugly laugh. "No, I don't think that's quite what I meant." He stares at her, gripping his pipe in his hand and his teeth as if it wants to twist free. He has very bright eyes, like some kind of bird or animal, and dark straight clearly-defined eyebrows. Even when his mouth is firmly closed it seems to be on the edge of smiling, not always warmly, sometimes with what looks like self-satisfaction. He's not ugly – not quite – but she doesn't find him attractive. Fascinating though. Quick and clever. And his fame – anybody's fame – *that* is attractive.

He removes the pipe and shakes it out on the grass. "But there's no doubt about who'd get the gold if there were such a thing."

"Wittgenstein?"

"If he survives the war."

"He's in France?"

"I don't know where he is. He's fighting on the other side."

She's surprised, shocked. "But that's terrible, isn't it?"

He casts her a glance that is firm, cool. She sees in it the strong Bertie, the unshakeable one. "It's terrible that such a brilliant man may not live to do his best work. Which side he's fighting on in the present disaster seems to me less significant."

"Yes, of course." And then, because she feels she's been rebuked: "So he doesn't share your view of war. Does that bother you?"

"That he might die bothers me."

She persists. "But that he's not a pacifist – not an objector – doesn't?"

"Ah." Bertie's answer comes carefully, without the aid of the pipe. "If I ever had the chance to argue with him about it, I can imagine it might trouble me a great deal. He will have thought about it very carefully. That's his nature. I'm glad I've been spared that ordeal. In the meantime I have my own moral certainties and the hope that he lives to do great work as a philosopher."

"A noble answer," Katherine says.

He looks up at her from under his dark eyebrows. "And a mocking rejoinder?"

"No, not at all. I think you're very brave."

"I assure you I'm not."

"Accepting your student's criticisms – *that's* heroic. Honest beyond the call of duty. Herr Wittgenstein might have been wrong."

Bertie shakes his head. "He wasn't wrong."

"It's hard to imagine. How did he go about it? What did he say?"

"He burst into my room, actually. Very agitated. He'd just read something I'd written about religion. He described my thinking as stale, careless, vague, inexact."

"I don't think I'd like him," she says.

Bertie smiles. "Probably not."

The grass has been mown recently and in a momentary breeze there's a smell of something like pennyroyal. An oak leaf makes its way down, sidling past, avoiding his head. He reaches out with his right hand. It's a silent request, and she responds, laying her own over his. He puts his left on top, stares into her eyes and says, "You and I could do great things together."

It might have been a touching moment but she is remembering something Brett has told her — that one of Bertie's techniques with women is "the hand sandwich". He's doing it now.

"What might we do?" She feels herself slightly breathless, excited despite herself, but also repressing a faint stir of laughter.

He presses the hand. "Will you have dinner with me later in the week? We can talk about it then."

There was more than one dinner, a number of teas, lunches, late-night talks. There was an understanding between them, at first undeclared, then spoken, that their friendship was to be of the spirit, "platonic". Passion, they agreed, might confuse, and sex spoil, their "marriage of true minds". That suited her. There was a little of the salt of danger in it, and the pepper of the unpredictable — enough to make it interesting, not enough to cause anxiety.

She knew the gossip about him — the long-since abandoned wife; his long and now cooling (or cold? or occasionally re-heated?

– the stories varied) affair with Ottoline; his "Chicago mistake" (as Carrington called it) – the young lady he'd carelessly bedded on an American visit, who followed him to London and had to be hidden from, and finally driven off like a stray dog that wouldn't go home. There were also the questions that hung over the "innocent" lunches, and even seaside holidays, he took with Mrs Eliot, the fluffy, clever, possibly unstable wife of the American poet. And what of his Irish actress-friend, Constance Malleson? What his relations with her had been, or continued to be, no one was sure, but Carrington said rumours were flying and Ottoline was anxious.

"With Bertie," Katherine told her, "I proceed on the principle that where there's smoke there's also burnt toast – or will be, or has been."

"It's like joining a club," Carrington said.

"Perhaps. But not just any old club. And mine is only associate membership."

Carrington didn't approve. "What does he want?"

"I don't know. That's what makes it interesting. Such a big brain roaming the streets at night. What does it do? Where does it go?"

"It'll be wanting a spoon or two of sugar, for sure."

Katherine shook her head. "It may be that it just wants another brain to talk to – because there's only so much a body can do. I don't care, really."

"You might fall in love with him," Carrington said. "Then you'd care."

But Katherine was sure that wasn't possible. "He's too small."

"Jack's small."

"Yes but Jack doesn't wear celluloid collars. And his breath's sweeter."

Carrington nodded briskly. "Glad to hear it, Mansfield." Then she smiled, becoming a different person. "And how's your little boy this morning? Did he have a good night?"

That autumn Bertie came and went. Her meetings with him increased her confidence. He liked to manage a conversation, to talk about some moral or social issue that was going to come up in one of his public lectures. She listened, commented only when she had something to say, and accepted his arguments – because she was respectful of his reputation, but also because they were clear and made good sense. His ideas were radical, but she was a free spirit and there was little in her personality that stood in their way.

"Your mind, my dear Mansfield," he told her once, "is uncluttered. There's not the usual lumber – religious, political, social." They were having lunch together in a restaurant not far from the British Museum.

"This is the nicest possible way of telling me I'm empty-headed."

"I would say unspoiled."

"An empty vessel into which you can pour . . ."

"*No*. A rational creature, to whom I can *offer* . . ."

"Well . . ." She smiled her gratitude for a compliment gracefully delivered. "I'm not sure it's true, but if it is, it's because I'm a citizen of nowhere. I learned very little in New Zealand; but because that's where I began, what I'm taught here I don't always accept or believe. Nothing ever seems gospel, you know?"

"The social imprint is thin." His eyes were bright, eager. "People of my sort – Ottoline, Brett, Huxley – we have a lot to unlearn. Too much is laid on us too early. We grow up fettered."

It was half true, she thought, and he half meant it, but it was also more than he meant and it made her uneasy. In a different mood, to a different person, he might say the same things about her, but to her disadvantage. She'd learned to be wary of these people, not to trust them entirely.

He nodded at the parcel, wrapped in plain grey paper, lying on the table at her elbow. "Will you open it?"

"You know what your presents do to me. They unman me." He'd bought her, at different times lately, perfume, a silk scarf, a book of poems by Aldous. "You promised you wouldn't."

"And I haven't. This time it's not for you. It's for me."

"So why am I to . . ."

"Please. Open it."

She did. It was a copy of her book, *In a German Pension*, now out of print. "I want you to inscribe it for me."

He took out his pen and unscrewed the cap for her. She looked up at the ceiling and out the window to the trees that lined the streets, trying to decide what she should write in a book she'd once been proud of and had since decided she must refuse to re-publish. Finally she wrote in a small neat dashing hand, "Bertie dear – Germans are not quite so funny any more, and the woman who wrote these stories is not quite so young and full of confidence – but you will recognise something of her here that can't be disclaimed. With love – Katherine Mansfield."

"Thank you, dear Katherine." He kissed her hand. "Now you must tell me about your current work. A new story, didn't you say?"

His lectures and his work against the war took him away again. The Government had put restrictions on his travel, not allowing him into zones of England that were declared militarily sensitive. This was no more than a means of obstructing him, and he worked his way around it, drew crowds, argued fearlessly, won some support for the idea of immediate and unconditional peace negotiations, and built up a storm of hatred against himself – a fact which only seemed to make him more cheerful and determined.

December, and he was back in London. Their conversations had become more intense, serious, with strange undertones she couldn't interpret, and she began to fear silences and dislocations. As his ideas about the war were more sharply defined, obsessive and insistent, she found herself avoiding the subject. It wasn't that she wanted to defend the war; only that she craved relief from it. She was in a mood to make jokes with him, to tease and mock, but there was something in Bertie's temperament that resisted. Her humour unsettled him, and she found herself choosing "solid topics" in advance, as if readying herself for a class. Lawrence was one – his books, his ideas, his personality. Lawrence was common ground for them. He'd wanted to share Bertie's lecture series, thinking that because they both opposed the war they could work together. Then, discovering how different their ways of thinking were, he'd rejected Bertie, calling him "a false prophet and an enemy of mankind".

"It was worse than that," Bertie told her. "He said I was a feelingless machine. He told me I should stop *doing* and start *being*. Lawrence knows how to hurt. He knows where one is vulnerable. One of his letters left me feeling I ought to kill myself."

She understood and sympathised. "He can be so unreasonable. And yet the good Lorenzo is *so* good. So charming and interesting." As she said this she was remembering the last visit he'd made to them at Mylor, and the sight of Jack rowing him off down the estuary towards Falmouth, the sun on his straw hat, his linen jacket, his red beard.

One evening when Jack was away, she and Bertie had supper

together at a restaurant and he returned with her to Gower Street. Over the meal, and walking back through the darkened streets, they made only small talk. She found herself telling him about Freddie Goodyear and then, when he nodded but seemed not to be listening, she fell silent feeling a terrible loneliness.

Settled in front of the fire, she asked him – as if she'd been a conscientious student making the most of her time with a senior professor – to tell her his latest thinking on the relative strengths of Mr Asquith and Mr Lloyd George, and the consequent balance of forces for and against a negotiated peace.

"Ah yes," he said. "Tweedledum and Tweedledee." And he discoursed – obligingly, seriously – on how things stood with the War Cabinet, and how the balance of forces there was likely to go in the coming months. It was interesting – and then it wasn't. All at once it seemed absurd to her, meaningless when set against the death of her brother and her fears for Freddie.

She stopped listening. She saw Bertie – a vision of Bertie – with his pipe and his gold watch chain, upright in his chair like a performing dog or talking parrot, his neck poking out of its white starched collar, his hands at his sides overlapped by starched cuffs. She focused on the chain and the heavy gold watch thinking she should tell him that if he was ever on a sinking ship they would take him straight down with it. She remembered a story Carrington had told her about how Mr Asquith had cornered her at Garsington, let her feel the weight of his gold watch and put his hand on her bottom.

And then she was jerked into renewed attention. Bertie had finished with the rise of Lloyd George and was speaking of her writing. He had found time on the train to "dash through her German stories".

"They're very sharp, Katherine. Very clever indeed."

"Thank you."

"You have such power to recognise the weaknesses in people. You're like Lawrence in that."

She knew that when someone had taken the trouble to read one's work, one shouldn't argue. "Yes," she said. And then, "Not *quite* like Lawrence."

"Without his preachiness," Bertie said.

"Without his genius."

"Oh well, there's genius and genius."

"Thank you for reading them . . ."

But Bertie hadn't finished. He'd noticed often, he went on, her quick insight into the mind of Ottoline, Carrington, Brett, young Huxley – and no doubt into his own; that and her *daring*, her willingness to *say* what she saw and to render it funny. "I find it terrifying. But of course my admiration is . . ."

"Is?"

"Oh unbounded."

"No," she said. "I sense a but there, as I'm sure there should be. You admire, *but* . . ."

He stared a moment at the ceiling. "Well as to that I would say only that I can see why you say you're keen to move on. Art of the very highest kind requires something more than . . . *penetration*. It looks to go beyond satire and towards . . . Towards compassion, certainly. But beyond compassion. To poetry, perhaps; or vision. Haven't you and I spoken often of the artist's necessary *vision*? That, I'm sure, is where your work will take you next."

But she'd stopped listening. It was too much, this talk about her work as if she were some other person, someone far away and unknown to both of them. She found herself standing and didn't remember having got up from her chair. "I'm dreadfully afraid I have a headache," she said. "I must be needing sleep."

It was like a spring, projecting him out of his chair. "Of course," he said. And then, "Of course of course." He fought his way into his heavy black overcoat like a man overcoming a bear. "How foolish of me. How careless."

He gathered up the papers and books he'd carried with him and shovelled them into his briefcase. "Shouldn't have come in. Supper should've been enough. Such a pleasure . . . and so on."

Such a pleasure . . . and so on. She said it over silently to herself, watching his fingers run like a bassoon player's up and down his buttons. It sounded so odd, so silly, so endearingly Bertie. She forgave him his comments about her stories, which, after all, only confirmed what she herself had said of them.

By now he was at the door, opening it . . .

And then he hesitated. He looked out into the street, and up at the stars, and back at Katherine. It was as if he'd forgotten – or remembered – something. His face seemed to cloud over, his eyes to lose focus. He swayed towards her, propelled (she could see) by something stronger than intellect. Her whole being responded without thought as she waited to be kissed. But in the same instant he recovered, steadied himself. "I'm so sorry," he murmured, and was gone.

She shut the door, leaned her forehead against it. Returned to her room, she stamped up and down, running fingers through her hair, throwing her arms about, groaning, letting out yelps of pain. Was she angry with him? With herself? She didn't know, but anyway it didn't matter. It was all over. She'd had enough. She wanted no more of Bertie Russell with his unforgivably starched collars and his bad breath. Let him get back to Ottoline, or on with Vivien, or forward with Constance. She, Katherine, was happy to have seen the last of him.

When the doorbell rang her first thought was that he must have found some pretext for coming back. She must tell him to go away – that he wasn't wanted. No, wrong. She must invite him in. They must make it right. No kisses, just friendship. She would tell him about Freddie; about her hopes for the future.

She hovered at the door, undecided. The bell rang a second time. It was a tentative ring, a light finger-stab. She opened the door slowly and peered out into the dark London night. The light from the hallway fell on the visitor.

It was her friend Ida Baker, only recently returned from a two-year visit to her home in Rhodesia. Ida was standing on the top step, somehow signalling in her expression, and in the way she held herself, that she was already leaving, not there on a visit, had no intention of coming in.

Katherine and Ida had been friends since their schooldays. They'd sworn eternal friendship and loyalty to one another, and for eternal schoolgirl Ida the promise was as binding now as on the day it had been made. To Katherine, Ida (who had once written "If your man fails *I am your trump card*") was "Aida", "the Albatross", "the Rhodesian Mountain", "the Dwarf", "the FO" (Faithful One). She was Jones. She was also "LM" (Lesley Moore), the secret name Katherine had given her, echoing the brother's. About Ida Katherine's feelings changed from one year, or one week, to the next, and even from moment to moment. She had often been a friend in need, but more servant than friend, more slave than servant. Ida was a fact of Katherine's life. Since her return from Rhodesia she'd been working in a munitions factory. Katherine had been keeping her at arm's length, but now, seeing her there, what she felt was something like relief.

She smiled. "Darling, it's so late."

"I know, darling. I'm not coming in. I'm staying with . . ." Mumble mumble. There was a name Katherine didn't catch. "We're just down the road – at the YWCA. I was passing and saw your light. I thought, I *can't* pass without saying goodnight. Is that too foolish, darling?"

Why would she be "just passing"? She must have come out hoping . . . Snooping . . . Perhaps she'd been lurking in the shadows and had seen Bertie leave.

Ida wavered there on the top step, cringing from the rejection she fully expected – perhaps even wanted – knowing that Katherine was likely to be at her most brutal when there was a man in her life.

Katherine stepped forward and wrapped her in a hug. "Of course not, silly thing. Goodnight, darling. Goodnight, dear friend. Now hurry back to Mumble before they lock you out."

"Oh," Ida said. "*Oh!*" It was almost too much for her, this kindness, this embrace. She wasn't used to it, certainly not from her "best friend".

"Go," Katherine said, kindly but firmly. She fluttered a hand in the gap, and closed the door.

She stood a moment in the passageway hearing the steps recede. She congratulated herself. The hug had been a tour de force. That was how she should have treated Bertie – wrapped arms around him. Smothered the little fellow.

She felt again a surge of affection for this famous absurd great man. She went to her desk, took out a sheet of her best notepaper, and sat thinking. She would write as if she'd let a day go by, and wouldn't post it until tomorrow afternoon.

She began: "I meant to write to you immediately after you left me on Friday night to say how sorry I was to have been such cold comfort and so useless to lift even ever so little of the cloud of your fatigue . . .'

She got up and walked about the room. Oh yes, she thought, *Such* a pleasure, and so on . . .

ELEVEN

Winter–Spring 1917 – Fred Goodyear

SECOND LIEUTENANT FREDERICK GOODYEAR, NEW TO HIS commission and still having to deal with unworthy sensations of pleasure at receiving salutes from men with the sergeant's third stripe he had never earned, crossed to France again early in March 1917. His parents and his sister saw him off at Waterloo. He'd missed Katherine but managed a quick exchange with Jack Murry, who shook his hand, wished him well and looked at once dismal and accusing, as if to say he knew bloody Goodyear would die on him too, the bastard, unloading another ton of misery on his already bent shoulders.

Katherine, Jack said, would be sorry not to have said goodbye. She was acting in a movie that day – a walk-on part in a beautiful dress. "She left early. She'd gone before I got your note."

Fred hid his disappointment. His notice to be ready for the crossing had come only hours before they were to be on the move. Katherine was the one he'd wanted most to be there, to see him off.

"Tell her I love her," Fred said, as if it was a joke.

"I think she knows that," Jack said, as if it wasn't.

Fred's unit reached Folkestone at dawn and he and his fellow-officers were put up in boarding houses along the seafront, commandeered "for the duration". The crossing, when it came, was in three cross-Channel packet-boats, painted black and numbered 1, 2 and 3, escorted by torpedo boats, also black, and (it was said) by submarines. The ships were crowded with men, about half new to the war, the remainder returning from leave, or from "a Blighty", which was what they called a wound serious enough to earn home leave. There was a great deal of noise, shouting of orders, cheerfully grim jokes, singing of popular songs, but for Fred, though he heard it, it was screened out. He was alone with himself, with the throb of engines, the surge of waves, the coldness of the breeze in his face. He stood at the rail, looked ahead, and saw nothing but grey water. Somewhere up ahead, beyond a coastline yet to appear, was where it was happening. It was his future, and might be all the future he was to have. Whatever was waiting for him there, he believed he was ready for it. His state of mind was, he thought, the equivalent of saying "Thy Will be Done", only there was no Thou and no Will, only the doing, most of it yet to be done.

They spent two nights in a Base Camp near Boulogne after which came a train journey lasting most of a day. There were tedious hours in sidings and alongside empty station platforms; and once or twice among fields and woods, with early spring flowers in the grass and birds in the trees. The number of uniformed men on the move was immense, but behind the lines France was France, going about its business as the season dictated, and scarcely less beautiful than in times of peace.

Fred imagined the huge country as God might see it if there were a God, an enormous map with what would seem, from up there, a snaking ribbon of devastation, narrow (though it might be five, and in places ten and more, miles wide), and on either side of this serpent, Lo! (as God was in the habit of exclaiming) the earth and the bounty thereof – crops planting or growing, cattle and sheep grazing, vineyards and olive groves flourishing, orchards flowering, peasants tending, feeding, culling, weeding. And towards that line, endlessly, God looking down would be seeing echelons of men in uniform, drawn from either side, willingly or against their will, to be shot, blown up, gassed, bayoneted, drowned in mud, buried where they fell or left to rot in no man's land. It was the European, the human, the Gadarene insanity, as apparent to man as to God, and yet *happening*; and he, Frederick Goodyear, was a party to it. The only rational posture was one of refusal. So why would he not refuse? Because he too was insane! When the whole world was mad there was a kind of propriety in madness. It took a peculiar temperament – one like Russell's – to insist on reason at such a time.

But what kind of a God would it be who could look down on His own Creation, see all this and not say, "There's a fault in the design. I'd better fix it"? This madness of "the Great War" was the final proof of something that needed no proving because it was known to every human heart, though it was in the nature of the human heart to deny what it knew. There would be no finality, no great explanatory outcome, no revelation of a Divine Plan. There would not even be an end to war. It was deeply depressing – and yet Fred felt a kind of excitement in accepting it. The pretences and deceptions of childhood were over. There was no Omnipotent and Loving Father, no Supreme Looker-on with a hand ready at the Wheel of Fate – only Generals and Politicians, men and machines, destruction and death. War was even (you could argue) a lot of people doing their best. That was the biggest irony of all.

The train brought them to a clanking hissing halt. There was pasture to one side, a cornfield and a patch of woodland on the other, and not far away a road along which horse-drawn limbers, artillery pieces and military cars trundled at intervals, with small detachments of soldiers. It was past the middle of the afternoon and the air, when they stepped down from the train, was cold, the sky heavy and grey. They formed up with their kitbags and marched. There were intermittent rumblings in the distance as of summer thunder.

As the march continued the rumbles grew louder, underscored by the visible red and white flashes of the guns. Now most of the trees were shredded or broken, some tilting, others snapped off like pencils. The road was pitted with shell-holes and in places completely destroyed. This was territory that had been fought over, won and lost and won again. There were hasty graves along either side of the route, some informal crosses, many sticks each with the dead soldier's cap, British, French, German. Here and there were dead mules and horses, inflated like balloons or decomposing in a cloud of stench and flies. Bones, that might have been human or animal, whitened among tall thistles where once must have been crops. Coils of rusting barbed wire lay about. The landscape was wet with recent rain and abandoned trenches were full of water. The litter of armies had been scattered in the wake of the most recent allied advances. Fred noted empty shell cases, a tunic pressed into the mud, several unrelated boots, a helmet, abandoned latrines and field kitchens.

The clusters of farmhouses, barns and outbuildings they passed now were wrecked and abandoned. They reached the ruins of a village not far from the town of Arras and were told this would be their stop for the night. Not a single building was still standing.

Bricks spilled into what had once been lanes and across the main road that ran through. Here and there a chimney stood, the house around it a heap of timber, bricks and mortar. Fred's platoon commander, Captain Johnson, who had trained with him at Newmarket, pointed out, in one still upright wall of the village church, a single stained-glass window depicting the sad face of the Virgin. The last light in the sky was coming through, making the colours glow.

"Hail Mary mother of God," Fred murmured. "And what are *you* doing here?"

The two officers were billeted with the captain's servant in what remained of a small basement, part covered, the rest open to the sky. For supper the platoon was served tinned sardines, thick slices of bread and Cheddar, and a swig of rum in their tin mugs. On the earthen floor the servant made a fire of bully boxes and timber from the collapsed roof. There was singing from the larger, adjoining basement in which most of the platoon was housed –

> And when we get to Ber-lin
> The Kaiser he will say
> "Hock hock mein Gott
> What a terrible lot
> What bloody use are they?"

They slept on straw-filled palliasses laid out close to the fire. In the night they were woken by a salvo of shells dropping somewhere nearby, long shots from behind the German lines. Fred listened for the sound they'd been taught would signal gas shells; but these were high explosives. There was nothing to be done except pray not to take a direct hit.

In the morning the platoon was led to a ruined house on

the edge of the village. Inside its roofless walls the first of the trenches began. Unseasonable sleet was falling, alternating with cold rain. In file they made their way out into a landscape hidden from them by the parapets, on a long slow trek up to the line, threading through busy parts of the trench system, passing weary soldiers going back for rest, and, now and then, wounded men carried on stretchers. There was a group of German prisoners, haggard, dirty, dead-weary, apprehensive. Stepping back to let them pass Fred looked into their faces, smelled their human closeness. He felt no animosity and detected none – only the strangeness that, lacking any very clear reason, the two sides were engaged in trying to destroy one another.

It didn't take many days to get used to the routines of trench life, to its boredom and its moments of sudden horror. Fred saw men die – one hit in the head by a sniper's random ricochet while sitting on a box reading a comic, one cut down by flying shell fragments, one gassed because too slow with his mask, one spectacularly exploded into a red shower under a flare at night in no man's land. He saw bleeding wounds, frothing lungs, fractured bones. He saw rats eating human corpses. He put up with the damp and the cold, and endured, hating it more than all the rest, the noise of their own "heavies". He remained mostly calm, as if drugged; but he'd been warned that that was how it would be if you could "take it": you began calm and only very slowly your nerves frayed, sleep became more difficult, and fear began to haunt you.

No attack was ordered, and none came at them. There were signs the Hun was "straightening his line", which might involve a pull-back from the area just east of Arras. But the war of attrition went on and the officers were warned a new offensive was planned for the spring. They should prepare their men for it and keep them alert.

The routine was four days in the front line, four in the support trenches, and four at rest behind the lines with the chance to take a bath, change underwear and sleep long hours. Sometimes it was possible to get a ride to a small town out of artillery range where cafés, shops and brothels were open.

On one of their rest days, when the weather relented, Fred and his friend Johnson took a long walk. They were some way back from the line, on a road that ran through woodland beyond the village of Mont St Eloi. Some of the trees were coming into leaf. The road stretched away westward. The boom of guns in the distance was a reminder. "We are very strange animals," Fred said. "Why are you and I going back to that when we could just keep walking?"

"Because we don't want to be shot," Johnson said, and they both laughed.

"Have you noticed," Fred said, "men pray for a Blighty, get one, and then chafe to get back, even though they know exactly what it's like and that they'll hate it."

Johnson quoted,

"And gentlemen in England now abed
Shall think themselves accurs'd they were not here
And hold their manhoods cheap whiles any speaks
That fought with us upon Saint Crispin's day."

To make it clear this wasn't offered as a solemn expression of feelings he added, "Enter the Earl of Salisbury with a sausage." But the lines caught at something. If you survived this ghastliness you wouldn't be sorry to be able to say, "Yes, I was there."

As they walked along Fred talked about food. He described

spicy rice and vegetable dishes he'd eaten in India, Norway's winter feasting on fish and savouries washed down with schnapps, a "best restaurant" meal in Paris, with Jack and Katherine, when Katherine had a gift of money from her family and decided it should be spent. Even the thought of Oxford's meat-and-two-veg with pudding, and the similar lunches and dinners during his time as a housemaster at Charterhouse, could be recalled, if not with nostalgia, at least with an upwardly revised contempt. "Come on, Johnson," he said. "It's your turn. Tell me about your favourite tucker."

For Johnson it was the childhood family Sunday roast lamb after church, with mint sauce, baked parsnips, carrots, onions and potatoes, and boiled green peas.

Johnson had a girlfriend he loved very much. He'd wanted to get married, or at the very least engaged, before going to France but she'd said there was no hurry. He was terrified he would lose her to someone else. He said it preyed on his mind, keeping him awake at night.

Fred told him about Katherine. "She's a writer. After the war we're going to travel together in Sweden. Up beyond the Arctic Circle." He said it as if he believed it. While he talked about it he did believe it — that he could survive the war, and that, surviving, he could take Katherine away from Jack.

A few days later, just before Easter, a letter came from her, a letter that bulged in its envelope, brought down to him from First Line Transport. It had gone the rounds, first to BEF HQ, then to his former meteorological unit, and finally, via his new regiment, the Essex, to the Front. It began without the usual preliminaries, as if she had just rushed into the room breathless, with something urgent that needed to be said:

141A Church Street
Chelsea
London, SW

It's important I talk to you, my dear Pa-man, because as ever I'm surrounded by little brothers. I attract them, I love them, I need them, just as I resist and reject Pa-men; but I have begun to suspect – have long suspected – it's a Pa-man I want and will one day find at my side.

I have been pursued by Bertie Russell. I have to say I put bird seed on my lawn and he flew down to peck at it, so I can't complain. But what bothers me is that he offered me advice (he is *of course* very intelligent and serious and clever) which was well meant and thoughtful, and so close to what you, my very Goodyear, offered, I have to give it my best attention. I don't altogether like it, you see; or I think it falls short. But to hear it twice in only a few months, and from two such sound gentlemen – well, you will understand, Prudence darling, I have to discuss it with you. I know you can't reply, and may not even receive this letter since I don't know where I should send it. And I know that if you do receive it you may be occupied with more serious, indeed life and death, matters, and not disposed to listen. But I believe that simply by writing to you I will be able to imagine your answers, to hear them in your voice (which is often in my head), and that will help me. So forgive, please, my frivolous intrusion, and if you are able for a moment to lift your eyes from the page of history you are helping to write, I will try to explain.

You remember what you wrote to me about my writing. We talked about it that day – that wonderful day, darling, beyond St Mawes. (It was your "republic of sounds and scents and grasses and dews and café mirrors" that made me love you!) Well Bertie has told me the same thing – that I'm too smart at the expense of common mortals, and that I have to get beyond "satire" in my writing, find "compassion", and "poetry", and "vision".

And, you see, I know all of that. But I know too that if I try to go there directly, by an act of will, like buying a train ticket to Aberystwyth or Brighton, it doesn't work. I betray something in myself. False notes creep in. I become the "good" Katherine. And when I read *that* Katherine I think, Better honest about what I see around me – even if I am "too clever" – than a gypsy violinist playing oh so feelingly off the note. I have a long way to go. Of course I have. But it's almost as if I had to *live* first – yes, that's it! – and wouldn't allow myself to write more (though I desperately wanted to, was burning with impatience to get on with it) until my self had grown up to the next necessary pencil mark on the back of the pantry door . . .

And that's all really. You see, Fred darling, I knew you would understand and say the right things, as you have done in my head, and that you would help me reach a new understanding of myself. How I love you at this moment! But if I'm dead wrong and you are out there somewhere and able to listen to me, and if you have a moment of freedom, then please, darling, write and tell me. Punish me. Put me straight.

As for my important little philosopher the Hon. Bertie – I tried to take him and his advice seriously. I mean *seriously* seriously. I wrote him nice little notes and talked to him like a good intelligent young woman. We were at Garsington together for Christmas. He and I talked late into the night, and next morning Ottoline came down, looking like a ginger Brownhilda recently released from her bed of fire, and told us that our conversation had been audible from her room, that she had heard what we'd been saying (I didn't believe her). She was jealous. Bertie is *hers*, even though she's tired of him and in love with a soldier poet called Siegfried (I am not joking). But she need not have been so wakeful and so anxious. I have no designs on Bertie, only a passing interest in his brain.

In any case I made up for my sins there by writing a play for the Christmas party and it was a tremendous success. I was Florence Kaziany, the rather dashing and horribly insensitive daughter of Lytton Strachey (Dr Keit – we gave him a big red beard). Carrington (Muriel Dash) was my love child. There were parts for Aldous and his Belgian friend Maria Nys. Jack was a sort of Chekhov character (called Ivan Tchek) who wandered about sighing heavily and saying things like, "And so it goes on." We had such a lovely time doing it I came away feeling reconciled to Ottoline and Garsington and that whole Bloomsbury crew who have made me so nervous and uncertain in the past. But now Lorenzo has thrown his huge and terrible spanner into the works. Not into *my* works. Ottoline's. She got wind from one of her spies that she's represented in his new novel and she asked to see it. He *sent it to her*! Why would he do that if the portrait is so terrible? My guess is because Frieda, who hates Ottoline, told him to. Anyway, Ottoline has been cast into torment and anguish (she is awfully good at t and a – it's one of her strongest roles) by the portrayal, which she says is cruel and unjust and undeserved and unkind; and her husband

(Philip Morrell – he's the MP, you know?) is threatening an action for defamation if it's published unchanged. Poor silly Lorenzo! What chance has he to publish anyway, after the suppression of *The Rainbow*? While the war goes on, none! Brett says Jack and I are in the novel too. That arouses my curiosity; but I wonder whether we will ever see it.

After Christmas I felt I had to get out of Gower Street. Too many people coming and going, too much happening. I wanted to work, had things to write for *The New Age*, and couldn't disengage (you know my weaknesses, Freddie) when so much was going on under my nose. And Jack was trailing clouds of gloomy from the Ministry. So I've taken this studio flat in Chelsea. Jack is in rooms in Redcliffe Road – not too far away, and he calls by when he feels like it.

Darling, I have to tell you one more thing (apart from the fact that I believe in you as a poet and beg you not to take risks and to come back safe and sound): it's about Bertie again. I persisted really because I thought – and I still think – his courage in opposing the war is remark-able, and I felt flattered (honoured, if that doesn't sound weak-womanish) that he paid me such attention, credited me with a brain, listened to my thoughts, laughed at my jokes (an awful loud laugh he has), and was interested in my writing. I tried to be "good", you know, and curb the sharp "too clever by half Katherine" who has been reproached and rebuked for most of her 28 years. But I kept hearing that false voice of mine, and I began to dislike Bertie not for himself but because of *my*self. So I've brought my relations with him to an end – not by saying it's all over in so many words. Just by adopting a cool tone and being always too unwell to meet him. (And I have been unwell – I didn't have to make it up. Winter chills and a frightful graveyard cough.)

And darling, after almost a year I'm *writing again* – I mean for myself, apart from *The New Age* work. That is the surest sign that some kind of interior correction has gone on. I needed you to know that; and to know that I think of you every single day, and that often when I do I see two figures, he and she together in a quite startlingly starched white landscape, going somewhere, getting somewhere, wrapped in furs.

Please believe me, dearest Freddie. I press your hands. I kiss your brow and your lips. Be safe, my soldier –

Katherine

PS The Siegfried poet's second name is Sassoon which seems rather disappointing. Do you know his work?

Fred read it once quickly, and then, over that Easter, slowly and often. So she and Jack were living apart. And she was writing again. In his head he drafted replies. He would write to her, but not until there was time and space for the right words in the right order.

Easter Monday was the start of the new offensive. Kitted up with gas pack, rifle and bayonet, the men waited in the cold pre-dawn light while the artillery bombardment that was to clear a path for them went on. Strafes like this had been delivered in the same way at the same time during most of the past week, so this one would not give a clear signal that an assault was coming. But those on the other side with experience must have read the signs. If it wasn't today it would be tomorrow, or the day after. The Tommies were coming, and the Hun must have known it.

It was to begin at 7.30, the artillery bombardment shifting away ahead of the first wave at a pace meant to match their own. Of course it never worked out quite as it should – everyone knew that. But that was the plan.

There was fear. Fred felt it – in himself, and all around him. The waiting was intolerable. There were no jokes now, and very little talk. The mouthful of rum passed to every man helped – did it? Or did it just add, after the first momentary burning shock, to that dryness of throat which, along with weak knees and an emptiness in the gut, was a symptom of terror? They had all heard about the first waves of attacks cut down by concentrated machine-gun and rifle fire. Some few were survivors of the last and didn't expect to survive a second time. They were to stay on their feet, not to go down unless hit. Men who dived for cover under heavy fire were too hard to coax back up again. They were to keep moving forward at a jog-trot, no matter what was happening to left and right. The big guns were supposed to punch holes for them and to be their protection.

The noise of their own artillery was terrible. The whole landscape shook. Fred looked at Johnson who was looking at the sky, frowning, chewing his lower lip. Fear had a tight hand on his shoulder, that was obvious, but he was steady. He would shake it off. Fred thought, We all know many of us will die, but no one can quite believe *he* will die.

At 7.30, eye on his watch, revolver in his right hand and ready to lead by example, Johnson blew his whistle. At that moment, up and down the line, the whistles sounded. The men went up on to the fire step, on to the parapet and over. The first wave of the assault was on its way. They were in no man's land, which all at once seemed unthinkably wide, lumbering forward into the smoke from their own exploding shells, and already, through the smoke as it cleared, came the stutter of the defenders' fire.

Fred didn't die that day; nor did his friend. Many did; but as attacks of this kind usually went on the Western Front, casualties were light. Why it went so well was unclear, at least to the men. There was little new in the strategy – the same that had failed so often and so disastrously before. Perhaps they were getting better at it. Perhaps that straightening of the German line was incomplete and left the enemy vulnerable, with reserves too far back. Whatever the reason, the defenders wavered, trenches were abandoned, there was panic, retreat and surrender. It was only one day in a very long war, but it was special: a victory of sorts. Much death had been dealt. A whole German trench system east of Arras had been captured, along with men and guns.

But now came the delay, the loss of momentum, the old stalemate. Orders were sent to dig in. German reinforcements, held in the rear, were rushed forward. The line had shifted some miles but the hoped-for "rupture" had not been achieved, and to make further gains was going to be difficult.

There was a fortnight of ugly, random skirmishing, with salvo and counter-salvo, gas attack and answering gas attack. It was as if the Hun, rattled at having lost ground, wished to assert that the loss was an accident and that he was as iron-clad invincible as ever; while those on the British side, having smelled a major victory and won only a minor one, felt they should keep pressing.

Fred kept Katherine's letter in the big thigh pocket in his

breeches so he could re-read it often. He was waiting for his four-day break when he would reply to her, but that was delayed while the Corps re-deployed on the new ground, digging new trenches, adapting captured ones to their own use and system.

Towards the end of the second week of May Fred's company was involved in an attempt to regain lost ground around the village of Fampoux. German artillery seemed to get a fix on them. As the shells dropped around them they took cover wherever they could find it. Alone in a small dugout, Fred prepared to wait until the shower had passed. He took out Katherine's letter. He knew it so well he had only to glance at it for the sentences to form themselves in his mind. "It's important I talk to you, my dear Pa-man, because as ever I'm surrounded by little brothers. I attract them, I love them, I need them, just as I resist and reject Pa-men; but I have begun to suspect . . ."

He didn't hear the explosion. There was a gap, a blank – he wasn't sure whether long or short – and then consciousness, first of the fact that his mouth was full of earth. Then that he couldn't move. There was a weight of soil and a wooden beam lying across him. He lost consciousness again, and when he next came to it was dark and someone was directing men to ease the beam off him and pull him from the hole. That was his first sensation of pain – so extreme he let out a loud cry. A German flare went up and his rescuers hid in shell-holes waiting for it to burn out, one holding a hand over his mouth. When he next woke he was in a tent, a field hospital. He reached down for the breeches pocket in which he had kept the letter. It was gone. So was the pocket. And the leg.

He was given morphine for pain, and passed several days in a floating hallucinatory sleep, full of fears alternating with dreams of escape, rescue, transcendent love. Five days after the wounding and the amputation he had some hours of lucidity in which, coaxed by a nurse, he wrote to his mother telling her what had happened and that he was all right.

"Is there anyone else you want to write to?" the nurse asked. "A girl?"

'There's a girl," he said, "but she won't want a man with one leg."

"Of course she will."

Fred didn't reply. The nurse said, "Come on. Let me help you."

He looked into her eyes. They were blue. She had ginger hair and freckles. She looked honest and jolly. "Will you marry me?" he said.

She laughed nervously. He closed his eyes.

It was night-time. Katherine was standing at the end of his bed. He could hear his mother's voice saying, "I don't believe she's suitable, Frederick."

When he next woke Katherine was gone, replaced by his sister, weeping. "Don't cry," he said.

Next day he felt he was clearer in his head, aware of his own feverish condition and that it had changed in the night, not necessarily for the better. He was still in the tent which he now knew was a Canadian field hospital not many miles back from the fighting. Johnson was there, sitting on a stool. There was a bandage around his head and over one eye.

"My leg's gone," Fred said.

Johnson nodded. "So's my eye."

"You've lost it?"

"It's still there." He touched the bandage. "But the sight's kaput." They gave their losses a minute's silence. "Never mind," Johnson said. "We live to tell the tale, eh?"

It was strange. Fred had thought often of being dead, never of being like this, alive and without a limb. Even when he'd watched Lawrence raging at the sight of the amputees on Hampstead Heath it hadn't crossed his mind that one day he might be like that. Half a man. Scissors with only one blade. A scissor.

"Where's my sister?" As he asked it he realised that she couldn't have been there.

"No sister," Johnson said. "Not yet. When they get you back to Blighty . . ."

Fred focused his mind on the platoon. It was difficult. Something had happened to his head; to his thinking. He asked about some of the men whose names he could remember. Dead was the answer. Missing. Dead. Yes him too. Dead. Dead.

Had they all gone in that one bombardment?

No. Some had died days, even weeks ago.

He drifted into something like sleep, remembering in a waking dream that while he was at Brasenose there had been a man in a wheelchair who came out, when the weather was clement, and sat drinking in Radcliffe Square. A bag that clanked with bottles hung on his chair, and he worked his way through them, becoming drunker as the day wore on. It was said he'd worked as a shunter on the railways and had fallen under a train, losing both legs. The undergraduates treated him as a joke. They called him "Leggie" and would buy him more bottles, but first he had to sing for them. "Louder," they demanded. "Louder." And Leggie would bellow, out of tune, putting such effort into it that he sometimes fell out of his chair and had to be hoisted back into it by the lads.

Why was he recalling this? He remembered now a conversation between doctors in the night. He had heard the word "gangrene".

He opened his eyes. Johnson was still there. "Am I losing the other one?" he asked.

Johnson patted his arm. "Be strong, old chap."

TWELVE

Summer–Autumn 1917 – Katherine

SHE IS FREE OF JACK AND SHE'S PLEASED. THEY ARE LIVING APART, he in two rooms in Kensington, she in a studio flat in Chelsea. She is writing. She is alone and she is writing.

She says it often, feels the pleasure of it, the guilt of it, the refreshment, the sense of escape, the fear of it. The terror . . .

There is, for example, a strange knocking when everything else falls silent. It is always there, she supposes, but muffled, needing unusual quiet to be heard. As if someone is coming up from under the ground. Someone or something buried. A life – or a love – that refuses to die . . .

But to say that (she tells herself) is fanciful. It is playing with words – and with feelings. Unserious. It's one of the things she has to avoid, or to go easy on, in her writing.

None the less it's true that the tapping, dull and steady, frightens her, as if those words ("something buried, something refusing to die") have meaning. It is perhaps the idea more than the sound: life-chances missed, time and energy wasted, and the self you might have been, down there in the dark, knocking, crying "Why didn't you give me a chance?"

As if . . . The phrase is as dangerous as its cousin, *if only* . . .

She's not sorry to have left Gower Street. She had good times there with Brett and Carrington; but the spying that went on was unsettling. Everyone had secrets and everyone knew them. The last straw was finding a letter, left lying about by Brett, enclosing one to Ottoline from Jack. Jack had written to Ottoline saying something typically silly about thinking perhaps he was falling in love with her (thinking *perhaps* – wasn't he sure?) and Ottoline had sent it to Brett asking what she thought it meant. Of course it meant nothing – Katherine could have told her that – except that Jack was hoping to make some kind of impression on the great lady. If Ottoline were not (as everyone – except Jack? – seemed to know) at this moment infatuated with the soldier poet Siegfried Sassoon, she might have been interested – in which case Jack might have had to run for it.

Katherine lights a cigarette and looks around again at the little flat with its enormous window that allows the heavens to glare down on her and her to stare back; and her to look down on the garden, and the garden to smile. In this weather she can go and sit down there in a deckchair with her notebook on her knees, drinking lemon juice and thinking green thoughts in a green shade.

Up here, minimal but functional furniture – worthy of Scandinavia perhaps. The sort of thing she might see on her travels with Fred – "after the war". *Danske møbler*. A bed and chair in a gallery behind a draw-back curtain. A clean service-able kitchen with table, chairs, another window, a tree looking in nodding its green head.

Jack can come when he likes; when she needs him or he needs her. He has a key – her idea, so he wouldn't feel rejected. They can still be lovers – are lovers, when she wants him and when he's not too dried out and pressed between the pages of his work at the War Office. But they are apart – living apart. They are not a couple. And she's writing.

Ida Baker can come too, when it's convenient (if it ever is), or necessary. She can catch a few hours' sleep here between shifts. She can brush Katherine's hair, since it pleases her and is not unpleasant (rather nice, in fact). But she is not permitted to kiss the hair, nor to kiss Katherine (though she will, from time to time, and retire, rebuked and blushing, behind the curtain).

Visitors can come.

And there can be whole days and whole nights with no one. Or (sometimes) with Fred, in imagination.

There's a notebook open on the bed, another beside the typewriter on the desk under the big window; and a writing pad on the floor. No virgin page is allowed to stare at the ceiling undefiled.

She is writing dialogue pieces for *The New Age*. That's where she made her start; and where she is making her re-start. Not so sharp, not so smart, not so brutal as those early pieces – but sharp and smart. And Mr Orage is taking them, and paying. She is a writer. She must earn her keep and not depend always and only on the allowance from her father.

She tries to make each piece different – a different character, different circumstances; but she has begun to notice that in one way and another they are mostly about finding love. Not so much finding someone to love you as finding someone you can love.

She is also writing a play – has reached the third act. And new stories. And revising "The Aloe", begun in Paris and continued in Bandol. That is to be a book for Leonard and Virginia Woolf's new press. She's cutting it down, refining it, giving it shape. Going back to it has not been a disappointment. It's good – so good it deserves to be better. The thought of it as a book has given new colour to her life.

How can one's talent, one's fluency, one's *will to write* (because that is what it amounts to) so desert one, and so return? Like a very large and noisy prodigal son, missing, wept over, searched for and unresponding. For a whole year all correspondence "returned to sender". And now back again, as loud and alive as ever, as healthy and pushy, brooking no questions about reasons for departure or reasons for return. Mind your own business and take dictation! She minds it, and takes it.

Perhaps it's just a matter of confidence returning like the swallows in spring, but it seems more mysterious; something interior and obscure. And anyway, what is more mysterious than a return of confidence?

Being approached by the Woolfs and asked for work to publish had been part of it. Meeting them wasn't easy. She sensed Virginia's fragility, but also her fastidiousness, her snobbishness. Virginia – hedged around, guarded especially by Leonard (half-protector, half-warder), but with an appetite at least to know about the life she was shut out from; and Katherine had played up to that. She set out to shock, and did shock, and might afterwards have reproached herself if it hadn't been for the memory of Leonard (at first sight grim and unapproachable) laughing almost uncontrollably as she told her stories (her "poker-face stories") about the adventures of her younger days. Leonard liked her. That too was dangerous, perhaps. Almost certainly Virginia would be competitive, and vindictive. Yet there was also, at moments, something gentle and distinguished about her. She was cat-like, a particularly well-bred, long-faced feline, with nice fur and perfect cat-manners, capable of purring and rubbing up against one, but with sharp unscrupulous claws.

Above all Virginia recognised intelligence, and responded to it. Katherine had never doubted her own ability to be clever when it was required, and with the Woolfs it was required. Virginia was preparing to review a volume of memoirs by Henry James, and brought the subject up as if to prove to herself that this raffish young woman from the South Seas could not be counted on to know, or to say, anything of consequence. It was a test, and Katherine was sure she passed; more than passed – took them by surprise. Henry James's staple subject, after all – the wickedly wise Old World against the naive and puritan New – was something she knew at her fingertips and in her bones. It was beginning to be a part of her subject matter, and might one day, if she lived long enough in Europe, become the whole of it. But she said none of that to Virginia and Leonard; said only that because of his position in England and Europe, James had to be observant and couldn't help but seem detached. "But he was deeply appreciative," she said. "He saw things fresh and felt them acutely."

As she spoke she saw that Virginia was listening, interested, intent.

"And his wonderful prose . . ." Katherine went on.

Virginia interrupted: "Even the last novels?"

"Even *The Golden Bowl*. It's such a *test*."

"You know the cruel joke about the three Jameses? James the first, James the second . . ."

"And the Old Pretender." Yes, Katherine knew it.

They were laughing together now, recalling the extravagances, at its most florid, of that prose which made weak minds faint and weary ones fail, but which, to writers who cared about craft and were excited by virtuosity, shone like no other's except Dickens's.

And now the Woolfs had read the typescript she'd left with them, and confirmed by letter that they were keen to publish it. Would she have the revised copy ready for them soon? Yes she would. It was on the typewriter now. It would no longer be called "The Aloe". It was to be re-named "Prelude" – because it seemed a prelude to what might be a larger work based on her childhood; and because the events it recounted were like a prelude to the child Kezia's life. Also because she liked to think there was, or there ought to be, something musical about the construction of a work of fiction.

She was in the kitchen now, preparing to make tea. There would be a very small cake with it, a reward for work, for application and concentration. This had been a good day and a reward was in order.

Outside a small bird took off from a large branch, and the branch shook and shivered. It was like the fuss Jack had made on being left alone. A little departure, a big cosmic shudder. She'd said to him, "At least you'll know the hair on your bread and honey is your own." He'd laughed his weary martyr's laugh and said he would rather find her hair than his in his honey. "I've none to spare, Tig."

In the afternoon mail there had been a note from him, and a letter from Ottoline. Ottoline's was lying on the kitchen table. Katherine had only allowed herself a quick skim over its surface. Now she would read it again, properly, going below the surface, looking for submarines, torpedoes, mines perhaps, while she drank her tea and ate her cake. Her friendship with Ottoline, bizarre, precarious, subject to alteration without notice, had been one of the adventures of these past months.

The letters Katherine wrote her were careful compositions. They were rather fine (she thought), and rather false – but not entirely false, and that "not entirely" was what she found interesting. They were like the translation of herself into another language – necessary, because Ottoline didn't understand hers. Her role was that of the clever foreigner. She could write Ottoline's language, and did it well – but with an accent.

She had been back to Garsington since Christmas but (frightened of breaking the spell that kept her working) not as often as Ottoline wanted. A weekend now and then – and letters back and forth – that had had to suffice.

Sometimes Ottoline came to London and they met at the Lyons Teashop near the Bond Street Underground. Sometimes they had disagreements, but these were never open arguments. They were oblique, even opaque, consisting of absences, silences, and the sending of signals that might or might not be understood. When Ottoline sent, for example, what seemed many armloads of jasmine and roses from her garden, and a message saying that her "dearest friend" would understand what they meant, Katherine pretended that the dearest friend did, and that no more need be said. It called for a special talent.

On one of her London visits Ottoline took her to a balalaika concert at the Grafton Gallery. It was eerie, mysterious music ("As if the earth *breathed*," Ottoline whispered), and they walked together afterwards, arm in arm through the streets of Piccadilly under a misty moon, feeling elevated, euphoric. "I was afraid you might not like it, darling," Ottoline said.

"Oh but I did," Katherine assured her. "I did." And it was true. The music was lovely; and everything Russian fascinated her. But she felt also that she was on a stage, acting a part. She enjoyed acting; but it was as if the circumstances were dictating to her, moment by moment, what she was to say.

"Katherine, dear," Ottoline said as they walked along. "You know about my Philip. You've heard . . . what he's done?"

Katherine had not. It was surprising but for once she didn't have to pretend. "Philip has . . . *done* something?"

"He has betrayed me," Ottoline said. "He has betrayed us all. He has betrayed . . ." (her voice dropped an octave) ". . . *himself*."

Philip (she explained) had come to her while she was in a nursing home undergoing one of her "cures", to tell her that he'd been having one affair with her personal maid, Eva, and another with his secretary, Alice. What was most inconvenient about this, and necessitated the telling, was that both were pregnant.

"Pregnant! Heavens." Katherine was impressed. "What will happen?"

"What will happen?" Ottoline was momentarily very tall, up on her mountain. "Nothing will happen. Babies will be born. Life will go on."

It was the scale of the thing that took hold of Katherine's imagination: the cuckolded, frequently mocked, almost always socially sidelined husband of the great lady, the backbencher in every sense, revealed not with one below-stairs mistress but two; and not one but both soon to be delivered of his child! This was carelessness with a certain grandeur. From one point of view you could see it as a triumph, as easily calling for champagne as for weeping and gnashing of teeth.

If at that moment in the dim light Ottoline's distress had not been so evident Katherine might have been unsure what was expected of her. But when she looked at her friend's face there was no doubt. She embraced Ottoline, making comforting sounds, murmurings, into her fur. The embrace was welcomed and returned.

"Oh darling," Ottoline said; and because she was weeping, Katherine wept too.

Katherine took her tea to the big window and set it down on the desk, reading Ottoline's letter and eating the cake. Then she lit herself a cigarette and stared down into the garden where a neighbour's toddler, a little boy, was being entertained by a nanny with a large red ball. His name, the name Katherine had given him, was Boy, and lately he had become her child. Often in imagination she tucked Boy into bed, told him stories, sang him to sleep. He was part of her inner life, the part she didn't confess to Jack.

Ottoline's letter was about a number of things, and included the names of a great many flowers. She'd been cycling in and out of Oxford and wrote of the scents of grass cut for hay, and elder flowers and honeysuckle. But it was chiefly about "darling, tiresome Siegfried".

"I have been finding him of late," she wrote, "almost unforgivably self-absorbed. He behaves as if I don't exist; or exist only to provide him with comfortable accommodation. He's an ungrateful fellow. But there you are. The important thing is that he wants to do something about the war."

Back on this side of the Channel only to recover from wounds, Sassoon had come around to the view that the war was being needlessly prosecuted by men who had no notion of the suffering of the common soldier, and no concern about the scale of the killing. His poems were revealing war as it really was; but poetry didn't reach out to a wide enough audience. "He wants to take a stand," Ottoline continued. "He has decided he should prepare a statement saying the war is no longer morally justifiable. Negotiations with Germany should begin at once." His statement would be cast in the form of a public refusal to return to the Front. Since he was a decorated officer it would receive attention in the newspapers. "Philip counselled caution. It's a risky business standing up to the military. He could be court-martialled and shot. But if he's quite determined, Philip will find a way to have it read in the House."

But the statement needed some refining. It was better that Philip should have no direct hand in it. Bertie was away in the countryside, out of reach. "Time's pressing," Ottoline went on, "so I'm sending Sassoon to Murry, with the request that he have a look at it – check that it makes its points well with no loopholes."

Jack's note to Katherine gave the same news. "I know you didn't much like Sassoon," he wrote, "but I think you should have a hand in this business. Come to my place this evening, if you would like to. I hope you will, dearest Tig. I'm going to grab a bite at the Good Intent first and then – to business! Say around eight?"

Katherine sat in her chair, the letters on her lap. She thought of Leslie, and the naïve idealism they both, brother and sister, had felt at his becoming a soldier, going to fight in a war. The "good cause" had been the protection of "little Belgium" from Prussian militarism, and she still felt it had been right. But the consequences had been so far beyond imagining, nothing was clear any more. If Sassoon wanted to make a statement of course he should do it. Someone in Valhalla might be listening.

She watched the toddler – Boy – down in the garden go after the big red ball, fall down in the grass, get up and go after it again, and again fall down. He was lovely, he was real. "The War" was an abstraction, a puzzle, a nightmare. She knew she couldn't write about it – not directly; but perhaps, if she could write about Boy, it would be there.

A few weeks later Jack came to her studio in the evening, carrying his battered little suitcase. He was going on to Garsington next morning but she would cook him supper first and he would stay the night. Ottoline had invited them both but Katherine, busy with her writing, had declined. Jack wanted to see his young brother Richard, who had joined the pacifist farm workers there; but he needed the rest for himself too, a break from the grind of sixty hours a week at the Ministry.

Over dinner they talked about their meeting with Sassoon. It had been a warm damp night, and Jack had lit candles in an attempt to give some kind of "atmosphere" to his dreary quarters. The statement of protest had been worked over and a final wording agreed. Siegfried's eyes had scarcely moved from Jack. He was a man's man, Katherine had thought, *decidedly*. She'd offered a few suggestions – matters of grammar and choice of words – but otherwise remained silent, feeling she couldn't stand either of them: Jack going on about how the war, and the deaths of friends, hurt his soul; Sassoon so full of himself, a hero in battle, and now a hero for peace. It wasn't that she didn't approve of what he was doing, and admire his courage. But it would have been better, she'd thought, if she could have approved and admired without meeting the man.

When it was done the three had walked down to the river in silence, watching the long stalks of light sweeping the sky, catching on cloud and probing into the black emptiness beyond. That walk had had for her a special, resonant kind of dreariness, like living in a moment of "History" when you would rather have been at a party. There was no escaping the war; it corrupted everyone, even those who opposed it.

She said now, "You know I didn't like you that night."

Jack looked up from his pork cutlet. "You didn't?"

"You were going on about the war in that way I can't stand. Saying it hurt your soul."

"Well, darling . . . it does."

"Does it? I suppose so. But why do you have to say those

things? We all have souls, Jack, but we don't all *bare* them as you do."

He shrugged and said, "I'm sorry," and she felt the old guilt at hurting him.

After a moment he said, "I suppose Ottoline told you about Sassoon's protest? It fell through. Collapsed. Came to nothing."

She hadn't heard and he explained. Sassoon's fellow-poet and brother-officer, Robert Graves, had got wind of what was going on and stepped in to save him from a court martial. "He persuaded Sassoon to go before a medical board. He's been classified as suffering from shell shock and sent to a hospital in Scotland for treatment. They're calling it a nervous breakdown."

"The hero's courage failed?"

"Well . . . I suppose you could say the military stared at him and he blinked."

"And so . . . On with the dance."

"The dance?"

"The war, darling." And after a moment, laughing at him: "The war dance."

She was first in bed and watched him in the half-light, naked, combing his hair and holding the comb up to see how many strands it had pulled out. He opened his suitcase to put the comb back and she saw his old felt hat, squashed down, and a very battered French grammar book.

She said, "You're not a tidy packer, Boge."

He frowned down into the case. "I've only got three hand-kerchiefs, Tig. Do you think that will do?"

She felt herself on the brink of laughter. She said, "So long as you don't catch cold, darling, and *take care to make them last*."

He was small, bow-legged. His bones stuck out. He looked so young without his clothes, like a boy who needed looking after. "Jack darling, you've lost weight haven't you?"

He said he thought he had. His usual weight was nine and a half stone.

She told him he must treat himself better, eat bigger lunches, and not work so hard. "Now come to bed and make me happy."

Next morning he was up before her. He had been out and bought *The Times*. As she went past him to make coffee she could see that he was going through the casualty lists. She filled the coffee pot and put it on the stove. Without looking, she felt something − a stillness, as if he'd stopped breathing. When she looked he was standing at the window, staring down into the garden. Light rain was falling. It drifted past the huge pane in sideways curves, catching the light. She thought, I know what's happened. She felt unnaturally calm.

"Jack?"

He turned to look at her.

"Who is it?"

"Goodyear, darling."

"Freddie?"

"Freddie."

"Killed?"

"D.O.W." There were tears in his eyes. He came over and hugged her. She remained stiff, couldn't respond, felt nothing, a blankness.

All day it remained the same. Jack caught his train. She did her work, stopping from time to time to say to herself that Fred Goodyear was dead, had died of wounds, was already under the ground, in France, with Leslie. For ever. She would never see him again, there would be no Scandinavia, no frozen north. The facts lay there, like something spilled, thrown up. There was no pain, no grief, but she felt hollow, awful, not herself. The work went on. There was no change from the day before, or the day before that.

When she'd finished, later than usual because Jack had been late leaving, she tried to go on behaving normally – except (she decided) she would have coffee, not tea. She would give herself the usual little cake for reward, eat it at the window, and smoke a cigarette.

She was filling the coffee pot when she heard the muffled knocking. She stood quite still. It was there, it was gone, it was back again. She strained to hear it, coming up, as it seemed, from below, deep in the ground.

Knock . . . Knock-knock . . . Knock . . . Very slow, faint, with long gaps so she would think it was over and then it would start again.

What seized her next was so sudden and violent it was only as she panted through the streets, half running, half fast-walking, that she was able to remember it. She had panicked, letting the coffee pot fall into the sink where it lay on its side, leaking from its spout and under the lid. She had grabbed up her bag under one arm, a pad of writing paper and pen in the other hand, and had run out.

Even now, stumbling along through the evening crowds, she was struck by that – why the pad and pen? Only because it had been her habit lately never to go out without them.

She saw that she was heading towards Redcliffe Road and Jack's rooms. She would be safe there.

She got a key from Jack's landlady and climbed the stairs with their awful coir matting that seemed to make itself felt through the soles of her shoes. Once inside she drew the curtains, lit the gas and put the kettle on. She checked the clock and wound it. She looked into the bedroom at the huge high bed and recoiled from it, thinking how it would look with a corpse laid out on it. On the stand inside the door was Jack's black winter overcoat. She went to it, put her arms around it, her face against it. She stroked its flanks and felt her own tears between it and her cheeks.

She went to his desk. His journal lay there. She knew she shouldn't open it but did, going straight to the most recent entries, which were mostly about his work at the War Office, and turning back until she found her own name. It was an entry about the nature of love. It had to do with beauty, and the war, and "the very shipwreck of every human hope" – the kind of soul stuff she didn't like but forgave for the moment. What took her attention was the sentence, "I don't dare tell Katherine that I am losing all belief in love; that my childish faith in its human duration is gone."

The effect of this was strange. It put an end to her panic. It seemed to call for action; for correction. She turned forward to the most recent page. She would write him a letter there. It began with a lie: "My darling, Do not imagine because you find these lines in your private book that I have been trespassing. You know I have not."

She told him, in many different ways, that she loved him – and as she wrote it down, as the words and the examples came so readily and flowed so effortlessly from her pen, the conviction that all this was true caught up with the words. It was like the letters she'd written him sometimes from France. She *did* love Jack. In a final paragraph she wrote, "I have perfect faith in us. I want nobody but you for my lover and my friend. I am yours for ever,

– Tig."

THIRTEEN

Autumn–Winter 1917 – Katherine

"DARLING?" HER VOICE IS DROWSY. IT IS SUNDAY AFTERNOON and they are in bed together.

"Yes," he says but he's asleep – and so, after a moment, is she.

Later – one deep sleep later – she turns over and fits herself to the curve of his back, putting arms around him. "Bogey, darling."

"Mmm?"

"Do you . . . ?"

"Mmm."

"Sure?"

"Sure."

And once more they are asleep.

When they stir again London is growing dark. She gets up, puts on the Harrods dressing gown Ida got for her in exchange for the one sent by Aunt Belle at Christmas. It's still some sizes too large, but wearable. "I'll grow into it, darling," she told Ida, who was ready to go back and make a further exchange.

Katherine makes tea and brings it to the bed on a tray. "Will you miss me?"

"Too much." And then, "Don't go."

"But Dr Ainger . . ."

"Yes, and he's right. You must."

She shakes the pot, and pours. "You know, Bogey, France

again, Bandol – if it weren't for your having to stay here, I'd be looking forward to it."

"You are, aren't you?"

"Yes, but I'm sad too."

"Don't be. Enjoy it. Write, get well, and come back to me in the spring . . ."

"April. A spring wedding. Doesn't that seem nice? Silly and nice. I'm trying awfully hard not to be girlish about it."

George Bowden has at last asked for a divorce. The decree nisi has been granted. By April Katherine will be free.

"No more jibes from Virginia about my names. Beauchamp-Mansfield-Bowden-Murry. What was it she said?"

"Virginia's such a prig."

"No more problems with passports and hotel registers. Not to mention my family." She runs her fingers through his thinning hair. "When we're married and rich I'm going to take you on a visit to New Zealand. It will make your hair grow."

"Will it really?"

"Really."

"Are there no bald men in New Zealand?"

"None at all, darling. Not one. It's something in the water."

He looks doubtful, but interested. "Your pa . . ."

"Hair like a wire brush. Ginger."

"I don't think I'd like that."

"Hair's hair, Bogey. You have to take what you get and be thankful."

They go on with their tea and biscuits. "What about the Maoris?" he says.

"They're very nice. They sing very nicely."

"I thought they shouted and stamped and poked out their tongues."

"Sometimes. And roll their eyes. It's called a haka."

"You said they were cannibals."

"Yes. But I'll teach you a secret Maori word that will keep you safe. Aroha. Can you say that? A - ro - ha."

He says it. "Aroha."

"There's my lad. Now you've got Maori as well as French and German. What a linguist you are!"

"What does it mean?"

"Aroha? It means, 'Please don't eat me.'"

He lies back among the pillows, staring at the ceiling. "Aroha," he murmurs. "Aroha."

That is their private world. In the public world hope and fear and helplessness go hand in hand. Field Marshal Haig insists that one more big push is what's needed to break the German line in the West and the German will in Berlin. Prime Minister Lloyd George doesn't believe him, is alarmed that Britain is simply running out of young men to feed the fight, but afraid to assert his authority against the advice of his military experts. In France the French army has pretty much given up, and its mutinous soldiers are told to sit tight in their trenches and hold the line, the only order they can be counted on to obey. A revolution has occurred in Russia, giving the German and Austrian armies the possibility of relief on the Eastern Front and another whole army that might yet be brought over to the West. The Gallipoli assault – meant to open another front through Turkey – has long since been abandoned. Along the Italian Front the Austrians are making advances. But America has entered the war on the side of the French and British, and it's hoped that soon its troops will begin to arrive.

At Ypres, Broodseinde, Passchendaele, the British infantry

regiments that have taken such losses are pulled back, to be replaced by Anzacs; and when they have been thoroughly mauled, it is the turn of the Canadians. Enormous artillery bombardments destroy German defences, kill large numbers of men, and weaken the German will, so that the infantry, following up, make gains on the ground. Then comes the counter-attack (preceded by equally heavy bombardment) – German troops, held back beyond the reach of British artillery, now brought forward. The ground gained and insecurely held is re-taken. Thousands have been killed on either side, and the map is hardly changed. Yet still the Generals ask for more – more men, more tanks and guns, more time, more death.

In the trenches the men no longer care about the Cause. They want it over. They don't much hate the enemy – share rations with him when he is captured – but the two sides go on killing one another as and when they can. They are loyal, not to the Cause, and only half-heartedly to their nation, but to their comrades and to the experience of war.

Rain is falling. Not just ordinary seasonal rain. Exceptional rain, as if a bored deity, a god in the style of a Roman emperor, no longer sufficiently entertained by the spectacle of men destroying one another, has decided after all to intervene in a novel and interesting way. On low-lying plains and water meadows of Flanders, where all significant vegetation has been destroyed by incessant bombardments and roads have all but vanished, the rains fall on a scale hardly equalled since the ones that had Noah and the animals becoming sailors. Trenches become watercourses and mud rises above duckboards meant to keep feet and legs dry. Field guns and horses sink in it and can't be got out. Tanks, the new terror of modern warfare, are immobilised. In battle, men flounder, sink to their waists and wait, helpless, for the bayonet or bullet that will bring their part in the story to an end. Others, wounded, fall or roll, as before, into the shelter of shell-holes where their cries of pain and groans of despair fade as they slide into rising water, and drown. In places it is said the mud is ten feet deep. Wheels of gun carriages press the recently dead down into the ground in one place and in another turn up the bones and skulls, boots and helmets, of last year's corpses, and the year before's. The battlefields have become enormous, hungry cemeteries, the earth itself a man-eating monster.

South of Flanders at Cambrai, on dryer, higher ground, the tanks are given their best chance. Three hundred and eighty-one of them, with infantry close behind, break through German defences and for the first time since the war began, bells ring out in London celebrating a victory. But the bells are premature. There has been an oversight. The god's thirst for entertainment is not yet slaked. There are no reserves to secure the gains. Ten days later the Germans have re-taken every inch of ground lost.

At home there are the beginnings of restlessness, discontent, complaint. Too many deaths. The lives of too many good young fellows thrown away for nothing. Food is short – everything, including patience, is short – excepting only queues, which are long. Prices rise ahead of wages. People who read the better papers begin to notice and remark on the fact that the new revolutionary government in Russia is willing to negotiate "peace without annexation or indemnities", while France and Britain are still insisting they will have their pounds of flesh.

Labour is organising itself. There are signs, though still faint and hesitant, that that sad trio, hope, fear and helplessness, working so hard to keep the malign god's entertainment running, might yet be replaced by reason, the acknowledgement of mistakes, and a will to bring down the curtain. Bertie Russell keeps up his campaign against the war. He has been attacked and beaten by a mob during an anti-war meeting at the Brotherhood Church in Hackney, and knows it is only a matter of time before he will be jailed.

In Lawrence's kitchen garden at Zennor the same rain that falls on Flanders is beating his vegetable crops into the ground. Propelled by squalls and gales, it drives up in huge heavy volleys from the sea. His peas are destroyed, the marrow vines have lost their leaves. Even the kohlrabi that so impressed Katherine is looking defeated. No one will publish his offending novel, *Women in Love*, so he has offered a book of poems and received a promise of twenty guineas. It is called *Look, We Have Come Through*. But he and Frieda have come under suspicion again. The lights in their windows that look seaward have not always been blacked out. Mrs Lawrence has been overheard speaking German and seen waving a scarf towards the sea. Lawrence has been saying unpatriotic things about the war.

Late in October the cottage is searched. Some of Lawrence's papers are taken away. Soon an order comes that he and his wife are to leave Cornwall. Like Bertie Russell they are banned from all "prohibited areas", and instructed that wherever they next take up residence they must report themselves to the local police.

They make their way back to London, where they must survive on little more than the charity of friends, among whom, since the offence given to Ottoline in the new novel, the generous Morrells can no longer be numbered. Lawrence chafes at the greyness, the ugliness, the death watch of wartime London, with its endless talk of air raids at home and battles abroad, and its rain that is so much dirtier, less wholesome and refreshing, than the rain that sweeps in over the Cornish coast. He believes there are spies on the stairs, agents set to watch him. He hates his fellow-man with a new ferocity and misses his garden, his cottage, the wild air and wild sea, and the handsome smile and quiet burred speech of his Cornish friend, farmer Hocking.

He has been told more than once a story about Katherine that has restored his affection for her. Hearing three people at a table in the Café Royal reading out some of his poems and speaking of them disrespectfully, Katherine (so the story goes) asked politely to see the book and then walked out with it. Lawrence is touched and has put the episode into his new novel. He thinks of calling on her; but he hasn't forgiven the Murrys for their defection from Higher Tregerthen. In particular, he hasn't forgiven Jack, and doesn't want to see him.

It was in September 1917, while the rains fell on the Stalemate to end Stalemates, that Katherine and Jack began to talk about living together again. They would find a place in London in the short term. They would also look for a place in the country-side, like Leonard and Virginia's house in Sussex, but with some farmland. The house would be an ancient one, with walls three feet thick, ancient beams, an orchard, a meadow, good farm build-ings including a barn (it was Jack who got carried away with these details) where the printing press could be housed. House and press would both be named "The Heron" after Katherine's brother whose full name was Leslie Heron Beauchamp. They would love one another, perhaps have a child – and if that didn't happen, well, each was in any case the other's child and would remain so. They would live close to the earth with their cats, their hens and livestock, growing flowers and vegetables, breathing the fresh air of the countryside. They would live by their writing and become famous. When they were rich they might have two homes, one in the English countryside, the other in the south of France. They would visit New Zealand, and she would show him her magic places.

Did she believe it? Was it possible to believe anything so wholly desirable for more than a moment? Sometimes, when she tried to imagine Jack Murry, the boy from Peckham, being the countryman, she remembered watching him use a spade at Mylor and thinking he dug as if exhuming a hated body or making a hole for a loved one. She laughed of course – it was one of her jokes against Jack. But why should that not be their future? They were still in their twenties – had decades of life ahead of them. Time and talent would work for them so long as they retained confidence and maintained a steady path.

In November Jack became ill. It was a cold, 'flu, pleurisy – and possibly worse. His lungs were affected. He was feverish, weak, underweight, suffering from exhaustion and depression, and his doctor told him he must take six weeks off from the War Office. Alarmed, Katherine wrote to Ottoline. Would she take him at Garsington? Ottoline's telegram came winging back. Of course she would be delighted to have them both. They should come soon – why not today?

Katherine saw him off at Paddington, instructing him that he must go slow, drift, eat, sleep, keep warm and not forget how much she loved him. She planned, she told him, to turn herself into "a female Balzac", house-hunting by day and writing by night. She was in charge of herself, still writing strongly, full of good intentions.

A week or so later she went to visit him at Garsington, caught a chill there, caught whatever he had, returned to London and had to take to her bed. It gave her at first a feeling of luxury because there was nothing to be done but give in to it.

She had begun to feel pain – that sinister aching in the bones she called her "rheumatiz", and a burning sensation in the chest; but she remained cheerful, lying awake at night in a state (she wrote to Jack) of "*furious bliss*", watching the firelight flickering on the walls and listening to the air raids which had started up again. People came and went, giving her, without knowing it, secret entertainment, as if she were sitting alone and unseen in a theatre, the only one who saw the joke, or knew there was a joke.

"Have you had a good day, darling?"

This was Ida, the Rhodesian Mountain, the Faithful One, come to see her settled for the night.

"I've had visitors."

"Nice ones?"

"No, darling. Boring ones. Except Johnny Fergusson. He was nice."

"Jack's friend. I thought you said he was gloomy."

"He is gloomy. He's a Scot, you see? But he doesn't pretend things are *quite splendid* when they're not."

"And who else?"

"Mrs Maufe."

"Oh your neighbour. She's very nice."

"She's boring, Ida."

"Surely not. She was telling me about something the other day . . ."

"About . . . *something*. About what?"

"I don't remember, Katie. But it was very interesting."

"Jones."

"Yes, dear?"

"Mrs Maufe is boring."

"I see. I'm sorry to hear that, Katie."

Last night they'd quarrelled over whether she should have Oxo or warm milk before going to sleep. Katherine had been for Oxo. Ida was hell-bent on warm milk. It was strange how persistent Ida could be, especially if she thought it was for your own good. A jelly with a whim of iron. She should try not to quarrel with Ida, but it was difficult.

Ida was smiling now – a sort of Malvolio smile, with yellow stockings and cross garters. "And who else, dear?"

"My boring sister. My boring aunt."

There was a reproachful silence.

"Ida, I know you think I'm unfair and capricious. But if I hear the word *splendid* one more time I think I might spontaneously combust, like Mr Krook."

"Mr?"

"Krook." And after a moment's wait. "Mr Krook . . . Of *Bleak House*."

Silence. It was clear that Ida didn't understand and wouldn't pursue it – had fallen into too many of her best friend's well-laid traps. Katherine went on: "I had to hear that Mr Lloyd George is doing a *splendid* job. That the King is being absolutely *splendid*. That the courage of the men at the Front is simply *splendid*. What is it about those women? Chaddie had a brain once. And Aunt Belle – well, half a brain anyway. It's as though their heads have been squeezed in a vice."

"It's well meant, Katie-love."

"Well meant but not well said."

"You mean . . . some other word? Like . . . excellent?"

"No. I mean words attached to something real and particular. Statements preceded by observation and thought."

Ida stared at her, awaiting further illumination. How that look

228

irritated Katherine! "It's meaningless, Ida. Don't you see that? If everything's splendid then nothing is."

"I'm sure you're right, Katie."

This was the meek Ida, the one who expected to inherit the earth; and she was probably right – she would, if that God person who was arranging the Universe had anything to do with it. You had to be exceptionally sanguine and short-sighted not to spontaneously combust these days. While Ida fussed, straightening bedclothes, pulling up blankets that had half slipped to the floor, Katherine amused herself with the thought of Mr Krook alcoholically exploding, the air of Chancery Lane and the Inns of Court filling with black flakes and becoming "greasy". Didn't Mr Weevle and Mr Snagsby speculate on what the smell might be, and one suggested "Chops" and the other said "Well if it's chops, she must have burned them, and they can't have been *fresh*"?

She began to laugh. Ida's face was sulky. It said to her, "This is unfair," and it was. She pulled herself together. "I'm not laughing at you, darling. I was thinking about Dickens."

"Oh Dickens." Ida shrugged, as if to say, "*Him!*"

"Dr Ainger came," Katherine offered. She pulled the top of her nightdress down to reveal the new binding he'd put around her chest.

Ida leaned forward like a bird. Her hand hesitated towards it, as if to check it was satisfactory, but she restrained herself. "I'm glad," she said. "He's so conscientious. And I know you don't think *he's* boring, Katie."

"I don't. Indeed I don't. We talked about Tolstoy. And Taupo."

Dr Ainger was a New Zealander and this was another trap. Ida stepped into it – deliberately (Katherine was sure) because she'd decided her friend was in a mood to torment her. "Who is Taupo?" she asked.

But Katherine didn't spring the trap. She took Ida's hand. "Why am I so cruel to you?"

Tears came to the Faithful One's eyes. She shook her head, denying that Katherine was cruel, but for a moment couldn't speak. Then, "Did he listen to your lung, darling?"

"He did. He listened and it spoke. It told him it's living under a shadow and it needs the sun."

"Really?" Ida's face brightened.

"It's not the first time he's suggested it. But this time he was much more emphatic. He really means it. He said Tenerife or Madeira would be ideal. But Spain or the south of France would do."

After Dr Ainger had left, and in the gaps between other visits, Katherine had dwelt on that advice, dozed on it, dreamed of it. Slowly the wet green English countryside, The Heron with its beams and beans and wellington boots, had receded, replaced by a pink house with two cedars in front and hills behind, a compact walled garden and a view of the pale blue Mediterranean. A small house like the Villa Pauline would be the ticket, the size you could get for fifteen pounds a year, but big enough for friends to come and stay. Jack was bound to the Ministry until the war was over; but the war would soon end – had to, surely.

Looking out into the cold fog that came down over London, hearing the rag-and-bone man down in the street with his cry that might as well have been "Bring out your dead", she'd thought, not for the first time, but for the first time seriously, that she would take Dr Ainger's advice. The necessity, if it was a necessity, was frightening; but she could also see it as a stroke of wonderful luck. Her lung needed the south of France? Very well, she would take it there.

"I'm not sure that I believe in this illness," she told Ida, "but I begin to believe in the cure."

Christmas came and went. Ottoline sent a pink eiderdown. Aunt Belle sent a green padded silk dressing gown many sizes too large. Jack (still recovering at Garsington) sent a jacket to go with all her other jackets. "My Jack jacket", she called it. Ida gave her a petticoat the colour of raspberries or currants, which Katherine thought of as a coal of fire but knew, or thought she knew, it was not meant to be. Even Ottoline's daughter, 11-year-old Julian, sent her a pretty Calendar Book. "I shall have to send you my present for the New Year," Katherine wrote, "for I am still in my cage."

Dr Ainger gave her the necessary certificate that would secure permission to travel. Jack wrote to the Beau Rivage ordering her "a room with a view" (it was the title of one of Morgan Forster's novels). Ida came and went, helping her get well and ready for travel.

At the year's end she was improved enough to make another quick visit to Garsington. She and Jack returned to London together. They were both recovered, though both still coughing with an end-of-illness cough that sounded in the night, Katherine told Ida, like the bark and answering bark of a pair of back-country farm dogs.

"Aroha." Jack says it again. "Tell me what it *really* means."

"It means love, darling."

"Aroha. That's nice. Noun or verb?"

"Noun. I don't know what the verb would be."

Jack tries it as a verb. "I aroha you very much. He aroha'd her on Sunday afternoon."

'So he did," she says, and squeezes his hand.

He has been looking over a sheaf of her letters written to him at Garsington. "Tig, why do you spell cream with a b?"

"Oh." She shrugs and bites into a biscuit. "It's the kind of cream I like best." She says it, sounding the b. "Creamb."

"I wish Ida could have gone with you."

Ida has been a last-minute addition to the plan – to help Katherine on the journey, to ease her passage – but her application for a visa has failed.

"No, really, Jack, I'm glad. I don't need her. She was dead keen, but Ida's such a mixed blessing."

She looks at him, and reaches out to run fingers over his brow, smoothing his frown. "Stop fussing, darling. It's going to be all right."

Next day, a Monday, they say their tearful goodbyes on the platform of Waterloo Station. Her luggage stowed, she pushes down the window of the carriage door and leans out, holding Jack's eyes as he holds hers while the train pulls slowly away – keeping him in sight until distance and a curve in the rails take him from her.

It is the first week of 1918, a week in which the German High Command is hard at work on yet another plan to punch decisive holes through British and French lines along the Western Front.

EPILOGUE

Winter 1918

SHE IS LYING IN BED IN THE HÔTEL BEAU RIVAGE, HEARING THE sea speaking French out there, saying "*'issh 'issh*", running up the sand dropping its aitches. Her shutters are open and she can see beyond her windows the elegant downward curves of a single palm tree. It is still quite early in the morning but people are about, she can hear them speaking to one another in their forth-right – almost harsh – way, *using* their voices, their throats too, the women especially. Life goes on in France, but it is changed, it has taken a battering.

She is half awake, slipping in and out of a dozing dreaming remembering half-sleep by means of which she is recovering the past few hectic, exciting and sometimes terrible weeks, the highs and the lows. She wants to repossess them, add them to her store. The pile of work she is able to think of as "good" – or good enough, publishable – is growing. Of course there are ideas which fail, stories which somehow "miss it", and she doesn't let herself, or them, off lightly; but she feels more in control now. Her next book will be better than the *German Pension* collec-tion. After the Woolfs have published *Prelude* as a book she will think about putting it into a larger collection with a regular commercial publisher. She is working towards that. The list of titles is something she jots down in margins and notebooks and on pieces of blotting paper, playing put and take as the options increase. That is what she is here for in Bandol – to recover her health, yes, but also to work.

The principal scenes of these last weeks play over as in a movie. She sees herself taking a turn on the ferry deck before retiring, standing at the rail feeling as if she is on a mythic journey again, the ship sailing into the softness of a snowstorm. She is shivering, but she has eaten a big supper – such a *whack* of beef, with bread and butter and tea. The snowflakes flutter like moths in the ship's lights, catching fire there and taking it down with them on to the dark heaving glossy-animal flank of the sea.

Then there was the day in Le Havre and the journey to Paris, revealing that though the "War to end War" could put the heating out of action on the SNCF, slow its trains, make a joke of its timetables, and allow snow to come sneaking in without a ticket through its broken windows, it could make no impact at all on the glories of French bread or French cheeses.

The next day was Paris, making her way "*comme un poulet malade*" – like a sick chicken – on the icy pavements, having her visa stamped, trying to send messages, get money, arrange that she and her luggage should arrive at the same place, discover to which train at what time on which platform she should change at Marseilles – all of this done, so to speak, against the odds, against the grain of the war, and yet through it all finding herself simply loving France and the French and the French language. It must have been (she tells herself now) some kind of saintly madness bestowed on her by the fact of being at last on the move, let out of her cage, relieved of the boredom of illness – so she was seeing, not quite "France and the French", but a mirror, a reflection of her own unreasonable, unseasonable happiness.

It couldn't last of course, and didn't. She was not well enough, and the way ahead was too tough. The long delays, the uncertainties, the cold, dirt and discomfort of the train, the lack of food, hot drinks, pillows, working wash-rooms – all of that together with the aching-and-burning in her lung that got worse by the hour . . . And then, late in the long cold night, somewhere south of Lyons as the train crawled through the blacked-out landscape, two French women talking about the Mediterranean coast, agreeing that the popular idea that it was good for people with damaged lungs was a myth, and surely contradicted by the facts. The Protestant cemeteries down there (did nobody notice?) were full of English, Germans, Scandinavians, who had come south to get better and had only dug their own graves. It was something in the air . . . Something fatal . . . They didn't stand a chance . . . One had known an American girl, beautiful, suffering only from bronchitis, expected to get better in three months, hadn't lasted six weeks . . .

It was all in French, in an undertone, but she heard it and understood it as clearly as if it had been a bell tolling distantly but getting nearer as the hours passed and the train closed on that fatal coast. She tried to dismiss them from her mind, joke them out of existence. Bubble bubble toil and trouble. Where's your sister, Sisters? Missed the train, did she?

She dropped back again into an exhausted sleep, but took them with her there, still talking about lungs and death and the graveyards of the Côte d'Azure.

Then came Marseilles, the effort of it, the gathering of her luggage, the long queues, getting her visa stamped again, the uncertainty about where from, and when, the train to Bandol would leave, the bruising rushes with the crowd as announcements and contradictions sent it surging from one platform to another . . .

Simply to be on board, seated, with a compartment all to herself, as it turned out to be, and to hear the doors banging shut and the whistle blowing, was such a relief it almost cancelled the disappointment she felt at having eight Serbian officers and their two dogs push in with her at the last moment.

"Madame does not object?" one asked in French, bowing and baring a set of exceptionally white teeth under his black moustache.

She felt it would not have made any difference if Madame had; and in any case they were handsome animals, all ten of them, and, ill or not, this side of death she was not going to be indifferent to manly good looks. "Not at all," she assured him. "More bodies means more warmth, *n'est-ce pas?*"

In their own language they discussed what this meant, seemed to come to an understanding, and all smiled at her together. Even the dogs smiled. She felt she had recruited a palace guard. It was a piece of good fortune. The train was not moving, despite a second whistle-blast from the guard and a wave of his flag. Out there on the platform a contingent of French soldiers were holding up the departure, demanding places on the train. The shouting grew louder. All at once they attacked. It was no outburst of good-humoured high jinks. These were angry men just back from the war zone around Verdun, bitter at what they had been put through while these civilians had sat at home. Why did people need to travel while there was a war on? Were they going on holiday?

They burst into the train, shouting, dragging passengers, men and women, old and young, man-handling them out on to the platform and taking their places. The Serbians were ordered out but refused. They too were fighting men, they insisted. They had been fighting for France, and had earned their places in blood.

Coriolanus-like, they uncovered their scars. They were staunch, determined. Also, they were armed.

"Well, *she* must go," a French soldier said, grabbing Katherine and dragging her towards the door.

The Serbian who had first spoken to her intervened, holding the Frenchman by the shoulder, towering over him. "*Non, Monsieur. Elle est ma femme.*"

The Frenchman, who smelled strongly of wine, tobacco and stale sweat, hesitated, then let her go. He didn't know whether to believe it, but it might be true (she was a foreigner), and clearly it would have been folly to intervene between such a large man and his wife. The Serbians eased him out of the compartment and secured the door with their dogs' leather collars. As the train began to move she could see civilians, some weeping, others angry and bruised, some with their luggage and some with nothing, all helpless on the platform. Up and down the train the French soldiers burst into a triumphant "Marseillaise".

She had been frowning hard, concentrating on the thought that whatever happened she must not cry. Now she smiled at her protector.

"Thank you," she said. "*Merci beaucoup, Monsieur. Danke schön.*" And then, searching among the bits and pieces of several languages she'd learned in Germany, she added, not feeling quite sure it was the word she wanted, "*Hvala!*"

They laughed and applauded. "My wife is a linguist," he said in French. "Madame is welcome. Now she will have a small brandy and a cigarette?"

Bandol, when she reached it at last, she found changed by war and weather. At the Beau Rivage the management were new, there was no heating, the service was skimpy, the food basic and the prices high. There were few guests; its verandahs and pale public rooms with their white cane furniture seemed empty and battened down like a ship in a gale, whispering and gasping with sudden gusts and draughts. She had to buy wood for the fireplace in her room. In the town she was not immediately recognised by shopkeepers who had been her friends. When she reminded them who she was they told her, with a combination of kindness and frankness alien to the Anglo-Saxon, that she was *changed*, that it was clear she'd been unwell, that she'd lost her pretty-girl look.

She found herself homesick, alternately grieving for Freddie and missing Jack, loving them both in a way that seemed wild, extravagant. Every day she wrote to Jack; every day she looked out for his replies and felt panicky and bereft if none came. But she was working. The weather improved. And the maid, Juliette, who had little to do in this lean time, was the rare kind of being whose good humour and goodwill could make it seem the sun was shining even when it wasn't.

The sea out there is still speaking French under its breath. "*'isshsh*" it says to the sand, "*'isshsh*." She slips in and out of sleep, but the sound stays with her. She knows where she is. The recollections that come to her are real, are dreams, are real again. Leslie, still a small boy, is playing with the cat on the floor beside her bed. Her mother sits fanning herself in a white basket chair with a pink cushion on the hotel verandah. Her father is the man at the *bar-tabac* along the seafront, speaking excellent French. Now Fred is standing at the window, looking out at the sea and laughing. But these surprises force her awake again.

She is remembering the day, soon after settling in at the Beau Rivage, when she decided she would visit Madame Allègre. She went up from the seafront, away from the shops and cafés, turning on to the gravel road that climbed steeply above and beyond the town. There was the sea coming into view again away to her right. She passed the olive grove, its trees blown silver in the wind, and the grassy field that had been their short-cut to the market. She passed the wall where they had seen "the last lizard of summer" sunning itself. There were tiny puffs of yellow blossom on the feathery grey-green mimosa. Now she could see the Villa Pauline up ahead, pink, looking over its own wall towards her. For a moment the greyness of the day made no difference. She saw it as it had been on good days; as it had been when the weather had meant next to nothing – when every day, warm or cold, wet or dry, had been good.

She stopped because something was happening to her. At first she thought she must be ill, it was so strong; then she recognised that it wasn't physical. What she was feeling was an emotion. Regret? Nostalgia? No single word quite described it because it involved pleasure as well as pain. Intensity. Something of the mind but so powerful it was felt in the body, at the fingertips and the nerve ends; in the scalp and at the throat. Her life and Jack's met and were joined for ever at this point, in this place. Robert Louis Stevenson, she remembered, had written, "Happy? I was happy once. That was in Hyères." Why did it only occur to her now that Hyères was just along the coast, and that they – she and Jack – could write the same of Bandol?

She pushed open the gate and heard its familiar creak, and the crunch of the gravel under her feet. It was strange how so many gates and doors had voices as distinct as a human voice. If she'd been blind, brought here from anywhere on earth and asked where she was, hearing that sound she could have answered correctly without a moment's pause.

She walked up the path past the almond tree and up the steps to the door which was slightly ajar. She knocked, pushed it open (it stuck, as always), and was greeted by Madame Allègre who was airing the house, getting it ready to let again when the spring arrived. The greeting, once she'd been recognised, was fulsome, noisy. The kisses went from cheek to cheek and back again, as if she were a tennis match. She was peered at, reviewed, kissed again, led indoors. They sat on either side of the table where she'd worked on "The Aloe". They talked about the war, the great battles now starting up again; about the weather, about Jack in London, and the Allègres' son who was wounded – thank God, because he wouldn't have to fight any more.

Through all of this, and especially when she saw her own photograph still on the shelf where Jack had propped it, it was as if she were holding her breath, fighting back tears at the knowledge that something invaluable had been cast aside, casually, and could never be recovered.

The tears didn't come until she was walking down the hill again. Rain had started to fall, a light misty shower blown in from the sea, and she said over to herself

Il pleure dans mon coeur
Comme il pleut sur la ville.

Back on the waterfront she leaned over the wall looking at the grey sea and watching North African soldiers kicking something about on the sand. She thought of it, that soft object doing service for a football, as herself, kicked about by Fate. It was a bad moment, a moment of self-pity, and she went into combat with it. Whatever was left behind when she and Jack answered Lawrence's summons, the decision, she knew, had been as much hers as his. And self-reproach was no use. It had to do with what was called "free will". She had never thought of her will (though

240

she knew she had one) as "free". Decisions of that kind were not "choices". They were just events, happenings. They were what you found yourself *doing*, in the circumstances, being the person you were. If you had been another person you might have done different, but you were not.

So the best had to be made of whatever was the case; and if the moment ever came when regret and nostalgia seemed to be taking control, then it was time to remember Freddie's advice: burn your boats every morning; live, not as if there were no tomorrow, but as if there were no yesterday.

She has arranged her days into a routine which allows plenty of rest, a certain amount of walking, and some hours of work. Her best hours for writing are after her mid-afternoon walk and before dinner. She has written a long story about the French and the English, told by a Frenchman, a writer – partly Carco. She began it as an exposure of this character's corruption and cynicism and, day by day, wrote herself into his voice, into his consciousness, until she ended up *being* him, enjoying him, liking him. There is an Englishman in the story, based partly on Jack (at least he has Jack's rolling gait and some of his mannerisms). And there is an Englishwoman called Mouse, a pale shadow of herself, who in a crisis says very little and demands *tea*. It is so new in technique and content she feels everything that comes after must take it into account or seem a step backward. She has also dreamed a small story, even its name, "Sun and Moon", and next day written it straight down. And now she's writing another – about London, middle-class marriage, infidelity.

The weather which began so bleak and cold has changed in a way the locals tell her is characteristic of the region: one moment winter, with cold wind and rain, the next a sky and a sea like silk, the mimosa exploding into gold, jonquils yellow and white everywhere, windows and doors wide open, a smile on every face that says, even if no word is uttered, "*Fait beau, n'est-ce pas?*"

There are shadows, of course: her fears; the difficulty of sleeping through the night when she is writing; her anxiety about Jack in London; the burn in her creaking lung and the uncertainty about what it might mean . . . And now there is Ida, the Rhodesian Mountain, who has fought her way past every obstacle, every wartime restriction on travel, and come hurtling south convinced by some ghoulish intuition that she is needed. Katherine is hating her at this moment – unreasonably, she knows, and therefore holding her hatred in check. The woman loves her; wants to eat her alive; is disappointed (or so Katherine persuades herself) that her darling is not worse, seriously ill, dying, so she would be needed *really*. Since she can't eat her friend she eats everything else (they take meals together) in amounts that seem to Katherine excessive, even disgusting. Ida is submissive but also single-minded, focused, determined. It is a war, Katherine tells herself (everything is war!), in which Ida's strongest weapon is the guilt her devotion and subjugation cause Katherine to feel.

Katherine is trying not to be cruel. This means she *has* been cruel, but not as she might have been if she did not put a brake on herself. She knows Ida will help her get back to London when the weather is warmer. That will be fortunate; even perhaps necessary, if the expected spring offensive occurs and there are long delays on the trains and interruptions to the journey. So she will make use of Ida, as she has done in the past – and should be grateful, shouldn't she? She thinks not. She should acknowledge Ida's devotion, and does. But at this moment she can't think of it as other than a burden, an imposition, and Ida as the leech on her life.

She's not well. She has not had her Aunt Martha since leaving England and would love to believe (remembering that Sunday afternoon in bed with Jack before her departure) that she is pregnant. But she doesn't believe it. There are none of the other signs (sore breasts, vomiting) she remembers from the far-off pregnancy that ended with so much blood and unhappiness in Wörishofen.

She must take comfort in her work. It's what matters now in her life – that and her love for Jack. There is nothing else. Her new story has kept her awake last night, suffering a kind of nervous excitement at the thought of what may happen when her second book is published, the success it may bring.

She must get up now, have breakfast, begin. She remembers lines she learned at school from Shakespeare's *Venus and Adonis*, and says them over to herself:

> Lo, here the gentle lark, weary of rest,
> From his moist cabinet mounts up on high,
> And wakes the morning from whose silver breast
> The sun ariseth in his majesty;
> > Who doth the world so gloriously behold,
> > That cedar-tops and hills seem burnish'd gold.

In a rush of energy she throws back the bedclothes, jumps from the bed and runs three steps to the window. It causes her to cough, deep in her lungs – a coughing fit that drives her backward to the edge of the bed where she collapses for a moment, recovering. Something tastes strange. She puts her hand to her mouth. There is blood. Not just a fleck or spot. A lot – a bright thick smear of it across and between her fingers.

There is something she remembers now. On that last quick dash to Garsington she picked up Colvin's life of Keats which Jack had borrowed from Ottoline. She sat on his bed skimming it for an hour or more. One thing that stuck in her mind was Keats noting the bright red blood – arterial blood – of his first haemorrhage, and saying he knew what it was, and that it would be fatal, because he'd seen it in the case of his brother. He knew it was his death warrant.

That is the colour Katherine sees on her hand, and goes on seeing as it creeps through her fingers. The seconds tick by, and the minutes. There is no great rush of blood, but nor is it the merest trace. She coughs and it is still there. She remains sitting on the bed. She thinks of Chekhov. She was always too close to him in her imagination – borrowed his style in her earliest work, even pinched a story from him. Is she now going to die his death? What would that be? A punishment? Or just an ordinary old irony?

After a time there is only a very faint trace – but she knows this is not an end. It is a beginning. Why else has there been that burning sensation? And Dr Ainger speaking of a "spot" or "shadow"? At the time she let her mind slide over it. Pulled the blind down on it.

This is tuberculosis. Has to be.

She is calm. There is a fear so deep – much deeper than panic – that dulls and anaesthetises; that simply waits for the worst to happen. It must, she supposes, be what a person feels being led to execution. She was told that her brother's wounds were too terrible for him to feel pain. She guesses there must be a parallel protection against fear. When you *know* you are going to die perhaps you are beyond fear. Perhaps you only fear when your death is less than certain, or when you can't believe in it.

I must work, is what she tells herself. The book must be finished, and perhaps (this kind of dying sometimes takes several years) there will be another. If I have to go (she's remembering Fred's resolve not to argue with his fate) I'll go quietly – but not quickly, and I will leave my fingerprints on things.

She goes to the window again and looks out. She closes her eyes and summons Wellington Harbour, and the hills behind it, and the sea beyond. They are there. She can count on them. They will always be there.

She opens her eyes and sees Bandol. It too is there – the town, the port, the Mediterranean all blue and turquoise in the morning light. There are three fishing boats being mended and tarred under her window, and one getting a new coat of paint. Not far from the shore fishermen are out in pairs in their smallest boats. One sculls lightly, little flicks of the oars, so the boat inches over the water. The other stands in the prow with a spear, waiting to strike.

She notices that the two submarines have gone from the harbour; have crept out at night to do their underwater work. The destroyer is showing signs of getting up steam. Death must go on.

She will have to find a way to break this news to Jack. That will take a very careful choice of words. Yes, for words on the page, she *does* consider herself responsible. *Those* are her acts of will!

But first, she had better have breakfast.

Subsequent Facts

KATHERINE MANSFIELD MARRIED JOHN MIDDLETON MURRY (JACK) IN
May 1918. She published two further collections of stories in her lifetime and died at Fontainebleau in January 1923, aged thirty-four. Further
collections of stories, and volumes of letters and journals, were published
after her death. Virginia Woolf, whose mature style owes a great deal to
Mansfield's, confided to her journal, "and I was jealous of her writing –
the only writing I have ever been jealous of". Elizabeth Bowen wrote
of her, "Had she not written, written as she did, one form of art might
still be in its infancy. [. . .] We owe to her the prosperity of the 'free'
story: she untrammelled it from conventions and, still more, gained for
it a prestige till then unthought. How much ground Katherine Mansfield
broke for her successors may not be realized. Her imagination kindled
unlikely matter; she was to alter for good and all our idea of what goes
to make a story."